continued . . .

AGONY OF THE LEAVES

Tea Shop Mystery #13

LAURA CHILDS

BERKLEY PRIME CRIME, NEW YORK

THE BERKLEY PUBLISHING GROUP
Published by the Penguin Group
Penguin Group (USA) Inc.
375 Hudson Street, New York, New York 10014, USA

USA / Canada / UK / Ireland / Australia / New Zealand / India / South Africa / China

Penguin Books Ltd., Registered Offices: 80 Strand, London WC2R 0RL, England
For more information about the Penguin Group, visit penguin.com.

AGONY OF THE LEAVES

A Berkley Prime Crime Book / published by arrangement with Gerry Schmitt & Associates, Inc.

Copyright © 2012 by Gerry Schmitt & Associates, Inc.
Excerpt from *Sweet Tea Revenge* by Laura Childs copyright © 2013 by
Gerry Schmitt & Associates, Inc.

Berkley Prime Crime Books are published by The Berkley Publishing Group.
BERKLEY® PRIME CRIME and the PRIME CRIME logo are trademarks of
Penguin Group (USA) Inc.

For information, address: The Berkley Publishing Group,
a division of Penguin Group (USA) Inc.,
375 Hudson Street, New York, New York 10014.

ISBN: 978-0-425-25196-6

PUBLISHING HISTORY
Berkley Prime Crime hardcover edition / March 2012
Berkley Prime Crime mass-market edition / March 2013

PRINTED IN THE UNITED STATES OF AMERICA

10 9 8 7 6 5 4 3

Cover illustration by Stephanie Henderson.
Cover design by Lesley Worrell.

ALWAYS LEARNING   **PEARSON**

For Pat and Gary, dedicated
purveyors of mystery

ACKNOWLEDGMENTS

Heartfelt thanks to Sam, Tom, Bob, Jennie, Dan, and all the fine folks at Berkley Prime Crime who handle design, publicity, copywriting, bookstore sales, and gift sales. A special thank-you to all tea lovers, tea shop owners, bookstore owners, librarians, reviewers, magazine writers, websites, and radio stations who have enjoyed the ongoing adventures of the Indigo Tea Shop gang.

1

Elegant green tendrils of kelp swayed in graceful, undulating motions as grouper and sea bass peeked out from their leafy sanctuary. Bullet-shaped tuna, the Indy car drivers of the sea, zoomed through the vast tank like silver streaks.

"Fabulous," Theodosia murmured, as she watched, fascinated, separated from the five-hundred-thousand-gallon tank by more than fourteen inches of tempered glass.

It was the grand opening of the Neptune Aquarium in Charleston, South Carolina, and Theodosia Browning, proprietor of the Indigo Tea Shop, had been tapped to cater tea, scones, and tea sandwiches for the opening-night private party to honor dignitaries and big-buck donors. Except, right now, she'd briefly escaped the black-tie party and retreated to the Ocean Wall exhibit, where she was off in her own sweet reverie, marveling at the kelp garden and coral reef. She was aware of distant voices and slight chatter somewhere overhead, but right now, in this particular space, Theodosia was able to pretty much block them out.

"I thought perhaps I might find you here," a genteel male voice called to her.

Theodosia pulled her attention from the enormous tank and spun on her hot-pink suede stilettos. "I felt the need to escape," she said, smiling and shaking her head. "But if you need me . . ." She smoothed the front of her short black cocktail dress as Drayton Conneley, her catering manager and master tea blender, tapped his foot and smiled a benevolent smile. Probably, Theodosia decided, Drayton had come to fetch her and drag her back to the festivities, which pretty much involved all the donors heartily congratulating each other for the enormous checks they'd written to finance this state-of-the-art aquarium. Although Theodosia was a huge believer in supporting museums, arts organizations, and various charities, she was not so enthusiastic when it came to boasting about it.

"Actually," said Drayton, "Haley's managing the tea table rather nicely." Drayton was six feet tall, graying, and sixty-something, impeccably dressed in a narrow European-cut tuxedo with a red-and-midnight-blue tartan cummerbund. "Besides, there are three other restaurants serving tonight as well. All plying the aquarium's donors and dignitaries with excellent canapés, pâtés, and fresh seafood." Drayton posed and cocked his head in a quirky magpie gesture. "Although seafood appetizers *do* seem like a strange contradiction, considering our surroundings." He moved a few steps closer to the tank and peered into the dark, briny depths. "Amazing, isn't it? To actually recreate the ocean floor and reefs?"

"It's mesmerizing," Theodosia agreed, as she caught a glint of her own reflection mirrored in the tank's outer wall. Blessed with masses of auburn hair, a fair English complexion, high cheekbones, and full mouth, Theodosia cut an eager, elegant figure. Her inner workings, however, were a bit of a dichotomy. While Theodosia possessed a Southern lady's gentility and grace, she was also fiercely independent and courageous. She wasn't afraid to stand up for her rights, take her place in the business community, accept any challenge that was thrown at her, and champion the occasional underdog. It was this unflagging courage and disdain for inertia that made her cornflower-blue eyes fairly dance with excitement. "I could gaze into this tank forever," she murmured, partly to Drayton, partly to herself.

Theodosia had been born with a love of the sea as well as all living sea creatures, from enormous humpback whales to minuscule anemones. And each year, when tiny leatherback hatchlings crawled out of their nests on Halliehurst Beach, Theodosia helped shepherd these newborn turtles across the treacherous sand, where hungry shorebirds hovered, and into the safety of the sea.

And, of course, living in Charleston, a city built on a grand peninsula that enjoyed the crashing, lashing waves of the Atlantic, put Theodosia in almost constant touch with water. If she wasn't speeding across the dizzying Cooper River Bridge, she was enjoying the local bounty of briny shrimp and fresh oysters, or jogging with her dog, Earl Grey, at White Point Gardens on the very tip of the peninsula. At the very least, Theodosia was able to inhale the intoxicating scent of sea salt on the warm breezes as she bustled about her little tea shop on nearby Church Street.

"Haley's been giving me some rather stern lectures concerning sustainable seafood," Drayton smiled. "Apparently, it's acceptable for bluefish and yellowfin tuna to be served in her luncheon crêpes and chowders, but Chilean sea bass is strictly verboten."

"Contrary to what people have believed for centuries," said Theodosia, "there just isn't an unlimited supply of fish in our oceans."

"Pity," said Drayton, "how we humans tend to muck things up." He touched an index finger to the thick glass, then turned even more serious. "You know, don't you, that the folks from Solstice are here tonight?" Solstice was the restaurant that

Theodosia's former boyfriend Parker Scully owned and ran. A popular bistro that offered tapas and a wine bar.

Theodosia nodded. "I know."

"I hope that's not why you're dodging all the champagne and merriment."

"It's not," Theodosia told him. She gave a shrug, easy to do in her cute one-shouldered number. "Parker and I are just fine." She and Parker had had their talk, a very frank discussion about ending their two-year relationship, and now things were simpatico. At least she assumed they were. "I'm cool, he's cool," she told Drayton.

"Excellent," said Drayton. He peered down his aquiline nose. "Then I suppose you've already spoken with Parker tonight?"

"No, just to Chef Toby." Toby Crisp was the executive chef at Solstice, the one who created tapas for the bar and low-country cuisine for the dining room and kept the kitchen humming. "But I'm positive Parker's around somewhere. I'm sure I'll run into him."

Drayton stepped away from the glass, then hesitated. "Our bursting-his-buttons executive director, David Sedakis, is slated to give a welcoming speech in another ten minutes or so." He glanced down and tapped his watch, an antique Patek Phillipe. "Actually, five minutes."

"And you're thinking it would be politically correct if I were there," said Theodosia, "since Sedakis also sits on the board of your beloved Heritage Society?"

"Your applause would be most welcome."

"Then I'll be there."

Drayton gave the short half bow of a fencing instructor and quickly departed, while Theodosia, in no hurry to rejoin the boisterous crowd, turned her attention back to the Ocean Wall.

What was the hypnotic pull, she wondered, that the sea had on her? She bent forward and touched her cheek against the coolness of the glass. Probably, she decided, it harked back to sailing on her dad's J-22—sluicing through the waves, running the slots between Sullivan's Island and Patriot's Point. She could practically picture the yellow spinnaker booming and billowing like mad, feel her hands on the wheel, recall that her dad's strong hands had hovered just inches away.

Good times.

Theodosia was alone now, both parents long dead. In fact, her only living relative was her Aunt Libby, who lived at Cane Ridge Plantation. But she had Drayton and Haley, who were practically family, as well as an entire contingent of dear friends and customers who congregated almost daily in her tea shop.

I'm lucky. I'm one of the lucky ones.

Her eyes closed and a smile drifted across her face as a wave of gratitude swept through her, stirring her heart.

Because these days . . .

Something pecked at the glass. A gentle tap. Theodosia didn't so much hear it as sense a vibration.

Her eyes opened slowly, her curiosity roused. She stared into the tank.

For a few seconds, Theodosia couldn't quite figure out what she was staring at. Or what was staring back. The thickness of the glass magnified and distorted whatever creature was peering at her.

She tilted her head, curious. Then, like a morning mist suddenly burning off, her eyes focused and she was able to see exactly what was happening.

A face bobbed close to hers! A human face! Papery white skin leached of color, eyes rolled back so far that only the whites were visible.

Theodosia clapped a hand to her mouth, horrified but unable to look away. Her rapidly darting eyes took in the entire bizarre scene of a man gently bobbing in the tank, hopelessly entwined in some kind of net. His facial expression was a death grimace. Then, a floating, almost disembodied hand seemed to slowly rise up and scratch tentatively at the glass.

Oh no! Please, no!

Theodosia's world suddenly lurched crazily on its axis. Because bizarrely, horrifically, she *recognized* the signet ring on the dead man's left hand!

If she hadn't, Theodosia wouldn't have known it was her former boyfriend!

"Parker?" she gasped.

Her legs turning to jelly, panic coursing through her, Theodosia sank to her knees as the horror of what was happening, here and now, closed in around her like a dank rag dripping with chloroform. Her respiration came in short, biting gasps, but the air didn't seem to be getting to her lungs. She felt close to blacking out as a strange darkness, oppressive like a damp, threatening fog, threatened to overtake her.

Balling both hands into fists, Theodosia beat futilely against the glass wall. How could this happen? How could this *be* happening? Her former boyfriend bobbing like a cork before her very eyes!

Clawing at the glass now, Theodosia let loose a low moan as Parker's body twisted in the netting that wrapped around him, scattering fish like frightened lemmings. Could they sense his death, too? Did they feel her shock and dread? Were they absorbing the sound waves of her desperate beating against the glass?

It was only when a moray eel made a lazy circle about Parker's head that Theodosia thought to scream out loud.

2

It was your basic nightmare aftermath. And even though the Charleston Fire Department's rescue squad arrived in record time, there was no rescue, only a sad recovery.

"I can't believe it," Theodosia told Drayton. "We were just talking about him." Her lips felt stiff, as if they'd been shot with Novocain, and her entire being felt completely detached from what was happening around her. Probably, Theodosia decided, she was in the throes of mild shock.

Of course, I'm in shock. Who wouldn't be?

Drayton, along with Haley, her young baker and chef extraordinaire, tried to lend support. Drayton, in particular, was a brick.

Balling her fists up, Theodosia wiped at her eyes. She saw shiny sparkles and felt hard grit. "Tell me this isn't happening," she muttered in a hoarse voice.

"It's happening," said a glum Haley. Usually saucy and cute with her stick-straight blond hair and pert nose, Haley looked like she'd been dragged through the mill. Her shoulders slumped, her normally bright and mischievous eyes had lost their sparkle. Instead of looking like she was in her early twenties, she looked like she'd aged twenty years.

There was a clank of metal and then Drayton said, "Come on, let's find an office or someplace where we can regroup. Maybe have a cup of tea." He put a hand on Theodosia's shoulder, trying to pull her away.

But the clanking had gotten louder and Theodosia knew exactly what was going on. The same fire and rescue squad that had hung down over the tank and pulled Parker out had loaded his body onto a gurney and were now wheeling him out into the corridor where they were standing.

"You really don't want to see him like this," said Drayton, in a tone that was sharper than usual.

But Theodosia had other ideas. "Please," she told him. "I want to. I have to."

As the gurney rolled closer, she shook free of Drayton's grasp and rushed over to it. Wrapping a hand around its cold metal railing, she said to the two firemen who were wheeling it, "Please wait, I need to see him."

One of the firemen, an older man whose name tag read MORLEY, said, "No, you really don't, ma'am."

"Please," Theodosia said again, "I promise I won't fall apart."

An EMT, an earnest-looking young African American in a navy-blue jumpsuit with red-and-white shoulder patches, had been following a few paces behind the gurney. Overhearing snips of their conversation, he shifted his medical bag from one hand to the other and said, "It's not a pretty sight."

"I know that!" Theodosia snapped. "I'm the one who found him."

There were a few moments of hesitation on the part of the men, and then Morley gazed at Theodosia with sympathy-filled brown eyes. "Your call," he told her.

Theodosia nodded.

Morley grimaced, then reached for the zipper tab on the black vinyl body bag. His big hand fumbled for a few moments, and then he gave a short jerk and tugged it down until the body bag was halfway open.

"Oh jeez!" Haley clapped a hand to her mouth and stepped back. "Oh man!" she cried out again, spinning away. It was just too much for her.

But Theodosia, her back ramrod stiff, stood next to the gurney, staring down at her ex-boyfriend. She took in his papery skin, closed but slightly bulging eyes, and white lips. And found it inconceivable that this relatively young man, always so full of life and big ideas, could suddenly be dead. And dead from drowning. A shudder passed through her and Theodosia wondered if poor Parker was resting safely in the Lord's arms now. She certainly hoped he was. Believed he was. When she was alone tonight, back in her little cottage where she could grieve in private, she'd light a candle and offer some special prayers.

"Okay?" asked the EMT. He seemed worried that she might faint. Didn't know the steel she had in her. "Okay to take him now?" he asked.

Theodosia continued to stare down at Parker's body, even as she felt Drayton step up behind her. He was offering both sympathy and strength, and she appreciated that. But at the same time, he tugged on her arm, urging her to back away. To let Parker go.

"Theo?" said Drayton.

Reluctant to just turn her back on Parker's body, Theodosia let loose a sigh of resignation. And noted that Parker's mouth had been frozen into an O, almost as if he'd been surprised to be rescued, after all. Even though it had all come too late.

The firemen and EMT shifted back and forth, nervously, restlessly. Probably, they just wanted to complete their job and go home.

Finally, Morley said, "Just slipped off the overhead walkway, I guess." He, too, seemed in need of an explanation.

The other fireman nodded. "There's a whole tangle of walkways over that main tank. All metal. Probably slippery as heck."

"Never should have allowed people to take behind-the-scenes tours," added the EMT.

Morley bent forward to rezip the bag, but now the zipper was jammed. It didn't want to close. He tried a second time, unsuccessfully. Frowning, he quickly unzipped the bag all the way down, creating a ripping sound. He meant to start clean from the bottom, but in so doing, revealed Parker's hands, which were folded loosely across his chest.

Instead of stepping away and letting the fireman fuss, Theodosia cocked her head and stared intently.

What . . . on . . . earth?

Her heart gave a lurch and a tiny hit of adrenaline surged through her as she studied Parker's body in situ now. And what she saw made her suddenly question the grim circumstances of his death.

"What if he didn't fall?" said Theodosia. Her voice was quiet and even, practically drowned out by the mumble of the EMT, firemen, and now some nervous-looking aquarium employees who had edged in to join them.

"What?" said Drayton, leaning in close to her. "What did you say?"

Theodosia turned and gazed wide-eyed at Drayton. There was a flash of anger as well as incredulousness in her eyes. "We need to call the police," she told him, in a hoarse, barely audible voice. Then she gathered herself together, put a hand back on the gurney, and said, in clear, firm tones, "Please don't move him one more inch."

"What?" Drayton said again, still not understanding. "What on earth are you . . .?"

"I don't think Parker fell into that tank," said Theodosia.

"I think he might have been pushed. And then he was somehow . . . I don't know . . ." Her voice wavered for an instant and then she found her strength. "He was held under."

Now the second fireman spoke up, his voice filled with professional interest, but skeptical at the same time. "How do you figure that?"

"Look at his hands," said Theodosia. "They're all cut up."

The fireman shook his head. "I don't quite . . ."

"The wounds," said Theodosia. "I think they might be *defensive* wounds!"

Detective Burt Tidwell wasn't Theodosia's most favorite person in the whole world, but he was smart and dogged, and he headed the Charleston Police Department's Robbery-Homicide Division.

Tidwell was also aggressive, demanding, and often petty. He was rough and gruff and had bright, beady eyes and a bulbous body with a stomach that resembled an errant weather balloon. When Tidwell had first arrived in Charleston, fresh off his stint of apprehending the Crow River Killer, the detectives and officers under him had been thrown into a state of shock. He didn't look like a brilliant investigator. Rather, he resembled a slow-moving buffoon. Big mistake, for they soon learned, sometimes the hard way, that Tidwell was as predatory as they came and that his moods could shift instantaneously from genial cop to angry snapping turtle.

Tidwell had arrived at the Neptune Aquarium, spoken a few curt words to Theodosia and Drayton, then disappeared for a good thirty minutes. Now he was back, talking to Theodosia.

"One of the marine biologists I talked with," said Tidwell, "surmised that your friend was exploring where he shouldn't have been."

"Possibly," said Theodosia.

Tidwell went on, his jowls sloshing sideways. "Then he slipped and fell into one of the large nets that covered the top of the tank."

"He was wrapped in it," Theodosia told him. *Like the poor dolphins that get hopelessly entangled in commercial nets. Only this was Parker.*

Tidwell went on calmly. "Stands to reason. When Mr. Scully fell from the catwalk and hit the safety net, it tore loose and plunged with him into the tank."

"But Parker could swim," Theodosia told Tidwell. "So why wouldn't he just kick his way to the surface?" She thought about all the sailing Parker had done, the boogie-boarding he'd enjoyed at his favorite beaches on Hilton Head. "He wasn't afraid of the water."

"Again," said Tidwell, "the initial theory is that the deceased, obviously tangled and somewhat disoriented in the net, banged his head against the protein skimmer. Of course, the ME will have to render a definitive answer." He paused, a look of regret on his broad, pudgy face. "Perhaps your friend's fall was caused by a brain aneurysm or cardiac incident? It's rare in someone so young, but it happens. Again, the ME will—"

"Did you look at his hands?" Theodosia asked. "They were completely cut up!"

"And did you see the enormous coral reef inside that tank?" Tidwell asked, but in a kinder, gentler tone. "I don't doubt the deceased struggled mightily and gashed his hands rather badly against the sharp coral."

Theodosia digested this information for a few moments. "I suppose he could have. Still . . ."

"All in all," said Tidwell, "a terrible way to—"

"Please don't call him *the deceased*," said Theodosia.

"What do you want me to call him?"

"He was . . . Parker."

Tidwell peered at her. "Tell me, if you can, what do you

suppose Parker Scully was doing up there? Climbing on the catwalk that stretched across the aquarium tank?" Tidwell had put his investigator's hat back on.

"I don't know," said Theodosia. It was true. She didn't have a clue. How could she?

"You didn't have words with him?"

Theodosia was stunned. "No! I never even saw him tonight!"

"But you knew he was present," said Tidwell.

"I *surmised* he'd be here," said Theodosia. "I knew that Solstice was one of the caterers. They were; um, doing appetizers and small plates. Tuna tartare and spring rolls." What was she doing? she suddenly wondered. A recitation of the menu? Surely, her overtaxed brain was spitting up information that was decidedly unhelpful. Better stick to the subject.

"And you didn't have any sort of disagreement with him?" Tidwell asked.

Theodosia jerked as if a hot coal had been pressed against her flesh. "No!"

"Old boyfriend-girlfriend issues?" Tidwell prodded.

"What are you implying?" Theodosia asked. She didn't like his line of questioning. Not one bit.

"I bring this up," said Tidwell, "only because someone mentioned seeing the two of you together.

Theodosia practically bared her teeth. "Who said that?"

Tidwell drew back from her. "I'm afraid I'm not at liberty to say."

3

❧

Theodosia stared into the mirror and saw a crazy woman staring back at her. Quickly bending forward, she splashed cool water on her face and blotted herself with a paper towel. Then she dug in her clutch purse for a comb and a tissue, patted down her hair, and blew her nose.

There. Better? No, not really. Not by a long shot.

As she exited the ladies' room, she wheeled left and ran smack-dab into Chef Toby Crisp, Parker's friend and executive chef. At which point they pretty much collapsed against each other.

"How could this happen?" Chef Toby cried. The sorrow on his plump and usually garrulous face was palpable. "I was just talking to Drayton and he . . ." His face crumpled. "Well, he said you were there."

"I was," said Theodosia. "It was awful."

"He drowned," said Chef Toby, shaking his head, brushing away tears. "In that big tank."

"Apparently," said Theodosia.

Chef Toby stared at her. "How could he have drowned?" he asked, his voice practically a growl.

Theodosia gazed at him through a veil of tears. "You think that's strange, too?"

"Yes, I do," said Chef Toby. "Sure. I mean Parker pretty much grew up on Hilton Head, something like a mile from Sunset Beach. He surfed, he did boogie boards; Parker even took dive lessons. He was *certified*, for gosh sake."

"You're thinking Parker didn't just fall into that tank and drown," said Theodosia. She was believing this more and more. Trying to convince herself of what really might have happened? Yes, probably.

Chef Toby scratched at his curly sideburns. "It just doesn't seem in character that Parker would launch into a full-blown panic, even if he was wrapped in a net. Seems like he'd just . . ."

"Kick," said Theodosia. "He would have just kicked his way to the surface."

"You'd think so."

"Unless someone held him under," said Theodosia.

"Huh?" Chef Toby looked surprised. "What are you saying?"

"Parker's hands were all cut up," she told him. "I saw him. I looked at the body just before the rescue guys took him away."

Chef Toby looked confused. "You mean like he cut himself trying to climb out?"

"More like he was fighting with someone and got . . ." She took a deep breath. "Got stabbed."

Chef Toby waggled his hands in a questioning gesture. "You mean . . . murdered?"

She nodded. "Something like that." *Exactly like that.*

"And you talked to the police about this?"

"Yes, but they don't seem all that interested in my theories right now," said Theodosia. Even though she felt angry and frustrated, she fought to keep any note of hysteria out of her voice.

Chef Toby stood there frowning, hands thrust deep into the pockets of his white jacket, his chef's hat canted at a crazy angle atop his head. "Is there somebody else we can get to pursue this? Like a lawyer or something?"

Or me, thought Theodosia.

"I'm not sure," she said.

"But why? *Who?*" Chef Toby cleared his throat. "That's the better question. Who would push him in, or push him under?"

"That's the real question," said Theodosia.

"You really think . . . ?"

"Possible." *Probable.*

Chef Toby was having trouble wrapping his mind around it. "So what would prompt . . . ?"

"I don't know," said Theodosia. Her mind whirred in a million directions. But she knew if she was going to find an answer, Chef Toby was as good a place as any to start. "What was going on in Parker's life?" Theodosia asked. "Recently."

"You mean businesswise?" said Chef Toby. "Or with his personal life?"

"Let's start with business," said Theodosia. She decided that looking in that direction might offer the most possibilities.

Chef Toby let loose a deep sigh. "Parker was mostly negotiating to buy a second restaurant."

"The one in Savannah," said Theodosia. She was aware that Parker had been working on that for some time.

Chef Toby shook his head. "No, no, that fell through a while back."

"Really?" This was news to Theodosia. "Why?"

Chef Toby grimaced. "I don't know the exact details. But I did hear there were some scary guys involved in that deal."

That remark sparked Theodosia's curiosity enough to lead

to another impertinent but necessary question, "Scary enough to commit murder?"

Chef Toby considered her words. "I don't know. I never met them."

"Do you know who they are? Do you know their names?"

"Yes, but that's about it. All the negotiating was happening out of town and Parker was planning to hire a different executive chef, so I didn't pay all that much attention."

Theodosia thought for a moment. Was this something she should tell Tidwell? Or would he think she was too emotionally involved and simply trying to send him on a fool's errand? She let those questions percolate in her brain for a few moments. Finally, an answer bubbled up. Yeah, probably, Tidwell would think she was grasping at straws. Tidwell was a bearish old boy who, like so many men, was a little distrustful of female emotions and intuition. So he'd probably listen politely, then blow her off. So . . . back to square one. What to do?

"Can I take a look in Parker's office?" Theodosia asked.

Chef Toby stared at her, then said, "You realize, if the police *do* suspect foul play, they'll probably start combing through his office first thing tomorrow."

"That's why I want to look now. Tonight."

"Seriously?"

Theodosia gave a tight nod.

Chef Toby gave it about three seconds of consideration. "Okay, but . . . don't tell anybody, okay?"

"My lips are sealed."

"Theodosia!" She turned. Drayton was striding down the hall toward them. "You're ready to leave now?"

"Yes," she said. "I'm going to give Chef Toby a ride home and then go home myself." She offered a thin smile. "You can ride with Haley?"

"Of course," said Drayton. He shook hands with Chef

Toby, then gave him a pat on the back. "Sorry, just so sorry," he said in a gruff voice.

"Thank you," said Chef Toby.

Drayton focused his gaze on Theodosia. "Just crawl into bed and sip a cup of chamomile tea," he advised. "Try to soothe your mind."

"Good advice," she told him.

But when the two of them tiptoed through the back door of Solstice some twenty minutes later, wild thoughts still whirled in Theodosia's head.

"This way," said Chef Toby. He clicked on a light above the large gas stove and led her through the narrow kitchen. They passed the walk-in cooler and a storage room, then turned into Parker's small office. Chef Toby shuffled across the carpet, then turned on a light. A puddle of yellow spilled from the small brass lamp that sat on Parker's desk. "Okay. Here we are." He sounded a little unsure, as if they were suddenly trespassing.

Theodosia had been in Parker's office any number of times. But not for the last couple of months. She stood, hesitant, wondering where to look, trying to figure out what she was looking for. A clue? Something to point her in the right direction, to give her a hint of a possible suspect? Theodosia made a helpless gesture with her hands. "I don't know what I'm looking for."

Chef Toby nodded.

"I suppose I should just look around." Theodosia stood there, her eyes roving the small office, seeing posters, menus tacked on the wall, an old metal restaurant sign that said CRAWDADS SERVED HERE.

"Maybe start with his desk?" Chef Toby suggested.

Theodosia plunked herself down in Parker's chair. She pulled open the top drawer and found the usual mishmash of guy clutter. Pens, stamps, a half-eaten Snickers bar, business cards, loose change, ticket stubs for a Stingrays game last winter.

"Who's going to run the restaurant now?" Chef Toby wondered.

Theodosia looked up. "I don't know? Parker's brother?" Parker's brother, Charles Scully, lived right here in Charleston, somewhere over near Meeting and Broad. She figured he was probably the heir or beneficiary or whatever the legal descriptor was.

Theodosia pulled open the rest of the drawers. Nothing. An old Sony Walkman, a pocketknife, half-used yellow legal pads, and two blue plastic binders, which proved to be empty.

The top of Parker's desk was fairly neat. Pen and pencil set. A few stray papers, mostly supplier invoices. A sign that said IF YOU WANT TO MAKE A MILLION, START WITH $900,000. And a four-year-old iMac computer.

Theodosia tapped a finger against the keyboard. "Did he use this much?"

Chef Toby shook his head. "Hardly ever. He was a jot-it-down-on-paper kind of guy."

"My impression, too." Theodosia spun the chair around, almost knocking her knees against an old green metal four-drawer file cabinet. Testing the top drawer, she found it was locked.

"Do you have a key to this file cabinet?"

"No. I didn't even know it was locked."

"He didn't usually lock it?"

Chef Toby looked thoughtful. "Parker was a pretty trusting guy. The only thing he was extremely mindful about was the cooler. We serve a lot of seafood here, and you know how expensive that stuff is. Costs an arm and a leg these days. So he was always telling us to keep it locked. In any restaurant there's always a bit of what you'd call . . . lateral transfer." He sighed. "But the file cabinet . . . I've got no idea."

Theodosia considered this. Maybe, if she could tiptoe through Parker's files, there might be some little nit or nat that would point her in the right direction. Maybe. That was, if she wasn't making a mountain out of a molehill. If Parker really *had* just fallen into that enormous fish tank and drowned.

Her eyes roved across the top of his desk and landed on a ceramic mug with a pinched face sculpted into the side, the kind of mug amateur potters sell at street fairs. She reached out, tipped over the mug, and was shocked when she detected a tinkle of metal against clay and an actual key slid out into her hand. But closer inspection revealed that it was a large brass key, way too large to fit the lock on the file cabinet.

"Back to square one," Theodosia sighed.

"Got an idea," said Chef Toby. He grabbed a metal letter opener off the desk and stuck the tip of it into the lock. Then he proceeded to wiggle it back and forth, very gently.

"If you do that, if you force the lock or leave marks, the police are going to know we broke in here," Theodosia told him. Part of her wanted the file cabinet open; part of her feared they might be tampering with evidence. Which was never a good thing in the eyes of Detective Tidwell. "So maybe you should . . . be careful."

Chef Toby poked and prodded for a few moments, picking and probing with just the tip of the letter opener. "There's a little metal tongue here and I think if I . . ."

A metallic *pop* finished his sentence.

"Holy buckets," said Theodosia, a little in awe of his lock-picking skills. "You did it!"

Chef Toby slid the top file drawer open with a self-satisfied smile. "And without breaking the lock."

Theodosia leaned forward anxiously and let her fingertips fly across the tops of the plastic file tabs. She wasn't exactly sure what she was looking for, but had a vague, unsettled notion that she'd know it when she found it. If that made any sense at all.

She pawed rapidly through the hanging folders, finding files marked PAYROLL, BENEFITS, INSURANCE, and MENUS. Finally, toward the back of the drawer was a file marked CURRENT PROJECTS. "I think this is what I might want to look at," she murmured softly.

"You think Parker was killed because of a restaurant deal?" Chef Toby asked.

"No idea," said Theodosia. "I'll admit it sounds ridiculous. On the other hand, if we can find just a nugget of information . . ."

But when she lifted the file folder from the cabinet, it flopped loosely in her hand. And when she flipped the file open on the desk, there was just a single blank piece of paper inside.

"That's weird," said Chef Toby, beetling his brows together. "From what I recall, Parker was negotiating on three or four different deals."

His eyes slid over to meet Theodosia's unsettled gaze. "Do you think, um, somebody could have . . . ?" His words trailed off.

"Stolen his files?" said Theodosia. "Yes, it's possible. It really is."

4

❧

Monday morning dawned sunny and bright in Charleston's historic district. Early-bird traffic meandered up Church Street, then made a small semicircular detour around St. Phillips, the landmark church that blipped out into the street, giving Church Street its well-deserved moniker. Wisps of pink-and-white parfait clouds scudded across the sky, heralding the start of another lovely and warm spring day, and a faint whiff of sea air wafted in as the Chowder Hound Restaurant and Cabbage Patch Gift Shop geared up for business with well-placed sidewalk placards advertising their specials.

But down the block, inside the Indigo Tea Shop, Theodosia sat at a small wooden table, feeling morose and a little lost.

It didn't seem possible that Parker was gone. He was young, a couple of years younger than she was. And the last time she'd seen him, at a chamber music concert two weeks ago, he'd seemed bursting with life.

So who'd been in his office? Well, according to Chef Toby, there'd been a veritable parade of people over the past couple of days. Vendors, commercial real estate agents, possible business partners, bankers, his new girlfriend. A couple of dozen people. So if she wanted to narrow it down, try to ferret out a suspect or two, Theodosia knew she'd probably have to get Parker's date book or access his computer in order to figure out where to start looking. Or, rather, *who* to start looking at.

A tea tray clattered discreetly as Drayton bore it solemnly across the empty tea room, dodging tables that were only half set.

"How are you feeling?" he asked. They were scheduled to open in another half hour and he was obviously worried.

"Awful."

"I brought you a cup of black rose tea." He set the tray down without waiting for an answer. A clear glass teapot held freshly steeping leaves. "And Haley's going to be out in a moment with some nice hot scones."

"Okay," said Theodosia. She watched the tea leaves dance and twist in the teapot. The agony of the leaves, it was called. The tea leaves doing their dance as they gave up their essence to the steaming water. But today, the twisting leaves only reminded her of poor Parker struggling for his life in that awful tank. And then losing his battle.

Drayton waited a few moments for the tea to brew, then poured a stream of amber liquor into Theodosia's teacup. "Have you talked to Max yet?"

Theodosia blinked. "No. He's still in New York, visiting galleries and schmoozing the media." Max Scofield was her new boyfriend, the one who'd pretty much replaced Parker. No, Theodosia told herself, that wasn't it at all. She'd met Max and then kind of eased Parker out of the picture. Now, of course, she felt awful about the whole thing. Maybe she hadn't really given Parker enough of a chance. Maybe she'd been too eager to go a little gaga over Max.

Whatever. Now it's a moot point.

Haley breezed over with a plate that held two fresh-baked apple scones. "Here you go," she said with an eager smile. "Still hot from the oven and amazingly fortifying. Along with a dish of the freshest Devonshire cream your taste buds have ever enjoyed." She paused, hoping either her words or her goodies might cheer Theodosia.

"Thank you, Haley," said Theodosia. She glanced at Drayton, who looked on tenterhooks. "Thank you both for being so kind and understanding and . . ." She'd somehow run out of words.

"Oh, Theo," said Haley, her sunny manner crumbling. "We both feel so awful!"

"It's a terrible thing," echoed Drayton.

"At least Detective Tidwell is working the case," said Haley. She gave a tentative frown. "You guys know that Tidwell's not my most favorite person in the world." Indeed, Haley didn't care for Tidwell's brusque manners one iota. "But he's a smart guy. A tenacious guy. So, all things considered, I'm pretty sure this whole investigation is in good hands."

"Is there an investigation?" asked Drayton. His eyebrows rose in twin arcs.

Haley looked startled. "Well . . . yeah. I think so." Now she wasn't so sure. "Isn't there, Theo?"

Theodosia took a sip of tea. A lovely Keemun with a slight top note of rose petals. "I don't know."

"The thing is," said Drayton, "just because one *suspects* foul play doesn't mean there actually *was* foul play."

"Spoken like a true doubter," said Haley. "Me? I'm with Theo. Something about Parker's death seems fishy to me and it's not just the fish. I find it hard to believe he just tumbled haphazardly into that tank!"

"Accidents happen," said Drayton.

"Then what was he *doing* up there?" pressed Haley. "I

mean, the aquarium people were leading tours last night, but I don't think that was one of the stops. I mean, seriously. Jellyfish Grotto, okay. Maybe Starfish Cove. But tiptoeing across a dangerous, slippery catwalk over a huge tank? Be serious." She shook her hair back for emphasis.

"It's a mystery," agreed Drayton.

Knock, knock, knock!

Someone was beating on the front door.

Drayton glanced over in annoyance. "Whoever's out there is way too early." One of his pet peeves was tourists who banged on the door, demanding to be let in. Especially when he was in the middle of setting out teakettles and strainers, or measuring out tea. Then he practically blew a gasket.

"Maybe somebody from the neighborhood?" asked Haley. The local shopkeepers were always anxious to swoop in for their morning cuppa-and-scone fix. She tiptoed to the window and slid a red chintz curtain aside. "Oh, poop," she said, "it's Delaine."

"Don't let her in," Drayton rasped. He had a love-hate relationship with Delaine Dish, one of their neighbors and the proprietor of Cotton Duck Boutique. In other words, he loved Delaine's prodigious fund-raising skills but hated her sharp tongue and gossipy nature.

"You have to let her in," said Theodosia. "She'll just keep knocking and battering at the door. After all, she knows we're in here. Knows we're going to open in twenty-five minutes."

"Twenty now," said Drayton.

Haley scampered over to the front door and turned the latch. "Delaine!" she cooed. "What a surprise!"

Delaine barely acknowledged Haley as she barreled her way in.

"Theodosia!" she exclaimed. Her stiletto heels made rapid-fire *click-clacks* against the pegged wooden floor as she headed for Theodosia. Her eyes blazed and her shoulder-length dark hair flew out around her heart-shaped face. She wore a tomato-red suit with patent leather blue-and-white spectator stilettos. When spring's warm weather came barreling into Charleston, Delaine and her wardrobe were good to go.

"I'm so sorry about your friend," said Delaine. She thrust a yellow gift bag into Theodosia's hands and plunked herself down in the chair across from her. "I tried to talk to you last night, but you were . . . how shall I put it? *Occupado?* Talking to that awful man Tidwell."

"What's this?" asked Theodosia, focusing on the gift bag. A gift? From Delaine? Surely this had to be a first.

"Just a little something," Delaine told her, as she reached into her navy Chanel bag and pulled out her cosmetics purse.

A bouquet of yellow daffodils poked out of the bag Delaine had handed Theodosia. Along with something else.

Theodosia stuck a finger into yellow tissue paper and plucked out a small tube of essential oil. She held it up and read the label. "Lavender."

Delaine swiped a smear of red across her full lips, then snapped the cap back on her lipstick. She tapped an index finger against her inner wrist. "Essential oil to dab on your pulse points," she explained. "Lavender is supposed to be . . ." She glanced into her pocket mirror, then nodded approval at her newly rouged lips. "Soothing."

"Thank you," said Theodosia, "how very kind of you."

Delaine forced her face into an overexuberant smile. "What are friends for?"

"A lovely gesture," said Drayton. He plucked another cup and saucer from the serving board, set it in front of Delaine, and filled it with tea.

Delaine turned bright eyes on Theodosia. "But you can't feel all that bad," she trilled. "After all, it's been a good while since you broke up with Parker. And you do have a wonderful *new* boyfriend."

"That's not really the point," said Theodosia. "Parker and

I were still friends." At least she thought they were friends. On the other hand, she didn't know a whole lot about what Parker had been up to in the past couple of months. Maybe he'd hadn't missed her at all; maybe he'd gotten on wonderfully well with his life post-Theodosia.

Delaine took a sip of tea and said, "Just think, Theo, now you're dating my old flame and I'm dating your next-door neighbor. It's like that old saying, politics makes strange bedfellows."

"How's that, Delaine?" asked Drayton.

"Just that we're both rapturously happy with who we ended up with," said Delaine. She reached across the table and patted Theodosia's hand. "Can you believe it, my Dougan right next door to you. Fancy that." Dougan Granville was Delaine's latest catch and Theodosia's next-door neighbor; also the former owner of her small house, which had once been part of Granville's rather grand estate. Delaine squeezed her eyes shut and said, "Just think, if Dougan and I ever decide to get married, we'd be neighbors! Wouldn't that be a scream!"

"It'd be a shocker," Theodosia agreed. *And I might even have to move.*

Delaine opened her eyes, tipped her head back, and gazed at Theodosia with a slightly accusing look. "But not as shocking as those headlines in this morning's paper."

"The ones about Parker drowning at the Neptune Aquarium?" asked Drayton. He pulled out a chair and sat down at the table with them.

"That's right," said Delaine. She pursed her lips. "Ghastly. Couldn't come at a worse time."

"What are you talking about?" asked Theodosia. Delaine seemed to be babbling more than usual.

"Just awful publicity for the grand opening of the Neptune Aquarium," Delaine lamented. "After all, Dougan is on the board."

So that's what this is about, thought Theodosia. *Her boy-friend being on the board.*

"Yesterday's events weren't so nice for Parker, either," Theodosia spat back.

Delaine seemed to realize that her words must have sounded a little cold and struggled to make amends. "I realize that, honey. I didn't mean anything by it." She suddenly looked confused. "I'm just talking silly, I guess. I'm not the best person in the world when it comes to offering soothing words and comfort. Just too doggone direct, I guess."

"I guess," said Theodosia.

"Really," said Delaine, batting her eyes and trying to look as sincere as she could manage, "I do apologize."

"Apology accepted," said Theodosia, thinking this was the first time she'd ever seen Delaine so solicitous. Except, of course, when she was cuddling and fussing with her cats.

Delaine stood up and smoothed the front of her jacket. "There's just one teeny-tiny thing I need to confirm before I take off."

"What's that?" asked Theodosia.

Delaine pulled her mouth into a hungry smile. "The scavenger hunt for City Charities kicks off Thursday afternoon. And I wanted to make sure you're still fielding a team." She held up an index finger and waggled it back and forth. "Remember, Theo, it's a *benefit*."

"I remember," Theodosia told her. How could she not? Delaine had been pounding away at her for the last month.

"And," Delaine continued, "you did agree your team would help raise funds for Tuesday's Child."

"Yes, but I . . ." Theodosia stammered. In lieu of what had just happened last night, how could she possibly go tripping off on a scavenger hunt? It was almost unthinkable.

But Delaine seemed to read her thoughts. "In fact, I'm bringing the executive director of Tuesday's Child here for lunch tomorrow. For the sole purpose of meeting you!"

Theodosia shook her head, tiredly. "I don't know . . ." Her brain was still numb from Parker's untimely death, she had two major tea parties to stage, the Charleston Coffee & Tea Expo kicked off this week, and now Delaine was haranguing her about a scavenger hunt.

Delaine's expression of concern suddenly switched to one of abject horror. "You *have* to participate, Theo! I'm *counting* on you! The at-risk *children* who benefit from Tuesday's Child are counting on you!"

Oh dear. "I suppose when you put it that way . . ." said Theodosia.

"Honestly, Theodosia!" said Delaine, jumping to her feet. "You've got to pull yourself out of this . . . this morass. And just get moving!"

Theodosia did get moving then, scurrying about the Indigo Tea Shop, placing bone china cups and saucers just so, arranging tiny silver butter knives, setting out glass bowls filled with sugar cubes, polishing silver sugar tongs.

"Splendid," said Drayton, as he fussed right alongside her.

Cozy and charming, the Indigo Tea Shop featured walls festooned with antique engravings depicting rice plantations and various views of the Charleston harbor, as well as Theodosia's handmade grapevine wreaths decorated with miniature teacups. Antique plates were propped on several wooden shelves along with collectible cup-and-saucer sets. A highboy held tins of tea, jars of Dubose Bees Honey, and Theodosia's selection of T-Bath products.

When Theodosia and Drayton finally arranged chairs, lit candles, and set three different pots of tea to brewing, they stood together and gazed about the little shop. It sparkled and shone to perfection while steamy notes of Darjeeling, Pouchong, and orange spice hung in the air.

"You don't think we're being too . . . futsy, do you?" Theodosia asked.

Drayton reared back. "Nonsense, this is perfection! Every aspect of composing a tea shop experience is akin to creating a perfect still-life painting. We do a splendid job and you know it. All our customers tell us so."

"That they do," Theodosia admitted.

"So why would you question our commitment to putting on an exquisite tea service?" asked Drayton, his feathers slightly ruffled.

"I'm just . . . having a bad morning, I guess," said Theodosia.

"Poor dear," said Drayton. "I do feel so bad for you."

"I'll be okay," said Theodosia. Draping a long black Parisian waiter's apron around her neck, she tied it from back to front, resolving to be positive. If only for their customers.

"Say now," said Haley, stepping out from the back. "You feel up to running through today's menu?"

Theodosia nodded. She knew she had to pull herself out of her blue funk and carry on. "Of course. What have you got for us?"

Haley flipped open a small spiral notebook and squinted at her left-slanted handwriting. "We'll be serving tomato basil soup with crostini spread with Brie cheese and fig jam. Chicken salad tea sandwiches on homemade cinnamon bread. And a citrus salad with oranges, mangoes, and walnuts."

"Quite an eclectic selection," said Drayton. "Makes me think today's the day to pull out all the stops and serve my new butter truffle tea."

Haley wrinkled her nose at him. "Run that by me again, mister. Butter truffle?"

"It's one of Drayton's new house blends," Theodosia told her.

"Black tea," said Drayton, half closing his eyes, the better to rhapsodize, "with bits of butter cookie, pistachio, almond, and orange."

"Sounds more like *dessert*," said Haley. "I mean, I'm sure it's tasty and all that, but it sure is different from your usual offerings."

Drayton peered over his half-glasses at Haley. "I like to keep you on your toes."

"You do, Drayton," said Haley, "in fact, sometimes you *step* on them."

"And for dessert?" Theodosia asked, trying to keep the discussion moving forward.

"Oh," said Haley, pulling herself back to the business at hand. "We've got pumpkin bread parfait, brownie bites, and I've got butter cake baking in the oven right now."

Tilting his head back, Drayton gave a tiny genteel sniff. "Ah, you do indeed."

Five minutes later, a clutch of customers came pouring in and, just like that, a busy Monday kicked off. Haley retreated to her fiefdom in the kitchen while Theodosia and Drayton did their whirling-twirling tea shop ballet of pouring tea, presenting plates of scones and bowls of jam, and whooshing away dirty dishes.

"We just received a call from the Broad Street Garden Club," Drayton told Theodosia, as he hung up the phone at the front counter. "The ladies made reservations for a tea luncheon on Thursday. They specifically asked for four courses, if we can manage it." He paused. "Usually that group is somewhat hoity-toity and opt for lobster thermidor at the Lady Goodwood Inn, so I'm a little surprised they chose us."

Theodosia paused at the front counter, a blue-and-white Chinese teapot in one hand, a plate of scones in the other. "After last night," she told Drayton, "I don't think anything can surprise me."

Which was exactly when the door flew open and a mournful face seemed to sway in front of Theodosia. A young woman stared directly at her and said, in a whispering voice, "Miss Browning? I need to talk to you. I'm . . . I mean I *was* . . . Parker's girlfriend."

5

It was a stunning conclusion to a rather strange morning, and Theodosia, completely taken aback, gasped sharply and simply stared. Then, upon seeing the sad, stricken expression on the girl's face, hastily gathered her wits about her and said, "I'm so sorry for your loss."

That seemed to break the initial tension between them. The girl touched an index finger to her chest and said, "Shelby McCawley. Nice to finally meet you."

Theodosia nodded. "Theodosia Browning. But then, you knew that, didn't you?"

Shelby bobbed her head. "Could we . . . is there someplace we can talk privately?"

Theodosia led Shelby through the celadon-green velvet curtain into the back of the tea shop. Past the postage stamp–sized kitchen and into her cluttered, crowded office where stacks of red hats, boxes of teapots, and tea catalogs threatened to overrun the place.

"Please," said Theodosia. "Sit down." She gestured toward

the oversized brocade chair that faced her desk. The one they'd dubbed "the tuffet."

Shelby sat down while Theodosia did a quick hop across a stack of wild grapevine wreaths and slid behind her desk. She moved a stack of tea catalogs, which were stacked too high and threatening to topple over, out of her way. "Now . . . what did you . . . ?" She paused, regrouped, and said, "How can I help you?" Then Theodosia decided her words still sounded a little brusque, so she said again, "I'm so sorry about Parker."

Shelby bobbed her head as tears sprang to her eyes. "It's awful. Shocking." She dropped her head forward and fine, straight light-brown hair fell like a curtain over her face. Then she pulled it together and smiled at Theodosia. Shelby was young, twenty-six, maybe twenty-seven, with dazzling dark eyes and a pale oval face. She was model-thin and dressed in skinny jeans with a well-cut white shirt tied at her waist.

"So you two were, um, going together . . . dating?" said Theodosia.

"For the past two months," said Shelby. She pulled a hanky from her woven leather bag and wiped at her tears. "I was really crazy about him. We were pretty crazy about each other." She paused, sniffled, and said, "But he told me about you."

Theodosia flapped a hand, as if to dismiss her past relationship with Parker.

"He really thought the world of you," said Shelby.

"Oh, I don't know about that . . ."

"No," said Shelby, "Parker was always very complimentary about you. In fact, that's one of the things I admired about him. Some guys, they'll grab any opportunity to slam their old girlfriends. Parker never did that."

"He wasn't like that," Theodosia murmured, almost to herself.

"No, he wasn't," said Shelby. "And he told me something else about you."

"What was that?" asked Theodosia.

"He said you were smart. And not just smart-smart, but clever, too."

"Kind of him," said Theodosia. She was beginning to get a funny vibe in the pit of her stomach. Probably, Shelby hadn't come here for a purely social call. And she wasn't here just to commiserate, either.

It took only a few moments for Shelby to drop her bombshell.

"I was hoping you could sort of . . . investigate," said Shelby. She shook her head sadly. "This whole drowning thing, I'm having a hard time buying it."

You, too? Theodosia thought.

But Theodosia's next words pretty much pooh-poohed Shelby's request. "I'm sorry, but you're talking to the wrong person. You should be trying to persuade Detective Tidwell to delve into this more thoroughly. To develop some sort of case."

"I did try," said Shelby.

"Okay," said Theodosia, playing it cool.

"And he believes it was an accident."

"Which it probably was," said Theodosia. It pretty much killed her to say that. Especially since she didn't believe it.

Shelby stared across the desk, her limpid brown eyes swimming with tears. "But you don't really believe that, do you?"

Theodosia's reply was practically a whisper. "No."

"Then could you sort of nose around? I know you've done investigations before. Parker told me all about it."

Still Theodosia hedged. "I don't know. Detective Tidwell would probably get awfully upset." Then again, when *wasn't* he upset?

Shelby gave a little shudder. "Tidwell. That man is definitely not a nice person. In fact, I had the dubious pleasure of meeting him last night."

Theodosia peered at Shelby with renewed interest. "You were there last night? At the Neptune Aquarium?"

Shelby bobbed her head. "Yes, but only for about thirty minutes. I helped Parker set up the tapas table and then I . . . I left."

"You went home?" asked Theodosia.

"That's right."

"Then how did you meet Detective Tidwell?"

Shelby wrapped her arms around herself and hunched forward. "He came to my house. With some other police officers. To deliver the bad news."

"Kind of him."

"Not really. He was basically deadpan about the whole thing." Shelby let loose another quick shudder. "*Dead.* Ooh. What a terrible choice of words."

Theodosia had a decision to make. She could put a commiserating arm around Shelby's shoulders, lead her to the front door, and bid the young woman good-bye. Or she could ask a few questions. Maybe probe a little deeper into what Parker had been involved in lately.

The choice was easy.

"Shelby, if I did explore a few angles, would you be able to tell me what had been going on in Parker's life?"

"I think so. I could try."

"Were there problems with his restaurant? With Solstice?"

Shelby nodded. "Some. Why?" She brightened. "Oh, you're looking for clues? For suspects?"

Theodosia let that question slide by her. "Was Parker involved in any disagreements that you know of? Personal or legal?"

"Mmm . . . maybe."

"I'm talking about vendors, business partners, or even customers," said Theodosia.

Shelby considered this. "I know for a fact that Parker was upset with a couple of people."

"Can you tell me who?"

"Joe Beaudry, for one," said Shelby.

"The lawyer," said Theodosia. She knew Joe Beaudry purely through his obnoxious TV commercials: cheesy thirty-second messages that promised Beaudry would handle your divorce, debts, or DUI. "What about Beaudry?" Theodosia asked.

"It had to do with financing," said Shelby. "Parker needed additional funding and Beaudry kind of led him on. I mean, Beaudry was coming into Solstice practically every night, rhapsodizing about their hot new partnership while he guzzled two-hundred-dollar bottles of Cristal or Château Latour. Then, after all the meetings and free dinners, Beaudry finally dropped the hammer and told Parker he wouldn't be able to finance his new restaurant after all."

"What new restaurant was that?"

"Parker wanted to open a seafood restaurant called Carolina Jack's. He'd drawn up plans for a raw bar as well as fine dining. He also hired a restaurant planner and had scouted a location."

"Where was that?" asked Theodosia.

"Fairly close to here," said Shelby. "The former Portofino's Pizza over on East Bay Street."

Theodosia knew the location. It would have made a fine choice, close to tourist areas, in a fun section of town. "Was there anyone else Parker might have been upset with? Or who was upset with him?"

Shelby put a hand to her forehead, as if trying to recollect some long-forgotten snippet of information. "There was another restaurant owner."

Theodosia felt another little twinge deep down in her gut.

"Do you know who it was? Someone local or . . . perhaps one who was located in Savannah?"

Shelby frowned. "I don't know." She swiped at her eyes again with her damp hanky. "Are you . . . will you still look into things?"

"I'll have to think about it," Theodosia told her. But deep in her heart Theodosia told herself, *I really do need to look into this.*

Theodosia didn't return to the scene of the crime, but she did return to Solstice. Right after lunch, once she was sure Drayton and Haley had customers and food service well in hand, she jumped in her Jeep and zipped across town. Bumping down a narrow cobblestone alley, she parked at the back door.

And wondered how many times in the past couple of years she'd casually navigated this back street, then parked here and run in? How many times, in more recent days, had Shelby done the same thing?

The restaurant looked closed, but Theodosia pounded on the back door anyway, in the off chance somebody might be there. And just when she was about to give up, the lock clicked, the door opened, and René Martine, the sous chef, stuck his head out the back door.

"Hey," René said, a smile blooming on his handsome face when he recognized her. "It's you." He opened the door wider to let her step inside.

René was half French, half African American, a talented young man who'd emigrated from Montserrat in the Caribbean and just recently graduated from Charleston's Johnson and Wales culinary school. Theodosia figured in another two years or so, René would be executive chef at one of Charleston's premier restaurants. That was, if he didn't open a place of his own.

"You okay?" Theodosia asked, giving René a quick hug.

René's face crumpled. "Not so good. Just . . . still in shock, I guess."

"Of course you are," said Theodosia. "It's impossible to prepare for a tragedy like this." She glanced into the kitchen, where baskets of green goods sat on the counter. "You're not prepping, are you? The restaurant's not going to be open tonight?"

René made a *What can you do?* gesture. "His brother, Charles, he says we should stay open."

Theodosia was shocked. "That's just plain weird! You'd think Charles would want to close for a few days, um, out of respect."

"Maybe he thinks because we're all on the payroll . . ."

"Maybe," said Theodosia. She drew breath and said, "So, have the police been by?"

René nodded. "They just left, maybe twenty minutes ago." His voice carried a pleasing, languid Caribbean lilt.

That was a positive sign, Theodosia decided. It meant Tidwell had given some credence to her fears. So, hopefully, he was proceeding full speed ahead, treating Parker's death as a possible homicide. "Do you know . . . did they find anything interesting in Parker's office, or take anything with them?"

"Not that I could tell," said René. "Mostly they just nosed around the place and took a few photos."

"Did the police go through Parker's computer?"

"One of them sat down and took a look. Then he e-mailed whatever he thought was significant to their tech people. He also stuck a flash drive in and copied everything."

"They'll send it all to the forensic computer lab," Theodosia murmured.

"Parker's computer wasn't password protected or anything," René added. "In fact, I don't think he'd updated his software for a while. There was just an old Word program he used for keeping track of menus and recipes."

"Did Parker have a calendar?"

"Probably. But I don't know where it is."

"Mind if I take a look? Go in his office?" *Yet again.*

René cast an appraising eye at her. "I don't think Parker would have minded. You know, back in the day, he was pretty crazy about you."

"Thank you," Theodosia said, her voice sounding dry and papery, just this side of choked. "That means a lot to me."

Theodosia was sitting in Parker's desk chair, spinning listlessly from side to side, when Chef Toby walked in.

"Find anything else?" he asked.

She shook her head. "But the police were just here, so maybe they uncovered something."

"You think?" said Chef Toby. He seemed doubtful, especially since their search last night hadn't produced much of anything.

"I know I asked you this before," said Theodosia, "but do you know if Parker was having problems or issues with anyone?"

René poked his head in. He'd obviously been listening. "That guy in Savannah," he said to Chef Toby, who nodded immediately.

"The scary guy?" said Theodosia. The restaurant guy Shelby had mentioned?

"Manship," said René. "His name is Lyle Manship."

"And he currently owns a couple of restaurants?" said Theodosia.

"Chimera, a fairly fancy restaurant, and another one named Violet's," said René.

"Successful?" asked Theodosia.

"According to the grapevine, yes," said René.

"And maybe someone local that Parker was having trouble with?"

Chef Toby and René stared at each other.

"News to me," said René, while Chef Toby just shrugged.

"What about Joe Beaudry?" said Theodosia. Shelby's story about the freeloading Beaudry was still fresh in her mind.

"That's right," said Chef Toby, "the lawyer."

"I think Beaudry might have promised some financing, then pulled it," said René.

"But it sounds as if Parker had more cause to be angry than Beaudry," Theodosia mused. After all, what would Beaudry have been upset about? There didn't seem to be any motive.

"Still," said René, "Beaudry's a sleazy guy."

Theodosia gazed at a red-and-yellow poster tacked to the wall, thinking about Joe Beaudry, feeling a certain fuzziness. As her mind rambled, she noted that the typeface on the poster said FUND-RAISER in bouncy black letters. Then Theodosia's mind seemed to snap back into focus and she said, "Perhaps I should pay Beaudry a visit."

A quick Google search revealed that Joe Beaudry's office was located over on Columbus Street. Theodosia thought for a minute, checked her watch, and decided she had time. After all, right now was always better than later. When you just showed up to ask questions, it gave people little time to prepare.

Some ten minutes later, Theodosia was standing outside a tall, elegant red brick building with narrow white shutters and a white door flanked by shiny brass sconces. But that was where any class or elegance ended.

Inside was a small waiting room, filled with a half-dozen tired-looking people sitting on ragtag pieces of furniture, and a reception desk staffed by a tired-looking receptionist.

"Just sign in," the receptionist told Theodosia without bothering to look up.

"I don't have an appointment," Theodosia told her. "I'm here on personal business."

The receptionist looked up.

Theodosia offered a wistful smile. "I'm afraid it concerns Parker Scully."

The receptionist, a fifty-something woman with frizzy red hair, wire-rimmed glasses, and a very kind face, said, "Wasn't that awful? I was just reading about it in the newspaper."

Sensing a kindred spirit, Theodosia said, "I was there at the Neptune Aquarium last night. I can't tell you how bad it was."

"And he was such a nice man, too," the receptionist said in hushed tones.

Theodosia glanced across the receptionist's desk and saw a wooden sign that spelled out BETTY. "Betty," she said, "I just need a minute with Joe."

Betty considered her request for a moment, then held up a finger and said, "Give me a sec." She stood up, smoothed her tight black skirt, and disappeared into a nearby office with a swish of taffeta. Thirty seconds later, Betty was back at her post. "You can go in, but Mr. Beaudry says he's only got two minutes. I'm afraid he has a very full afternoon."

"Understood," said Theodosia. "And thank you."

Joe Beaudry didn't bother to stand up when Theodosia entered his office. Instead, he looked up, creaked back in his chair, and said, "So you were there, huh?" He was a slat-thin man with a long, thin face and piercing dark eyes. He had a shock of unruly salt-and-pepper hair even though he looked to be in his midforties.

"That's right," said Theodosia. She crossed his office swiftly and seated herself in one of the black leather club chairs that faced his desk. "And it wasn't a pretty sight."

Beaudry studied her for a few moments, then said, "Seeing as how it's not within my power to bring him back, how is it I can help you?"

"You can answer a few questions," said Theodosia.

Beaudry offered a thin smile. "A lady with questions. What kind of questions?"

"I'm a friend of the family," said Theodosia, "and I'm trying to straighten out a few matters."

"What matters would those be?"

"Concerning his restaurant."

"Are you in the restaurant business?" Beaudry asked.

"In a manner of speaking, yes," said Theodosia. "I own the Indigo Tea Shop over on Church Street."

"A *tea* shop," said Beaudry. He crossed his legs, jiggled his foot.

Theodosia had the feeling Beaudry might be playing with her. "That's right," she said. "But what I'm really interested in is knowing something more about the financing deal you and Parker had kicked around."

Beaudry shrugged his narrow shoulders. "There really wasn't a deal."

"But the two of you talked about a deal."

"Yeah, we talked," said Beaudry. "But we never came to any agreement."

"You were going to finance his expansion," said Theodosia. She gazed about Beaudry's office, saw a few framed photos, antique golf clubs crossed and mounted on the wall, some kind of citation from the Rotarians.

"Again," said Beaudry, "we talked about it."

"So he never expanded," said Theodosia.

"Mainly because Parker wasn't able to obtain financing."

"From you or the bank," said Theodosia. "Why was that exactly?"

Beaudry shrugged. "He hadn't done all that well in the past year."

"A bad economy, an economic slowdown," Theodosia prompted.

Beaudry nodded. "All the restaurants got hit. You should know that."

Theodosia smiled. In all honesty, and knock on wood, the Indigo Tea Shop hadn't suffered much in this tough economy. Whether it was loyal customers, an uptick in catering jobs, or people who came tumbling in because the cozy tea shop offered a momentary respite from hard times, the Indigo Tea Shop was more than holding its own.

"Tell me," said Theodosia, "just what kind of restaurant did Parker want to open?" She knew the answer; she just wanted to hear Beaudry's answer.

"Seafood," he said. "Parker wanted to pattern it after a little seafood restaurant he used to frequent on Johns Island."

Theodosia knew the place exactly. Houlihans. Great fresh oysters and cracked crab, with a killer cilantro-flavored hot sauce made fresh in-house. Parker had taken her there once when they'd driven over to Oak Point to play golf.

"But you two could never agree on terms," she said.

"No, we couldn't," said Beaudry. "And now . . ." Beaudry sighed deeply and shook his head. "Now he's gone."

"It must have come as quite a shock to you," said Theodosia. She decided Beaudry didn't look a bit sad. Just casual and relaxed. Was he too relaxed? Good question.

"Yeah, the whole grisly story's been played out in the news," said Beaudry, still leaning back in his chair.

Theodosia glanced at his desk and noticed the *Post and Courier* sitting there, folded to the front-page story about the drowning at the aquarium.

Except, right now, Theodosia was pretty sure it hadn't been a drowning.

6

When Theodosia arrived back at the Indigo Tea Shop, afternoon tea was well under way. A half-dozen or so tables were occupied and Drayton was buzzing about, teapots clutched in both hands. She smiled, feeling comforted and grateful that her little shop was in such good hands. But when she saw Detective Burt Tidwell's bulk hunkered at the small table by the stone fireplace, Theodosia's smile slipped from her face.

"Tidwell," she murmured.

Drayton nodded. "He's been waiting for you."

Theodosia hustled over and stared down at Tidwell with marked disapproval.

Burt Tidwell was sprawled at his table looking carefree and casual, like the lord of the manor who didn't have a care in the world. His bright eyes roved hungrily across the basket of cream scones and peach-pecan bread that sat in front of him as he methodically stirred his cup of tea. In his giant paw, the tiny silver spoon looked like something from a doll's tea set.

"How nice that you've shown up to enjoy a tasty afternoon repast," Theodosia told Tidwell, biting off each word sharply. "Instead of investigating Parker's death."

Tidwell ignored her until he'd finally finished his annoying stirring. Then he set down his spoon and gazed at her with beady bright eyes that revealed nothing. "You were right," he said, finally, in a conversational tone of voice.

Theodosia blinked and stared back at him. What was he being elusive about now? "Right about what?"

"Sit, please," said Tidwell.

Theodosia pursed her lips and slid stiffly into the chair across from Tidwell.

"Parker didn't drown," said Tidwell, lasering dark eyes on her. "In fact, I just received a preliminary report from the coroner and . . ."

"Oh, dear Lord." Theodosia put one hand to her chest, as if to still her suddenly lurching heart. Tidwell's words hadn't just sent shock waves through her, they were the harsh, final truth she truly wasn't mentally prepared for.

Tidwell leaned forward and spoke rapidly to her. "Do you want to hear this? Because it's nasty and it's rough. And if you're going to go all bleary-eyed and slip into a crying jag, I'm not uttering another word."

Theodosia squared her shoulders and pulled herself together. "I want to hear this, I really do." She folded her hands in her lap and clenched them tightly, preparing for the worst. For the raw, unadulterated truth.

"All right, then," said Tidwell. He plucked a cream scone from the basket and set it on his plate. "You were quite correct last evening," he told her. "Mr. Scully's death does appear to be a homicide after all."

Theodosia dug her nails into the palms of her hands so

hard, they made crescent-shaped indentations. "I knew it," she choked out.

"This morning," said Tidwell, "one of the marine biologists discovered an aquascaping tool lying at the bottom of the Ocean Wall exhibit."

"An aquascaping tool," Theodosia repeated. "What's . . . ?"

"An implement not nearly as pleasant as it sounds," said Tidwell. He took his butter knife and split his scone lengthwise. "Basically thirty-two-inch-long surgical steel scissors with a serrated blade. Of the type medical professionals refer to as a Metzenbaum. Only much larger. Obviously."

"Dear Lord," said Theodosia. This was even worse than she'd feared.

"The aquarium people fished it out and one of my men carted it over to the ME's office." Tidwell reached over and swooped up an enormous dollop of raspberry jam, then slathered it heavily onto his scone.

"And there was a match," Theodosia said, in a dull voice. "The blades being consistent with the injuries on Parker's hands."

"Yes," said Tidwell. "As you so eloquently put it, there was a match."

Theodosia grimaced. "I knew it."

Tidwell took a large bite and did an exaggerated eye roll. "There's more," he said as he chewed.

"What?"

"A note was found in Mr. Scully's pocket. A partially decomposed note." He fluttered sticky fingers. "I say *decomposed* only because it was written on paper and subsequently submerged in water."

"What did the note say?" Theodosia pounced on his words. "Was anything readable?"

Tidwell set down what was left of his scone and reached for a file folder that lay at his elbow. He dug in, pulled out a sheet of paper, then slid it across the table. "This is a copy of what was recovered."

Theodosia stared at the sheet of paper. It was a black-and-white laser print. Outputted, no doubt, from a digital photo taken at the police lab. What she saw was a ragged, partially decomposed typed note. Most of the words were missing; the ones still readable were badly smudged. But she could just make out the faint message.

Please meet me
easily explain my

"Meet me where?" asked Theodosia.

"I have to assume it was somewhere near the top of that enormous fish tank," said Tidwell. He picked up his scone and resumed nibbling.

"They were giving tours last night," said Theodosia, half closing her eyes, thinking back. "For the big-buck donors. The . . . what would you call it . . . behind-the-scenes tour."

"Unfortunate," said Tidwell.

"Easily explain what?" Theodosia asked, focusing again on the printout of the tattered note.

"No idea," said Tidwell.

"It sounds as if Parker had questioned something," said Theodosia. "And the murderer . . . we have to assume this note was written by the murderer . . . wanted to explain himself."

"Or herself," said Tidwell.

"So there's a distinct possibility that Parker was lured to his death," said Theodosia.

"A small possibility," Tidwell allowed.

"Have you spoken with Chef Toby?" she asked.

"Only for a couple of minutes last night."

"Did he mention that Parker had dealings with some guys in Savannah?"

"When questioned, Mr. Crisp mentioned that to one of

my investigators, yes," said Tidwell. "We dug further and discovered the key person is a man by the name of Lyle Manship who owns various restaurants, among other things."

"Did Chef Toby tell your investigator that Manship was kind of a scary guy?" Theodosia asked.

"I believe he alluded to it."

Theodosia drew breath. "*Is* Manship a scary guy?"

Tidwell glanced about the tea shop, as if to make sure no one was listening in on their conversation. Then he leaned forward and said, "I tell you this in complete confidence."

"Yes," said Theodosia. "Of course."

"In the past, Lyle Manship has been linked to smuggling and laundering money."

"Seriously?" What had Parker gotten himself into?

"Let me emphasize *linked*," said Tidwell. "No charges have ever stuck. The man is like Teflon."

"Smuggling what?" asked Theodosia.

"Narcotics."

"And laundering money? That sounds serious."

"Trust me," said Tidwell, "both the Justice and Treasury Departments are vehemently opposed to such things."

Theodosia watched Tidwell finish his scone, then reach for a second one, as she continued to turn things over in her mind. This investigation—because that was what it was now, an official police investigation—seemed to be careening off at a crazy angle. Could Parker have been involved in drugs? Or money laundering? Her instincts told her no. Absolutely not. That he had been interested only in a restaurant deal. Still, Parker could have been pulled into something unwittingly.

"I have a confession to make," said Theodosia. In light of what Tidwell had just shared with her, she felt the need to come clean.

One corner of Tidwell's pudgy mouth turned downward. "What's that?"

"I went to Parker's office last night and looked around."

Tidwell's expression never changed. "Doesn't surprise me."

Theodosia continued. "And I have to say, that empty file kind of threw me."

Tidwell chewed thoughtfully. "The Current Projects file? Yes, when I skimmed the officer's report I also found it strange."

"My guess is that someone stole the full contents."

"That someone being the murderer?" said Tidwell.

"Not sure," said Theodosia. "Maybe. If there was some kind of incriminating evidence in the file . . . about financing or property or something."

Tidwell swallowed. "All in all, a very large *if.*"

"What did your guys find in Parker's computer?"

"Basically nothing. It's almost as if he was a technophobe."

"He was, sort of," said Theodosia, smiling wistfully. Although Parker hadn't been as bad as Drayton, who eschewed cell phones and still played vinyl records. "So what's next?"

"For you, nothing. For me, I continue to investigate," said Tidwell.

"But you're going to keep me in the loop," said Theodosia.

"No," said Tidwell.

"Can I make a copy of the note?" Theodosia asked.

"For what purpose?" said Tidwell.

"Just my own . . . edification."

"No," said Tidwell.

"You're not being very forthcoming," said Theodosia. "After all, I'm the one who spotted the defensive wounds on Parker's hands. I'm the one who kicked off this investigation."

"And the Robbery-Homicide Division of the Charleston Police Department commends you for that," said Tidwell. "In fact, you have our undying gratitude." He reached for a piece of sweet bread, then changed his mind.

"Except . . . ?" said Theodosia.

"Except from here on, my dear Miss Browning, you are hereby relegated to concerned citizen status. And now, if you'll excuse me, I have an appointment with the Coast Guard."

"Are you serious about me staying out of this?"

"Please," said Tidwell. "Whoever committed this crime is a very dangerous and sick individual. Please leave any and all investigating to the professionals."

With Tidwell's words still echoing in her head, Theodosia grabbed a cup of carrot bisque soup and holed up in her office.

Licking my wounds, she decided. After Tidwell's warning not to get involved.

But Theodosia knew she was already involved. Her former relationship with Parker bore that out. Her discovery of his body. Her assessment of his defensive wounds.

She had a few spoonfuls of soup and drifted off into deep thought.

A few minutes later, Theodosia was aware of Drayton standing in her doorway. He was holding a cup of Darjeeling tea and a cream scone.

"Hey," she said.

Drayton took a step forward. "Come along inside . . . we'll see if tea and buns can make the world a better place."

"That's from *The Wind in the Willows*," said Theodosia, smiling.

"I thought that might elicit a favorable reaction from you," said Drayton. "A smile, anyway."

"You know me well," said Theodosia. "You know what touches my heart."

Drayton set the tea and scone on her desk. "You're going to do it, aren't you?" His lips were pursed and a hopeful look illuminated his lined face.

"Do what?" said Theodosia.

Drayton hesitated for a moment, then said. "Avenge Parker's death."

Theodosia drew breath and squared her shoulders. "That not only sounds quaint, it sounds positively medieval. As if I'm going to don a suit of armor and ride out to slay the black knight."

"That's pretty much it," said Haley, who'd slipped in behind Drayton. She set a small bowl of maple pecan butter on Theodosia's desk and added, "After all, Theo, you're the one who always sticks up for the underdog."

Lucky me, thought Theodosia.

7

Even though the evening was still warm, Theodosia had a small fire crackling away in her brick fireplace. Red and blue flames snapped and licked, dancing off the wall of beveled cypress and lending a distinct air of coziness.

Stretched out on her damask sofa, Theodosia surveyed her little cottage and, once again, felt she'd done the exact right thing in buying it. The money had been a stretch, of course, but all her life she'd been a renter. And now, this little cottage with the charming name of Hazelhurst had become her pride and joy.

And what a cottage it was! The exterior was quirky and adorable—really a classic Tudor-style cottage, asymmetrical in design and complete with rough cedar tiles that replicated a thatched roof. Cross gables, arched doors, and a lovely turret added finishing touches, along with lush tendrils of ivy that curled up the sides. If Hansel and Gretel were suddenly dropped into the historic district, they'd undoubtedly turn up at the front door!

The interior had also captured Theodosia's heart. The foyer featured a brick floor and walls of hunter green with antique brass sconces. The living room had a beamed ceiling and polished wood floor. Her own chintz and damask furniture fit in perfectly as well as her blue-and-gold Aubusson carpet, antique highboy, and tasty oil paintings.

A log popped loudly and Earl Grey, her trusty Dalbrador, lifted his fine head.

"How are you doing?" Theodosia asked him. "Digested your supper yet?" She had changed into leggings and a T-shirt and was planning to take Earl Grey for his evening constitutional. Generally, they strolled down the back alley, turned into the historic district, and ended up at White Point Gardens. There, with the surging Atlantic as a backdrop, they could run together while the wind pounded away, stirring up ions and intoxicating sips of salt air.

"Okay," she said, grabbing his leash. "Time to head out."

Which was exactly when the phone rang.

"Saved by the bell," she told Earl Grey, as she reached for the receiver. "Hello?"

"I leave you alone for a few days and look what happens. You get yourself involved in a murder mystery!"

"Max!" Theodosia squealed. "Hello!" Then, "How did you know?"

"Sweetheart," said Max, "you made the front page of the *New York Times*."

Theodosia was shocked. "Seriously?"

"Well," Max amended, "maybe it was only the second or third page, but the story was there just the same. With your name and everything."

"Wow," said Theodosia. *Doggone. Now what does he think of me?*

"It must have been a terrible shock," Max said in a quieter tone. He cleared his throat. "I mean, you knew him pretty well."

"You have no idea," said Theodosia. "The whole episode at the aquarium was . . . bizarre."

"And the police are investigating?" Max hesitated. "The news story wasn't entirely clear on whether the death was accidental or . . ."

"Murder," finished Theodosia.

"Huh?" said Max. "Is that what you think? That this was a homicide?" He sounded shocked. And a little nervous, too.

Theodosia decided it might be better to downplay that aspect. "I'm not sure what to think," she told Max. "Since the police are still investigating."

"Mmm," he grunted.

"So, for now, it's all kind of in limbo." She winced at her little white lie. *Why am I downplaying this? Because I'm talking to my new boyfriend about my old boyfriend's death? Yes, that's right. And trying not to sound too sad in the process. Awkward.*

Theodosia hastily changed the subject. "When are you coming home?"

"Not till the end of the week," said Max. "There's an auction at Sotheby's on Thursday when the Impressionists come up for bid. And I still need to meet with one of the editors at *Arts Horizon* magazine. I'm trying to sweet-talk them into doing a story about our collection of English furniture." He hesitated. "Or at least a sidebar. Donors always like to see a little publicity. They enjoy the notoriety and it helps reassure them that their money is being well spent."

"I'm sure they do," said Theodosia. She wasn't sure whether Max not coming back until Friday or Saturday was welcome news or not. On the one hand, Max's absence conveniently afforded her personal space so she could conduct her own brand of investigation. On the other hand, she was disappointed since she was truly missing him.

"I'll call you tomorrow," Max promised. "And try not to think about this drowning thing too much, okay?"

"Okay."

"Promise?"

Theodosia winced again. "I promise."

Theodosia kept her promise for all of about five minutes—
the time it took to scoot upstairs and plunk herself down in
front of her laptop. She wiggled her fingers above the keys,
then hastily Googled Chimera, the restaurant down in
Savannah. That brought her to Bumbershoot Incorporated,
the umbrella company for both Chimera and Violet's.

She clicked ABOUT US and scanned a short paragraph
about the company. It was owned, as far as she could tell,
solely by Lyle Manship. In fact, there was even a photo of
Manship, a tall, olive-skinned man with a barracuda smile.
The smiling, genial, glad-handing owner.

Or was he? If one of Manship's sidelines was laundering
money, then were these restaurants simply a front? Did his
real business involve shuttling money to offshore banks in
Grand Cayman or Belize?

And who did he shuttle money for? Tidwell had mentioned that Manship might be involved in narcotics, so obviously it had to be dope dealers. Or even some cartel.
Theodosia's heart sank another couple of notches. What had
Parker gotten himself into?

And what about the note the police had recovered from
inside Parker's pocket? Could Manship possibly have written
it? Theodosia's eyes fluttered closed as she recalled the frag-
ment Tidwell had shown her.

Please meet me . . . easily explain my

Earl Grey came up alongside her and poked his head in
her lap. Theodosia ran her fingertips absently across the top
of his furry forehead, thinking about the note, about Manship, his restaurants, and his unsavory activities.

So what now? Should she call Manship? Just ask him out-
right about his dealings with Parker Scully?

But that would be a tough way to get any sort of realistic answer. He'd probably just blow her off, lie to her, or worse yet, simply hang up on her. And it would be next to impossible to get any sort of gut read on Manship. Or intuitive read, or whatever you wanted to call it.

So what then? Just drive down there? Arrive unannounced and hope for a meeting? The idea was brash, and brazen, and . . . it just might work.

Theodosia shut down her computer and stood up. She let the notion swirl around in her brain, liking it more and more, deciding that acting on impulse might be the smartest, cagiest way to ferret out information.

In fact, she'd drive down to Savannah first thing tomorrow morning. If she got an early start, she could be back at the tea shop by noon. Drayton and Haley could easily handle things until then.

"Okay," Theodosia said to Earl Grey, praying she didn't lose her nerve, hoping it wouldn't evaporate come morning. "Time to take that walk."

The evening was perfect. Sixty degrees, stars twinkling in the inky blue sky, a light wind blowing in. Theodosia and Earl Grey wandered through the historic district for fifteen minutes, dodging down narrow brick alleys, peering through wrought-iron gates at elegant private courtyards, and tiptoeing between narrow buildings on old walks that had once been reserved for servants. This part of the city was magical to Theodosia. She loved to imagine how it had been one hundred fifty or even two hundred years ago, when coaches pulled by high-stepping horses rolled up to these massive mansions and disgorged fine ladies in hoop skirts and men wearing high collars and long jackets. It must have been magnificent. And ethereal, too. Because that life hadn't lasted.

Now, many of the Italianate and Greek Revival mansions that lined the Battery had been turned into B and Bs, the carriage houses (like hers) converted into small homes. The wealth generated by the old indigo and rice plantations had simply evaporated.

Yes, Theodosia decided, you still needed big bucks to live in these old homes. But now the money was earned in more traditional ways.

They ran along the shore then, waves crashing in, then receding with a whoosh and a hiss, the sound echoing and reechoing in Theodosia's head.

Twenty minutes later, muscles thoroughly warmed, both of them a little breathless, Theodosia and Earl Grey turned up the walk for home.

But they were not alone.

Someone was also striding up the walk to Dougan Granville's massive front door. A figure that looked awfully familiar.

Theodosia glanced back at the curb. Yes, there was a dark-green Jaguar parked there. So . . . it had to be Delaine.

"Delaine," Theodosia called out. "Hello."

Delaine jumped like she'd been singled out by an unruly lynch mob. She whirled in a three-hundred-sixty-degree circle, finally spotted Theodosia, then put a trembling hand to her chest.

"You *scared* me," she said, sounding petulant and out of sorts.

"Sorry," said Theodosia, "I didn't mean to." Theodosia couldn't resist. "I'm on the Neighborhood Watch committee, you know." Now she was grinning to herself. "And when I saw a stranger sneaking up the walk . . ."

"I was hardly *sneaking*," came Delaine's indignant reply. She raised a large white shopping bag and dangled it. "I was bringing *dinner*."

"Ah."

"Poor Dougan works such terribly long hours," Delaine lamented, "and there's so much turmoil going on at his law firm right now."

"Big case?" asked Theodosia. She knew Granville was always embroiled in some big criminal case.

"Bad partner," said Delaine. "Someone they're trying to oust." She said it like they were trying to flick a bug off the table. "Anyway, in the interest of Dougan's well-being, I've taken to picking up dinner for him at Aubergine."

"Lucky him," said Theodosia. She wouldn't mind having dinner delivered to her each night from a four-star restaurant whose specials included sirloin tips, poached salmon, and veal chops.

"Yes," said Delaine. "Dougan is always crashingly busy. Then again, he *is* one of Charleston's leading attorneys."

"It's kind of you to be so concerned about Mr. Granville's nutrition," said Theodosia. She figured that Delaine's bringing dinner to Granville every night was her sneaky way to keep a keen eye on her new beau. Granville *did* have a reputation as a ladies' man. Until he started seeing Delaine, he'd squired a different woman about town practically every week.

"I do what I can," Delaine said, in a tone that dripped with false modesty. She gave a curt wave and said, "Good night, Theo. Have a pleasant evening." Then she continued up Granville's front walk.

"Delaine?"

Delaine hesitated. "Yes?"

"Do you think you could get me a copy of last night's guest list?" She knew Dougan Granville would have one. He was on the Neptune Aquarium's board of directors, after all. Now, even in the dark, Theodosia could see Delaine frowning, calculating how much trouble passing on the list might cause.

"Why do you want it, dear?" Delaine's voice floated back to her.

"I'd like to satisfy my curiosity," said Theodosia.

Delaine hesitated at the front door of Granville's mansion. Shifting her black tote bag and her white plastic bag of take-out to her left hand, she arched her finely plucked brows and threw Theodosia a truly sanctimonious gaze. "I'll try, Theo. But you know what they say . . ."

"I know, I know," said Theodosia, "curiosity killed the cat." It was one of Delaine's favorite phrases. Spinning on her heels, Theodosia quickly led Earl Grey across the damp grass to her own front door. Then she stopped and gazed down at him, a smile playing at her lips. "But I'm safe," she told Earl Grey in a soft voice. "Because I have a dog."

8

❧

The one hundred miles that stretched between Charleston and Savannah was truly a little slice of heaven—a ribbon of road that undulated through pine forests and picturesque villages and took her past tiny white churches, often known as praise houses, and farm stands that sold peaches, asparagus, purple cabbage, and okra. The sun shone down in a powder-blue sky and, for a few minutes, Theodosia was able to forget about Parker. Life felt good.

When Theodosia passed the halfway point, what she figured was the point of no return, she pulled out her cell phone and called the tea shop.

Drayton answered. "Where are you? It sounds like you're calling from inside a garbage can."

"Just rolling through Ashepoo," she told him.

There were a few seconds of silence, and then Drayton said, "What?" It came out as a rather uncharacteristic squawk. "Are you serious? Does this mean you're not coming in today?"

"I'll be back in time for lunch," Theodosia assured him.

"But I have some business to take care of. And, well, I don't particularly want this to get out . . ."

"Okay," Drayton said, cautiously.

"But I plan to talk to that restaurant fellow in Savannah, the one Parker had been dickering with a few months ago."

"Savannah!" Drayton burst out. "That's a long drive. Why didn't you just phone him up?"

"Because then I wouldn't be able to read his face when I ask about his business dealings with Parker. I wouldn't be able to get a visceral feel for his body language."

"All that from a single meeting?" asked Drayton.

"Maybe," said Theodosia. Was she expecting too much? "At least I hope so."

Drayton digested this for a moment, then said, "Excuse me, but have you been studying law enforcement textbooks in your off hours?"

The question was so out in left field that Theodosia had to laugh. "No. Why do you ask?"

Drayton let loose a dry chuckle. "Because you sound suspiciously like an FBI profiler."

I wish, Theodosia thought as she clicked off. *I really wish I were that smart.*

Savannah was as charming as ever. Elegant homes festooned with lacy wrought iron, lush and large city squares, vest-pocket parks, and an abundance of pattering fountains. Though the architecture and ambience were somewhat reminiscent of Charleston, Theodosia definitely felt that the pace here was a tad slower. In fact, when locals pronounced their vowels, it seemed more like a leisurely exercise.

Checking the printout from her computer, Theodosia drove down Harris Street, turned on Abercorn, and immediately spotted a tasteful painted wooden sign for the restaurant Chimera.

Chimera was housed in an old mansion with Regency-period architecture along with plenty of fancy scrollwork and Greek motifs.

She climbed the front steps, knocked on the polished wooden double doors, and waited. Nothing. No footsteps, nobody front and center to buzz her into the inner sanctum.

Probably, she decided, because there was nobody here?

Descending the front steps, Theodosia followed a narrow brick driveway around to the back, past a tangle of magnolias where flocks of butterflies fluttered and random bees buzzed. She continued under a columned stone portico and directly up to a large wooden door, what had probably been the service entrance when this served as someone's grand home. What was probably *still* the service entrance.

Theodosia gave three sharp raps with her knuckles and waited. A few minutes later, a young woman came to the door. She had a distracted look and a cap of brown curls, and she wore purple horn-rimmed glasses that coordinated nicely with her mauve blouse and cream linen slacks. Maybe an office manager or bookkeeper?

Theodosia smiled a pleasant smile and said, "I'm looking for Lyle Manship?"

The woman offered a hesitant smile. "Were you supposed to meet him here?" Her nose twitched like a suspicious rabbit. "Did he mess up his appointment times again?" She looked like she might be planning to give Manship a good talking-to.

"No, nothing like that," Theodosia assured her. "I was just in the neighborhood and decided to drop by. Really," she assured the woman, "this is just an impromptu visit."

"In that case," said the woman, "he should be over at Violet's right now. That's where our main office is."

"Of course," said Theodosia, giving what she hoped was a brilliant smile, along with an Academy Award–worthy performance. "Violet's."

"You know how to get there?"

"Back down Abercorn and then . . ."

"Past Oglethorpe Square, turn left at Reynolds Square . . ."

"And then down St. Julian," said Theodosia.

"That's right. Almost to the City Market," the woman instructed. "Parking lot's in back."

"Thank you," said Theodosia.

Legend holds that General Sherman, after his brutal and infamous "March to the Sea," finally relented when he reached Savannah. He gathered his wits about him, called a halt to the senseless burning and pillaging, and decreed that the city of Savannah was far too beautiful, the women amazingly gracious, and the parties far too elegant for him to wreak any more havoc. Savannah, it seemed, was the perfect city in which to enjoy a little R&R.

Thus, street after street of antebellum mansions, Federal period townhouses, and entire districts of Victorian homes remained historically intact and too gorgeous for words.

Theodosia drove down St. Julian Street, past Mulberry Books, the French Bouquet Boutique, and the Blue Moon Tea Shop. If this were another day, a leisure day, she'd park her car and wander through City Market, on the lookout for local art, gourmet goodies, or some wonderful hand-thrown clay teapot.

But she was a woman on a mission and she'd just spotted her destination. Or so she hoped.

Theodosia was pleasantly surprised to find that Violet's was billed as a garden café. Better still, an outdoor café filled with trellises and arbors, abundant pots of bougainvillea and magnolias, and smaller pots of violets. And since the café was open for business, she figured she had a good chance of catching the elusive Mr. Manship.

Strolling into Violet's, Theodosia was enticed by the aroma of spices, citrus, fresh coffee beans, and flowers.

The hostess, a young woman in a tight blue T-shirt and long, diaphanous skirt, greeted her. "Table for one?"

"Actually," said Theodosia, "I'm here to see Lyle Manship. Is he in?"

"Just arrived ten minutes ago," said the hostess. "Did you have an appointment?"

"I'm sort of popping in," Theodosia told the hostess. She gave a quick smile, trying her best to project the air of an old friend dropping in for a quick visit, a fun surprise.

Obviously her ruse worked, because she was dutifully led back to Lyle Manship's office, where the hostess pushed the door open and said, as a hasty introduction, "Someone here to see you."

Manship glanced up from behind an acre of mahogany desk. He was forty-something, fairly good-looking, with olive skin and lots of white teeth. Two framed photos on his desk showed a pretty dark-haired wife posing with two sons, each with heroic sets of teeth.

"How can I help you?" Manship asked, a quizzical look on his face.

"I'm a friend of Parker Scully," Theodosia told him.

"Ah . . ." Manship was immediately on his feet, a look of sympathy on his face and his arm outstretched to shake her hand. "I just heard the news. What a tragedy. And such terrible circumstances." An overindulgence of Hugo Boss cologne wafted about him.

"I understand the two of you were business partners," said Theodosia, trying hard not to sneeze.

"And your interest is . . . ?" Manship was pleasant but guarded.

"Just following up on some business for his firm," said Theodosia. Ouch. There was another little white lie. And they were starting to add up. Good thing it was a brilliantly sunny day and no chance for a bolt of lightning to come crashing down from the sky and incinerate her.

"I see," said Manship. "Please sit down." Theodosia made herself comfortable in an upholstered armchair while Manship eased himself back into his desk chair.

"The fact of the matter is," said Manship, picking up a black Montblanc pen and lining it up against his iPhone, "we *weren't* business partners. Parker and I talked about a couple of deals, but in the end nothing came of it."

"You were going to open a restaurant together," said Theodosia.

"That's correct." Manship stared at her for a moment, then leaned sideways and pulled open a desk drawer. He selected a file, placed it carefully on his desk, then flipped it open so it faced toward her. "Azalea," he told her. "That was our working title. With a menu aimed at gourmet Southern food." He grinned, thinking about it. "Think Old South décor but with a contemporary spin on Southern cuisine. We even had an old warehouse space picked out and were planning to decorate with blowups of antique Mathew Brady photos."

"Neat," said Theodosia.

"With luxurious brocade chairs set around old wooden plantation tables," Manship continued. "And the menu . . . Parker had amazing ideas for entrées such as blackened catfish with caviar, crab tacos with ponzu sauce, and short ribs with grits and jicama."

"This is a very cool idea," said Theodosia, shuffling through the pages, picking up on his enthusiasm.

"Isn't it?" said Manship. "And there are lots more plans, specifics that Parker had worked out. It's just too bad we couldn't hammer out a deal."

Theodosia decided to be bold. "Why couldn't you?"

Manship's face remained placid. "Financing. Basically, I liked the idea of going into business with Parker. He had this incredible enthusiasm and was amazingly creative when it came to concept, menu, and décor. Well, you know him, so you know exactly what I'm talking about. Unfortunately, he wasn't able to come up with the working capital."

She glanced at the papers again, wondering if any of the typed words matched the typography on the recovered note. Hard to tell. "And you could."

There was just a brief hesitation. "Yes."

"So you let a terrific deal slip through your fingers? Just like that?"

Manship steepled his fingers together, then pulled them apart, making a small gesture of inevitability. "It's the nature of business," he told her. "There's always a raft of interesting opportunities out there, but not all of them work out. And, of course, not all of them align with my particular interests."

"And just what are your interests?" asked Theodosia.

Manship smiled a self-satisfied smile. "Making a profit, of course."

"Spoken like a true businessman," said Theodosia.

Manship held his smile.

"So, help me out here," said Theodosia. "You hadn't seen Parker or spoken to him since you cut off your dealings?"

Manship gave an offhand shrug. "Actually, I had dinner at Solstice last Saturday night."

"Seriously?" First and foremost in her mind sprang the question, *Could Manship have lifted the missing file? And if so, why? To steal Parker's complete plans for the concept of gourmet Southern and hijack it for himself? Hmm . . . possibly. Could have happened.*

"I was in Charleston for the weekend, visiting friends," said Manship.

Theodosia eyed him carefully. "Did you, by any chance, attend the opening at the Neptune Aquarium?"

Manship shook his head. "No, no, I was back home by then." He seemed to take a small amount of pleasure in her disappointment. "So," he added, "you've come into my office unannounced and asked a lot of very direct questions. I, in turn, have pretty much opened the kimono for you." He gave a genial smile, a philosophical shrug. Both visual cues that this impromptu meeting was over.

"I thank you for the information," said Theodosia, standing up to leave. She was disappointed but tried not to show it. After all her questions and efforts, she hadn't really discovered anything of value at all.

Manship stood up, too, then seemed to waver. It looked like he wanted to add one more thing to the conversation.

"What?" said Theodosia.

"You know, he said, "if you're trying to piece together your friend's recent business history, you really should be talking to Peaches Pafford."

"Excuse me?" said Theodosia. Peaches Pafford was the owner of the four-star restaurant Aubergine. The same upscale, au courant restaurant that Delaine had been frequenting for take-out food. Even though takeout from a white-linen, four-star, maybe even five-star restaurant seemed a little strange. "Why Peaches Pafford?"

Manship rocked back on his heels. "Because, not so long ago, Peaches extended a rather generous offer to your friend."

"Um . . . what?" said Theodosia, not quite comprehending.

"She tried to buy Solstice from him," said Manship.

Theodosia's jaw pretty much dropped to the floor. "I had no idea Solstice was even for sale!"

"I didn't think it was, either," said Manship. His hand reached out and swiped up the iPhone from his desk. "But if you've ever butted heads with the indomitable Peaches, you'd know just how persuasive she can be."

9

 ❧

Theodosia sailed in the back door of the Indigo Tea Shop, dumped her handbag on top of her desk, then slipped into the steamy kitchen, where lunch service was in full swing.

"Apologies," she said to Haley. "I thought I'd be back sooner."

"No problem," said Haley, without bothering to look up. She was busy slicing fresh mozzarella and plum tomatoes, in between peeks inside her oven where something wonderful bubbled away. As Theodosia looped an apron around her neck, she detected the mingled aromas of cinnamon, oregano, melted cheese, and tea.

Haley finished her chopping and slicing, then finally looked up. "We've got a great menu today," she told Theodosia.

"We have a great menu every day," said Theodosia.

Haley chuckled. "You know what I mean."

"Yes, I do," said Theodosia. "So today we're serving . . ."

"Caprese tea sandwiches, zucchini soup, and toffee bars."

"And some cheesy, bubbly goodness from the oven," said Theodosia.

"Red pepper quiche," said Haley.

"So how can I help?" Theodosia asked, staring at a dozen white luncheon plates that looked like they'd been dealt out in a card game.

Haley pulled a baking sheet of toasted flatbread from the oven and said, "You can start by slicing these into wedges. Six per flatbread."

"I need two more cups of soup," Drayton called out as he stuck his head in the door. Then he caught sight of Theodosia and said, "Oh, the prodigal owner returns."

"I told you I'd be back in time for lunch," said Theodosia.

"So you did," said Drayton. He peered at her, curiosity evident on his face. "So, did you sleuth anything out on your whirlwind trip down to Savannah?"

"Not really," said Theodosia. "Not as much as I'd hoped."

"Drayton and I were talking before," said Haley, as she expertly plopped lettuce leaves, pesto, and tomato slices onto her flatbread wedges. "And I told him I simply don't trust that girl."

"That girl," Theodosia repeated. "I take it you're referring to Shelby? The girlfriend?"

Haley let loose an indelicate snort. "Some girlfriend."

"Why do you say that?" asked Theodosia.

"Because I saw her Sunday night," said Haley. "When they were setting up at the Neptune Aquarium."

Theodosia nodded. "Shelby told me she'd helped with the tapas bar."

"No way," said Haley, putting some grit in her voice. "Little Miss Girlfriend stood around looking like a princess and never lifted her little pinkie. Parker and Chef Toby did all the work."

"Just because the girl remained idle or wasn't helpful," said Drayton, "doesn't mean she's a murderer." He inclined his head slightly. "Case in point, half the youth today."

"There's something about her," said Haley, who wasn't about to waver from her conviction, "that I don't like."

"You saw her for all of two minutes," said Theodosia. "So it's difficult to form a truly, um, *balanced* judgment." She wanted to dismiss Haley's suspicions, she really did. But she was strangely hesitant. For some reason, Haley had the uncanny knack of being spot on in her judgment of people. Most of the time, anyway.

"Haley," said Theodosia, hastily arranging strawberry slices and bunches of tiny purple champagne grapes on luncheon plates, "you have a lot of friends who are chefs and bakers. What's the local scuttlebutt concerning Peaches Pafford?"

"She's in the tea room right now," Drayton said, in a matter-of-fact tone. He placed a basket of blueberry scones and a crystal bowl mounded with Devonshire cream onto a silver tray and smiled.

But his words had just about bowled Theodosia over. "What?" she cried. "Are you serious?"

Drayton gave an offhand shrug. "She wandered in ten minutes ago and plunked herself down at Delaine's table. Apparently Delaine was supposed to meet someone here for lunch, but they canceled at the last minute."

"So now Delaine and Peaches are having lunch?" asked Theodosia. Wasn't that interesting? And possibly serendipitous.

"Well, Delaine's not actually eating lunch," said Drayton. "She's just pushing food around on her plate, mewling about how she needs to lose five pounds. So, long story short, I brewed a pot of that special black Nilgiri tea, the tea I ordered from the Chamraj Estate. And I told her it was dieter's tea." Drayton gave a perfunctory grin, then aimed a look of supreme exasperation at Haley. "However, Peaches and several other customers are *still* waiting for their red pepper quiche, if I may be so bold as to inquire when it's going to emerge from your oven?"

"Keep your shirt on," Haley told him, as she pulled open the oven door and peeked inside again. "Yeah, it's coming. Five more minutes."

"Five?" said Drayton.

"You can't rush cheesy goodness," Haley told him.

"And Peaches is out there having lunch?" Theodosia asked.

"Yes, she's having a cup of soup and a scone," said Drayton. "Why? Is there a problem?"

"No," said Theodosia. "I don't think so. At least I hope there isn't."

Peaches Pafford was one of those women who pretty much looked like somebody's fun-loving, amiable aunt. But she wasn't, by any stretch of the imagination. True, Peaches had pinkish blond hair worn in a dated shag, and a broad, flat face with carefully rouged lips, and she was the requisite twenty pounds overweight in a pink tweed Dior suit that seemed to stretch and strain at the seams. But Peaches was one tough nut. She was a woman who'd become a widow at forty, a business owner by forty-three, and a well-heeled, slightly feared tyrant two years after that.

Still, Theodosia bounded up to her table and greeted Peaches and Delaine with great enthusiasm.

"Theo!" cried Delaine, "I was beginning to wonder where you were. I so want to introduce you to Peaches."

"Lovely to finally meet you," Peaches enthused. She grabbed Theodosia's hand and gave it several hearty pumps. Then her eyes got serious, her mouth puckered into a downward cast, and she said, "I was very sorry to hear about your friend Parker. I understand you two had been very close." She patted Theodosia's hand. "In fact, he told me you two were practically engaged."

"The two of them were thick as thieves," Delaine chortled. Then she quickly blotted her lips with her napkin, as if realizing the inappropriateness of her remark.

But Theodosia saw her chance and grabbed it. "I understand you were fairly close to Parker, too," she said to Peaches.

"Oh?" said Delaine, suddenly looking interested. Delaine was a woman who greatly prized any and all nuggets of gossip.

Peaches flashed a radiant smile at Theodosia. "I was always quite taken with Parker's restaurant and thought, at one time, I might like to add it to my roster."

"You pitched him on the idea rather recently," said Theodosia. "Really just a matter of a few weeks ago."

Peaches gave an imperceptible nod. "Yes."

"But he was resistant to selling," said Theodosia. She sat herself down in the chair directly across from Peaches.

"Resistant," said Peaches, her smile slipping. "Ha ha, I suppose that's one way to put it."

"Though I've been told you're quite persuasive," said Theodosia.

Peaches gave her a sharp-eyed look and said, "I can be," in a cool, even tone that seemed to underscore her iron will.

Delaine, sensing a sharp, prickly feeling beginning to develop between the two women, suddenly piped up, "I brought that list you wanted, Theo." She fumbled in her bag, this time a red tote with clanking chains, and set a sheaf of papers on the table.

Theodosia reached over and towed the papers toward her using her index finger. But not before Peaches got a gander at it.

"Ah," Peaches said, "the guest list from Sunday night's aquarium debacle."

"That's right," said Theodosia.

"Looking for suspects?" Peaches asked, her tone carefully neutral.

"Just looking," said Theodosia. Every once in a while

Peaches had a slight lisp, which led Theodosia to believe those perfect front teeth might be plastic veneers.

"Don't be surprised if you find my name on that list," Peaches told her. "Since I donated generously."

Delaine's face lit up. "You certainly did!"

Peaches lifted a spoonful of soup to her lips and tasted delicately. "Such a shame about young Parker. And how awful to have our opening-night donor party ruined. Shattered, really."

"Awful," echoed Delaine.

Peaches enjoyed another spoonful of soup, then glanced at her watch, an enormous Rolex—the midsize, not the ladies' model—rimmed in diamonds. "Goodness, look at the time! I absolutely must run!"

"Your quiche is just coming out of the oven," Theodosia told her.

But Peaches had already grabbed her bag and leaped to her feet. "No time," she said, tugging at her suit jacket. "I have to finalize plans for my big Oyster Fest this Saturday night, then I have to interview a new pastry chef."

"Good luck with that," said Delaine.

Peaches fastened her gaze directly on Theodosia and gave a measured smile. "Unless, of course, you'd like to give me yours."

"You want to hire Haley?" said Theodosia. "Then I suppose you'd have to make her an offer."

Peaches's smile never wavered. "Perhaps I'll do that."

10

❧

Even though Theodosia was still fuming over Peaches's little power play, she shrugged it off. The Indigo Tea Shop's late luncheon trade had revved up like crazy, and the three sets of tables and chairs that Drayton had moved onto the front sidewalk were suddenly occupied. Clutches of locals, as well as tourists, still clattered at the tea shop's door, eager to grab a table, anxious to taste whatever smelled so heavenly.

Haley, careful planner that she was, had baked eight pans of quiche and cooked something like six gallons of soup. It stretched as far as it could, but by two o'clock, the food was gone.

"The cupboard is virtually bare," Haley cautioned Theodosia and Drayton. "So baked goods only from here on." She had a smear of flour on the tip of her nose, and her hair was tied back in a pink bandanna.

"By the end of the day we won't have a single crumb left," Drayton predicted, as he fussed at the front counter, brewing what had to be his umpteenth pot of Assam tea.

"Then we're doing everything right," said Theodosia. She fanned herself slowly as she sipped from a glass of lemon verbena sweet tea. "After all, leftovers don't contribute to our bottom line." She was still mindful that the economy was turgid at best. The Indigo Tea Shop was humming nicely, but many of her fellow shopkeepers up and down Church Street had experienced huge downturns in business.

"Still," said Drayton, "it's always lovely to take home a leftover scone or brownie." He popped a red gingham tea cozy onto a blue-and-white rice pattern teapot and handed it to Theodosia. "This goes to table three," he told her, then glanced sharply over her shoulder as the front door swung open. "Well, hello there," he suddenly enthused to their new visitor. "It's been a while since we've had the pleasure."

Theodosia whirled about quickly and immediately recognized Harry Dubose, the genial beekeeper who produced all the jars of Dubose Bees Honey that they stocked in their gift area. Her face crinkled into a welcoming smile.

Harry Dubose was short, jolly, and fifty with red hair fading to light gray. He wore his usual apiary garb of khaki trousers, khaki shirt, and khaki vest. A large white box that could only contain a couple dozen more jars of his precious wildflower honey was balanced in his hands.

"Honey direct from the grower," said Theodosia, as Drayton lifted the teapot from her hands and carried it to table three himself.

Dubose smiled.

"That's just grand," said Theodosia. "And I hope you've got time to enjoy a nice cup of tea and a slice of almond cake?"

Dubose slid his package onto the counter and waved a chubby hand. "I gotta keep moving," he told her. "I've got an appointment over at Silver Butter Knife, that new gourmet grocery on Calhoun Street. It looks like they're interested in carrying some of our products."

"Congratulations," said Theodosia.

"You know," said Dubose, pressing both hands flat on the counter and leaning in toward her, "we're still waiting for you to come down and see our operation firsthand."

"I'd like to come," Theodosia told him. Truth was, she just hadn't had time.

"After all," said Dubose, "you're not only one of our biggest retailers, you're probably our biggest booster, too."

"How do you figure that?" asked Theodosia, oddly pleased by his words.

"People slather our honey on your fine scones and breads and they pretty much get hooked!" Dubose declared. "So they buy a couple of jars here and then order even more from our website."

"I'm thrilled you're doing so well."

But Dubose wasn't done with his little pitch. "Maybe you could even drive down this week. Fact is, we just finished our spring harvest and we're rolling out our new melon honey."

"Sounds positively luscious," said Theodosia.

"What we did," Dubose explained, "was plant Catawba melons in the fields surrounding the hives. As the blossoms ripened, the bees took a liking to them and sipped their nectar. The end result, of course, is that our new crop of honey has been imbued with a lovely melon flavor."

"That's so amazing," said Theodosia.

"You gotta come down," Dubose urged again.

Theodosia thought for a few moments. She was always looking for new and unusual products for her shop and her website. *Maybe . . .* "On the melon honey," she said. "Would you be able to give me a three-month exclusive?"

Dubose chewed at his lower lip. "We could probably work something out."

"So maybe if I drove down Friday," said Theodosia. "I could get the plant tour?" *And some melon honey.*

"We'll keep a look out for you," said Dubose, pleased.

*   *   *

"Theodosia. Telephone," said Drayton.

Theodosia stopped stacking jars of cider cinnamon jelly and blueberry jam and hurried to the front counter. "Theodosia here," she said, grabbing the phone.

"Dear girl!" came a familiar voice.

"Aunt Libby!" said Theodosia. Aunt Libby was her only living relative and the dearest, sweetest human being one would ever want to meet. She was also a woman who had a soft spot in her heart for all creatures and single-handedly fed and loved every bird, deer, fox, chipmunk, raccoon, and baby opossum in a thirty-mile zone. Aunt Libby's own personal TMZ.

"I just heard!" Aunt Libby cried. "About Parker. How awful for you!"

"I know," said Theodosia. "It was a total shock for all of us." For some reason, she was suddenly tongue-tied. Probably because, at one time, she and Parker had been close to getting married, and Aunt Libby had been a big booster of that union. Parker had also been incredibly kind to Aunt Libby and, on more than one occasion, had sent a car to pick her up so she could enjoy dinner with them at Solstice.

"So a terrible accident?" asked Aunt Libby.

"The police are still, uh, looking into things," said Theodosia. She didn't want to upset Aunt Libby with talk about murder.

"And if I know you," said Aunt Libby, "you will, too."

Theodosia hesitated. "We'll see. But we're still on for tomorrow. That hasn't changed." Tomorrow Aunt Libby was hosting a special tea party at her home at Cane Ridge Plantation and she, Drayton, and Haley were providing tea, treats, and sweets.

"I'm looking forward to it," Aunt Libby cooed. "I've got tons of people coming."

"Excellent," said Theodosia. "And we'll be bringing tons of food."

Just as Theodosia set the phone back in its cradle, it rang again. She gave a distracted shrug and snatched it up. "Indigo Tea Shop."

"Do you have a pressing engagement or can I drop by?" came a low growl.

Theodosia stiffened. It was Tidwell. "You know something!" she said in a hurried whisper. "You found something out!"

Tidwell didn't answer. Instead he said, "I'll stop by in a half hour or so." Then the phone clicked in her ear. No polite good-bye, no hint of what news he might be bringing her. Maddening, to be sure. But at least he was keeping her in the loop. Not being so boorish and standoffish, as he had been yesterday.

With many of the guests departed now, Theodosia corralled Drayton and Haley at one of the front tables. "We need to run through the plans for tomorrow's tea party at Cane Ridge," she told them. "I just spoke with Aunt Libby and she's got umpteen guests coming."

"What's this for again?" asked Haley.

"It's a benefit for an animal rescue group over in Colleton County," said Theodosia.

"Isn't it heartwarming," said Drayton, "how people step up to the plate to help out these small charities?"

Theodosia grinned. "You won't find it quite so heart-warming if I tap you to go along with me on Thursday night's scavenger hunt. As you recall, the tea shop is competing to help win funds for Tuesday's Child."

"Oh no!" Drayton exclaimed, staring at her with a deer-in-the-headlights gaze. "A scavenger hunt?" He looked like he'd just been told he had to attend a Jay-Z concert. "Surely your friend Max will have returned by then, so he can serve as your trusty sidekick. Or you can take Haley."

"Let's hope so," said Theodosia. "For your sake."

"So about tomorrow," said Haley, tapping her pen. "I'm mixing up crab salad and chicken salad here, then assembling tea sandwiches once we get to Aunt Libby's."

"So two kinds of sandwiches?" said Theodosia.

"Mmm, actually there'll be three," said Haley. "I'm doing turkey with cranberry relish, too. And there'll be Swiss cheese quiche and strawberry scones. I'm able to get fresh strawberries now from Strawberry Hill up in Chesnee, so it looks like we're set for the coming summer."

"And, Drayton," said Theodosia, "you've settled on which teas to serve?"

"Strawberry Darjeeling," said Drayton, "to complement Haley's scones. As well as a nice Viennese blend of Earl Grey. Both teas have wide appeal and aren't too tricky to brew." He removed his half-glasses and polished them on the lapel of his linen jacket. "Since we'll be a traveling tea party, it's best to keep things simple."

"And we've got Miss Dimple and her brother coming in to handle the tea shop tomorrow," said Theodosia. She was a little nervous about this. Miss Dimple was their bookkeeper and often worked part-time in the tea shop. Still, it wasn't often that she left someone else completely in charge of her baby.

"But all they have to do is serve morning scones and tea," said Haley. "By the time lunch rolls around, I'll be back here to honcho things."

"So we're both running on skeleton crews," laughed Drayton.

Still, the day was far from concluded. Because twenty minutes later, Miss Josette and her nephew, Dexter, dropped by with a stack of sweetgrass baskets.

Miss Josette was an African American woman, probably in her late seventies, but who could easily pass for early sixties. She had bright, intelligent eyes; the skillful, facile hands of an artist, and smooth skin the color of rich mahogany.

Dexter, who drove his aunt around on her deliveries, was tall, thin, and athletic-looking. He'd had a basketball scholarship to Charleston Southern University and now worked as an elementary school teacher.

Theodosia greeted them warmly, then said, "Are these all for us?"

"Only if you want them," said Miss Josette, adjusting the pale-blue shawl that wrapped around her sea-green dress. Sweetgrass baskets were unique to Charleston and the surrounding environs, and Miss Josette was one of the premier basket makers. Elegant and utilitarian, her baskets were woven from long bunches of sweetgrass, pine needles, and bulrush, then bound together by strips from native palmetto trees.

"We want them all," said Drayton, joining them.

"I told her you'd say that," said Dexter, smiling. "She thought we'd be making three stops today, but I told her it'd be just this one."

"That's because we can't keep them in stock," said Theodosia. She took the top basket off the stack, a traditional round Gullah bread basket, and turned it gently in her hands. "We actually have a waiting list." Over the years, sweetgrass baskets had become celebrated pieces of art in the low country. A collection of them was even on display at the Smithsonian in Washington, D.C.

"I hope you can stay for tea," said Theodosia. "We may be a little light on scones and desserts, but tea we've got."

"We can't," said Miss Josette. "Dexter has to drive over to Wadmalaw Island, where he works at a golf course."

"Golf?" said Drayton. "I thought you taught here in town at Heritage Elementary."

"Now I've got two jobs," said Dexter.

"He's working the second job so he can earn extra money

to fund a kind of local clubhouse," Miss Josette explained. "For the kids. You know, to hang out at. After school and weekends."

"We already have a pretty nice space," said Dexter. "It's only three hundred dollars a month to rent and it's huge. But it's still just raw space, so we plan to fix it up as we go along. Plus we need to buy sports equipment, a TV, CD player, that kind of stuff."

"He's doing a bang-up job, too," Miss Josette said. "I'm so proud of him. He's keeping the kids active and out of trouble. Teaching them, too."

"What are some of your activities?" Theodosia asked.

"We just hang out and do interesting stuff," Dexter explained. "Sometimes we play soccer, sometimes we read books, sometimes we listen to music. And not just rap or rock, either, but good music like Charlie Parker, Earl Hines, and Beethoven."

Miss Josette beamed. "Last week Dexter borrowed a bus from the Gullah tour folks and took the kids to the Gibbes Museum."

"We had a ball," grinned Dexter. "Checked out the paintings by Thomas Hart Benton and Georgia O'Keeffe. Even saw some Japanese woodblock prints."

"You know," said Theodosia, "if you filed for 501(c)3 status, you could become an official nonprofit and be eligible to receive any number of grants and donations."

Dexter hunched his shoulders forward. "Takes money to do that," he said. "To file with the state and pay attorney's fees and accountants and stuff."

"I suppose you're right," said Theodosia. It was strange, she decided, that it cost money to become a nonprofit. Seemed like yet another concept at odds with itself. Like army intelligence or educational TV.

"When we were at the museum," said Dexter, "they had a

great big glass fishbowl practically overflowing with cash. And not just dollar bills, but twenties and fifties."

"Sure," said Theodosia, "their donation fishbowl." She'd seen that same fishbowl many times. In fact, this month the museum had adopted Tuesday's Child as their charity du jour. Very nice for Tuesday's Child, but tough for guys like Dexter, who also had his heart in the right place but wasn't quite as organized or skilled in PR.

"Well, good luck to you," said Drayton. "That club of yours sounds quite wonderful."

"*I know I* warned you to stay away from the investigation," said Tidwell. He sat across the table from Theodosia, looking slightly discombobulated. "But something rather bizarre has come up."

"You found the murderer," said Theodosia. Her heartbeat ratcheted upward and she felt a surge of excitement.

"No," said Tidwell. "Nothing quite that earth-shattering."

"Then what?"

Tidwell's mouth puckered into a slight grimace. "Mr. Scully had a will."

"Probably," said Theodosia.

"No, he definitely did," said Tidwell. "And only a few hours ago I became privy to the contents of that will."

Theodosia wasn't sure where this was going. "Is there a problem?"

"Yes and no," said Tidwell. He shifted his bulk in the chair and said, "As it stands now, Shelby McCawley stands to inherit Solstice restaurant and one million dollars in insurance money."

"Excuse me?" said Theodosia. She'd heard his words quite clearly, but they didn't seem to register in her brain. "What?"

"Shelby McCawley is the beneficiary," Tidwell told her.

"The girlfriend?" said Theodosia. "That's utterly bizarre."

"Call it what you may," said Tidwell, but that seems to be the state of affairs at the current time."

Theodosia's brows pinched together and she said in a rush, "But why wouldn't Parker have left the restaurant to his family?" She was practically shouting now. "His brother, Charles, in particular?"

"Who knows what neurochemicals are released within the brain when a man is besotted." Tidwell's mouth did a minuscule uptick at the corners.

His statement shocked Theodosia into silence. And also got her thinking. *Was that what Parker had been? Besotted? By Shelby? Seriously?*

"Interestingly enough," Tidwell continued, "you'd been his previous beneficiary."

Theodosia put her head in her hands and gently massaged her temples. "You're freaking me out," she told him.

"Not my intention," said Tidwell.

"But you have to agree this is all incredibly bizarre," said Theodosia. "Leaving a restaurant and bar business to someone who's completely inexperienced in the hospitality industry. Leaving it to such a young woman."

"She's twenty-seven," said Tidwell.

"Like I said," said Theodosia, sounding exasperated.

Tidwell pursed his lips. "All right, yes. Like you, I find Parker Scully's choice of beneficiaries a trifle strange. But certainly not illegal."

"But what was he thinking?" murmured Theodosia. She drew a deep breath and said, "In light of these new developments, would you indulge me by taking a closer look at Shelby? Run a background check or whatever?"

"I already have," said Tidwell, "because I knew you would ask."

"And?" Theodosia lifted a hand and waggled her fingers.

"Nothing," said Tidwell. "The girl appears to be squeaky-clean."

"Appearances can be so deceiving," said Theodosia.

"In some instances, that's true."

"But not in this instance?"

Tidwell tipped his head to one side. "Like I said, we've discovered nothing unusual about the girl."

Theodosia sat there for a few moments, thinking. Then she said, "Does this make Shelby a suspect?"

"It could," said Tidwell.

Tidwell's somewhat circumspect answer caused Theodosia's brain to tick back to her meeting with Shelby. The girl had come to her asking for help. Then, after she'd made a few inquiries, Shelby had subtly pointed Theodosia in the direction of Joe Beaudry. Had Shelby been setting up a smoke screen? Constructing a dandy alibi? Was she that smart, that diabolical, that guilty?

Theodosia mulled this over for a few minutes. "Shelby was probably seeing Parker almost every day. She was in and out of his office. Do you think . . . do you think Shelby could have removed the contents of the Current Projects file?"

"You mean stolen?"

"Yes," said Theodosia.

"I suppose it's possible," Tidwell replied. "We've asked her about it and she claims to have no knowledge of it."

"But she could have," Theodosia mused. She leaned back in her chair and put a hand at the back of her neck, at the root of her tension. Rubbing gingerly, trying to ease her sore muscles, she said, "The question is . . . why? What would have been in that file that Shelby so desperately wanted?"

"I don't know," said Tidwell. He peered thoughtfully at Theodosia, his dark eyes deep pools of contemplation. "But perhaps . . ." He drew a long breath. "Perhaps you might want to ask her that yourself."

11

Theodosia stuck a wooden spoon in her pot of chicken and rice soup and stirred thoughtfully. As she stood in the kitchen of her little cottage, her mind felt like it was buzzing in a thousand different directions. There was Parker's murder, of course, with no solid leads as of yet. Lyle Manship was perched at the top of her list, but Joe Beaudry, Peaches, and Shelby had also earned honorary mention.

Theodosia was also feeling a wave of helplessness and sadness. Which would no doubt intensify when she attended Parker's funeral tomorrow morning.

There was also the Coffee & Tea Expo to deal with. That event kicked off in just two days' time. As a reminder, and because her office at the tea shop was jam-packed to the rafters, she had umpteen cases of private-label tea and T-Bath products piled up around her kitchen.

Taking up precious space. And switching up the feng shui in my kitchen, too.

As if reading her mind, Earl Grey padded over and sniffed

at the boxes. Then he turned baleful eyes on Theodosia, as if to ask, *Why is this stuff cluttering our lovely home?*

"Are you bugged, too?" she asked. "Because I promise this will all be gone by tomorrow night. Haley has some new guy she's dating who drives a van. So they're going to come by and schlep it all away."

Earl Grey continued to gaze at her. "Rwwr?"

"Yes, tomorrow," Theodosia promised, "and it can't happen soon enough for me, either."

She poured her soup into a blue-and-white Chinese bowl, placed it on a wicker tray, then decided she might like a couple of rye crackers as a crunchy counterpoint. But when she went to grab some, the cupboard was bare.

"Great," said Theodosia. Her arms flew up and flapped at her sides.

"Woof!" said Earl Grey, letting loose a sharp, high-pitched bark.

At that exact moment, a loud knock sounded at her back door.

Somebody knocking on my back door? Came in the back way through my garden? That's a little strange.

Startled, Theodosia stood there for a few moments, just gazing at the curtain that covered the window, as if she could somehow divine who her visitor might be. Then she stepped briskly to the door and reached for the doorknob. But just before she tugged open the door, she looped the chain across. Couldn't be too careful these days.

Delaine was peering in. And looking slightly perturbed at being made to wait.

"Delaine!" Theodosia exclaimed. "What are you doing here?"

"Tiptoeing through your magnolias," said Delaine. "Though they're not the only thing in your garden that could use some judicious pruning. Oh, and that so-called fishpond of yours?" She rolled her eyes. "There's so much green gunk growing in there, it looks like the Okefenokee Swamp!"

Theodosia wanted to say, *What are you, the patio police?* But didn't. Thought better of it. Why provoke her?

"Anyway," Delaine continued, "I popped over to deliver a sort of impromptu invitation."

"Really," said Theodosia. Was she finally being invited into Dougan Granville's home next door?

Turned out she was.

"Dougan is holding an informal meeting with some of the Neptune Aquarium people," said Delaine. "And I thought that, in light of the *events* of two nights ago, you might want to come over and join us."

Would I ever.

"Thank you," said Theodosia, "I think I'd like that."

Delaine seemed to fumble a bit with her words. "I thought maybe you should meet some of the wonderful people who are involved with the aquarium." She cleared her throat. "Then you'd see that nothing particularly, um, *sinister* happened that night. And maybe you'll be able to enjoy some sort of closure."

"That's kind of you," said Theodosia, knowing that, for her, closure was one of those concepts that didn't really work. When it came to death, Theodosia held firmly that there was no such thing as closure. There was a sense of great finality, certainly. But not closure. Never closure. Only lingering memory . . . and pain that was gently assuaged by time.

"And there's food, too," Delaine added brightly.

After a quick walk across her backyard, Theodosia found herself ushered into Dougan Granville's inner sanctum—in this case, an expansive living room hung with enormous oil paintings in Baroque frames and dominated at one end by a Hepplewhite sideboard. At the other end of the room a dozen people mingled and chatted across a gigantic Sheraton table laden with food.

"Just make yourself at home," said Delaine.

But this was unlike any home Theodosia had visited before, except for Timothy Neville's palatial manor. Granville's living room had been built on a grand scale and furnished with precious antiques, fine furniture, and silk Oriental carpets. Theodosia had always known her neighbor was a successful attorney; she just hadn't realized how successful.

"Glad you could make it," Dougan Granville said, coming up to greet her. He was tall and beefy and wore his arrogance like a bespoke suit. One of his beloved Cohiba cigars peeked from the pocket of his finely tailored jacket. Knowing Granville's penchant for Cuban cigars, Theodosia figured the man couldn't wait to duck out of this meeting, kick back on his patio, and puff away.

"Thanks for the invitation," Theodosia told him. "And, I have to say, I adore this room."

Granville looked oddly pleased. "Decorators," he said. "They always seem to know what works. If it were up to me I probably would have stuck in some white plastic lawn furniture."

Somehow I doubt that.

"Who was your decorator?" Theodosia asked, trying to be polite.

"Those two gals from Popple Hill," said Granville.

"Marianne Petigru and Hillary Retton," said Theodosia. They were two firecrackers who handled all the society and big-buck clients.

"Oh, you know them?" Granville grunted. "They do your place, too?"

"We're fairly well acquainted," said Theodosia. She knew them but certainly couldn't *afford* to hire Charleston's elite decorators!

"Theo," said Delaine, interrupting them. "I'd like you to meet David Sedakis, the executive director of the Neptune Aquarium." She reached back, grabbed Sedakis's arm, and pulled him into their circle.

"Nice to meet you," said Theodosia, shaking hands with Sedakis. He was tall, thin, and slightly balding with a hawkish nose. He also looked unhappy about being introduced to Theodosia.

"I'll let you two chat for a while," Delaine murmured as she eased Granville away.

"You were the one who . . ." were Sedakis's first words.

"Found him," finished Theodosia.

Sedakis made an appropriately emotive expression. "I understand you two had been good friends."

"Something like that," said Theodosia.

"A terrible accident," said Sedakis. "You'll be relieved to know we've taken incredible steps to ensure nothing like that ever happens again."

"You mean murder?"

Sedakis's mouth twitched to one side and his face suddenly became a thundercloud. "You don't know that," he hissed.

"But I do," said Theodosia. "Have you spoken to Detective Tidwell recently? Or the medical examiner?"

"Excuse me," said Sedakis. He turned abruptly and walked away.

But sharp-eyed Delaine had caught their exchange and quickly came scuttling over.

"What did you *say* to him?" she demanded in a high-pitched whisper.

"Your Mr. Sedakis seems to be under the impression that Parker's death was an accident."

"Well, wasn't it?" said Delaine.

"Highly doubtful," said Theodosia.

Now Delaine's face bunched in disapproval. "Really, Theo, I invited you over here tonight because I thought it might afford you some *comfort*." Her eyes suddenly sparkled with tears and she looked like she was about to cry. "So do you think you could please try to just . . . get along?"

"You don't want me to rock the boat," said Theodosia, wondering if Delaine's tears were real or just crocodile tears. Of course Delaine didn't want Theodosia to mention Parker's death. Delaine wanted the evening to be nice and polite and social and tidy.

Delaine looked suddenly hopeful. "That's right, dear!" She grasped Theodosia's hand. "Please don't rock the boat. Just . . . be simpatico. In fact, why don't you help yourself to some food. We're going to begin the meeting in a few minutes, and I think ingesting a little protein might do you a world of good." Delaine was always a huge proponent of eating protein. Low carbs, high protein.

Theodosia shrugged. "Sure, Delaine. Why not?" What could it hurt?

But Delaine wasn't finished. "I know you're terribly upset by Parker's passing, Theo, but flinging accusations or being rude to people isn't going to bring him back."

Good point, thought Theodosia. *But you never know when it'll flush out a suspect or two.*

"I suppose you're right," said Theodosia. "I promise I'll fly under the radar from here on." *And keep my eyes and ears open during this meeting.*

Delaine patted her hand. "That's a good girl." She smiled, glanced around, and the smile died on her face. "Oh no," she said in a low moan.

"What?" said Theodosia.

"You see that skanky blonde over there?" She nodded toward a tall, willowy blonde who'd just sidled up to Dougan Granville. "It's that awful Simone Asher." Delaine gritted her teeth. "Dougan used to *date* her."

"The operative words being *used to*," said Theodosia. "Now he's dating you."

But Delaine had hit the panic button and was on full alert. "You never know," she hissed, "one of these women could easily sneak back into his life!" She gave a little shimmy and said, "Looks like I need to stage a radical intervention." She waved a hand and called to Granville, "Oh, turtledove . . ."

While Delaine galloped toward Granville, Theodosia sidled up to the buffet table. Grabbing a white china plate, she decided this spread was a whole lot more interesting than the soup she'd been planning to eat. Here were oysters on the half shell, a bowl of plump pink shrimp, slices of rare roast beef, a citrus salad, and a large silver chafing dish filled with what appeared to be steaming seafood risotto. Delicious!

"Be sure to try those oysters," said a man standing across from her.

Theodosia glanced up. "Excuse me?"

"They're first-rate," he told her. Then he grinned and added, "I should know, I brought them."

"Really," said Theodosia, smiling. "And you are . . . ?"

"Buddy Krebs," said the man. He was stocky, with a shock of white hair and a weathered, ruddy complexion that looked as if he'd spent a lifetime in the outdoors. "Krebs and Company Seafood. Perhaps you've heard of us?"

"I sure have," said Theodosia. She'd seen their trucks all over town. "Nice to meet you. And I *will* help myself to a couple of your lovely oysters."

"Are you a purist or do you take 'em with hot sauce?" Krebs asked. He winked, then said, "Just a straw poll I like to take. On consumer preference."

"I'm pretty much a purist," Theodosia told him, placing three oysters on her plate. "Although sometimes I enjoy a squirt of lemon juice."

"Got no problem with that," said Krebs.

"Are you one of the board members?" Theodosia asked.

"That's right," said Krebs, helping himself to several large spoonfuls of risotto.

"Excuse me for saying this," said Theodosia, "but it seems a little strange that a seafood purveyor would sit on the board of directors of an aquarium."

Krebs let loose a good-natured laugh. "I can see where you might say that, but I think of myself as a kind of watchdog, too."

"How's that?" asked Theodosia, deciding she needed a couple of shrimp as well.

"An aquarium is all about education," Krebs explained, "and one of my personal missions is to help teach people about sustainable seafood."

"We were just talking about that the other day," said Theodosia. *Drayton and I were, right before I found Parker. Only he wasn't so sustainable.* She shook her head, as if to clear it. "I think you've got your work cut out for you," she told Krebs.

"That's true," he said, "but any kind of ecology movement doesn't happen right away. Takes time to gain inroads."

"That's really the question, isn't it?" said Theodosia. "Is there time? For our oceans, I mean."

"I sincerely hope so," said Krebs, looking thoughtful, "if people wake up and smell the sea breeze."

"Well put," said Theodosia. She found Krebs to be quietly thoughtful and a little charming. Which made her feel better about local seafood producers in general. And, truth be told, feel a little better about the Neptune Aquarium.

Those good feelings lasted for about ten minutes. Because once the board members pulled themselves into a circle and had a quick discussion about finances, they moved on to public relations. In other words, damage control.

"We need to downplay this recent accident," Sedakis told them. He sat in an armchair, one leg crossed over the other, surveying the group. "And push our grand-opening events and activities. Exciting events like our reef experience, petting pond, and family day."

"Rather than downplay the accident," said Granville, "why don't you talk about how you've instituted new safety measures?"

"We really don't want to do that," said Sedakis. "Any time

you talk safety, it leaves you open to watchdog groups who have an agenda or TV stations who want to come in and do some kind of consumer report."

Delaine glanced sharply at Theodosia, as if expecting she'd stand up and put in her two cents' worth. But Theodosia remained mum, just listening and watching. Of course she was fuming inwardly, but outwardly she appeared cool as a cucumber.

The meeting dragged on for another thirty-five minutes, until someone brought up the subject of the new restaurant at the aquarium. At which point Sedakis stepped in and said, "We still have requests for proposals out, so why don't we table that discussion for a later date."

"Table," said Delaine, giggling, "how very apropos."

But Theodosia's mind was elsewhere—thinking about, and pretty much dreading, Parker's funeral tomorrow.

12

❧

The carillon's chimes rang out sweet and pure as Theodosia and Drayton stepped inside the Summerall Chapel at The Citadel.

"Oh my," said Drayton, glancing around.

"What?" said Theodosia, touching shoulders with him.

"So lovely," he said, accepting two programs from the young cadet in uniform who stood ramrod stiff at the door.

It had been quite a few years since Theodosia had paid a visit to The Citadel, and she was pleased to see that the chapel was as peaceful and simple as ever. Cruciform in design, the nonsectarian Summerall Chapel was a shrine to God, country, remembrance, and simplicity. Accordingly, all of the benches were hand-sawed Appalachian white oak, the ceiling and side timbers were pine, the lighting fixtures wrought iron. Flags from the fifty states hung on the walls; the windows were small stained-glass medallions that commemorated Citadel graduates and warriors.

As they took their seats on one of the plain benches,

Theodosia scanned the small printed program and noted that the carillon was playing the final stanza from *Andante from Pastorale for Organ* by J. S. Bach. The notes hung in the air, haunting and beautiful. Then again, the entire setting was quiet and evocative. It was no wonder Parker's brother had chosen this chapel at The Citadel as the venue for the funeral. Probably, Charles had been a graduate himself. Or one of their relatives had.

"The chancel window," Drayton whispered. He pointed a discreet finger at the great window located directly behind the altar, where various symbols and exemplars portrayed courage, sacrifice, duty, loyalty, faith, and prayer.

"It is spectacular," Theodosia whispered back to him.

And then the service was underway.

A minister in a plain black suit came out from the back, while Parker's brother stood up from the front bench and solemnly placed a small metal urn on a simple wooden stand.

"Oh!" Theodosia said, with a slightly audible squeak. She hadn't been prepared for this. Parker had already been cremated, his body reduced to simple ashes.

Drayton turned a sympathetic gaze upon her. "You okay?" he whispered.

No.

Theodosia nodded instead. Yes, okay. She had to be okay. After all, what choice did she have?

It turned out to be a lovely, simple service with fine words, heartfelt testimonials, and emotions running fairly high. Parker's brother, Charles, spoke at length about their growing up together, what a caring and socially conscious person Parker had been, and how he'd created such a successful and popular restaurant. When Charles finished, his voice nearly cracking, he stepped back to his seat and put his arms around Shelby in a warm embrace.

Drayton let loose a quiet *hmm* in the back of his throat, while Theodosia tracked the girl's movements with her eyes.

And then the service was concluded. Charles carried the urn down the aisle, while Shelby and the relatives followed him in a monochromatic flying wedge of white faces and black clothes. The carillon's bronze bells let loose their ringing notes for a second round, this time *Pastoral Symphony* from *Messiah* by Handel.

"Short and simple," Drayton declared, as they waited their turn to ease into the aisle. "Just the way I'd like my memorial service to be."

Theodosia nudged him. "Don't talk so gloomy," she said. "You're a long way from that."

Drayton hesitated as he turned kind gray eyes upon her and said, "That's what Parker thought, too." Then, when he saw sudden pain flare in her eyes, he said, "I'm sorry, I didn't mean it that way."

"I know you didn't," said Theodosia. "But you're right. I guess most people *don't* see it coming."

"No, they don't," said Drayton.

Which set Theodosia to wondering again. Had Parker seen the end coming? He must have. That was why he'd fought, why he'd struggled so valiantly. He knew what was happening and fought with everything he had. If only . . .

Theodosia let loose a deep sigh, suddenly realizing she'd been off in a daze, locked in place, not budging an inch. Pretty much everyone else had filed out of the church already.

"You okay?" Drayton asked again. He'd waited patiently for her to regain her composure.

"Let's go," she said, stepping out into the aisle. "I want to talk to Shelby."

"I thought you might," he said.

The line for paying condolences snaked down the front steps and out onto a grassy plot, which gave Theodosia ample opportunity to get a look at the other mourners who'd shown up today. In fact, there was Joe Beaudry, smiling and chatting with an attractive woman.

"Beaudry," said Theodosia.

"The lawyer," Drayton sniffed. He said the name as if he were referencing bubonic plague. "What's he doing here?"

"Good question," said Theodosia. Was Beaudry feeling a twinge of guilt for leading Parker on about financing? Or was something else afoot?

Theodosia and Drayton took their places in the condolence line. It wound its way slowly past Charles Scully; his wife, Monica; and several other relatives. They murmured kind words, shook hands, and said all the proper things you're supposed to say to the bereaved.

Finally they got to Shelby.

Theodosia didn't bother with a handshake or an *I'm sorry*. Instead she said, "He left it all to you." Her tone was filled with grit and veered toward the accusing.

Shelby looked suddenly stricken. "It's not what you think," she whispered. "Really, I can explain."

Theodosia aimed a level gaze at her. "I'd so love to hear your explanation."

Shelby seemed to consider this, then said, "Meet me later? We'll talk?"

"I think we'd better do that," said Theodosia, moving past her. "I'll call you. I'll be out all day, but I'll call you."

As Theodosia walked beside Drayton, on the way to her car, she turned back and gazed at the group of mourners who were still circling like some kind of oceanic gyre. She noted that Peaches Pafford was in the group. And, oh yes, there was David Sedakis. Looking quite composed.

Was Tidwell lurking somewhere? Theodosia certainly hoped he was.

They were back at the Indigo Tea Shop by ten fifteen.

"How was the service?" asked Haley. She was hunkered in the kitchen, packing plastic tubs of crab salad, chicken salad, sliced cucumbers, and wedges of Brie cheese into the large, industrial-strength metal coolers they used for their off-site catering jobs. A basket stuffed with French baguettes sat nearby, ready to go.

"It was very sad," said Theodosia.

"Mournful," Drayton echoed.

"I'm sorry I missed it," said Haley, "but I wanted to get everything set for Aunt Libby's event."

"And is it?" asked Drayton.

"Of course," said Haley, not missing a beat.

"How are things out in the tea shop?" asked Drayton, inclining his head. He was fretting over Miss Dimple and her brother, just as Theodosia and Haley had predicted he would.

"Miss Dimple and her brother are doing a bang-up job," Haley told him. "She's preparing and serving tea and he's delivering scones."

"And our customers appear happy?" asked Drayton.

"Of course, they are," said Haley. "And if you guys can stop obsessing for one minute that this place is going to go bankrupt, then you could start toting this stuff out to the cars so we can take off for Cane Ridge."

"My my," said Drayton, "aren't we wound tight today."

"Yes, we are," said Haley. She glanced at Theodosia. "We'll load all the food into your Jeep and I'll drive out separately in my car?"

"Works for me," said Theodosia. She was anxious to get going. Anxious to have something else occupying her mind besides Parker's death and funeral.

The three of them spent five minutes ferrying everything out the back door. Then, just as they were ready to take off, Drayton decided he needed two more teapots. So he ducked back inside.

"Drayton's gonna have a coronary," Haley observed. She was wearing her white chef's jacket over a pair of black leggings. She'd removed her tall chef's hat and was twisting it in her hands.

"Don't say that," said Theodosia. "He's just being mindful."

"I brought three, just in case," said Drayton, slipping out the back door, juggling his precious cargo in a cardboard box.

"Good thinking," said Theodosia, while Haley just rolled her eyes.

Drayton loaded his final box, then turned to Theodosia and Haley, almost reluctant to leave. "You really think Miss Dimple and her brother can hold down the fort?"

"Of course, they can," Haley snapped. "It's a limited menu. Just tea, scones, zucchini bread, and soup. All they have to do is ladle, slice, pour, and serve. Basically, it's idiot-proofed."

"They're not exactly idiots," Theodosia reminded her. "Miss Dimple is our bookkeeper, and her brother used to be an English professor at the College of Charleston."

"Apologies," said Haley, "then let's just say the food service has been greatly simplified. Is that better?"

"Much," said Theodosia.

"You know what?" said Haley, her eyes starting to twinkle. "When Miss Dimple told me she had an elf to help out, I didn't think she literally meant an elf!"

"Excuse me," said Drayton, "you're talking about her brother?"

Haley nodded.

"The man is merely short of stature," said Drayton.

"But did you see his shiny head?" Haley giggled. "Did you see his pointy ears?"

"Nonsense," said Drayton.

Haley nodded sagely. "Miss Dimple was right. He is an elf."

13

❧

Built in 1835 on Horlbeck Creek, Cane Ridge was a former rice plantation that now served as the genteel home for Theodosia's Aunt Libby Ravelle and her companion and housekeeper, Margaret Rose Reese. The property was set high on a vantage point overlooking a quiet pond and marshland, and the surrounding low flat fields, once crisscrossed with dikes and sluiceways, were now thick with brush and forest and blended effortlessly with South Carolina's old-growth piney forests.

The main house was a fanciful Gothic Revival cottage replete with soaring peaks and gables, a steeply pitched shingled roof, and a broad piazza extending around three sides. A now-unused stable, a smokehouse, and smaller outbuildings were adjacent and accessed via a rocky path.

"You're here!" Aunt Libby, tiny, silver haired, and always energetic, rushed out to greet the Indigo Tea Shop gang. "Theo, my darling. And Drayton!"

"You're looking lovely as always," said Drayton, bending down to give Aunt Libby a chaste peck on the cheek.

"And Haley!" Aunt Libby continued. She swept her arms open wide, and Haley rushed to greet her.

"Aunt Libby!" said Haley, giving her a gentle squeeze, "it's been ages!"

"Too long," Aunt Libby cooed. Then she straightened up, squared her narrow shoulders, and gave a delighted grin. But you're all here now and just in the nick of time. We've already had a few guests show up."

"This early?" frowned Drayton, who was struggling to lug two of Haley's metal containers.

Aunt Libby waved a hand as if to dispel his nervousness. "But don't worry your head over them. They're chatting away on the front lawn, enjoying the lovely view. I had my dear neighbor, Mr. Bohicket, bring in a half-dozen tables with chairs and they're all set up to allow for a grand view of the pond." Aunt Libby chuckled. "The cedar waxwings are out there right now, doing their aerial ballet to entertain."

Aunt Libby was a bird lover of the first magnitude. She went through fifty-pound sacks of cracked corn, sunflower seeds, and thistle like they were popcorn at a James Bond movie. And she could instantly recognize birds by the shape of their bill, tail, and wing bars, much the same as aviation addicts delighted in identifying aircraft.

"Come along, come along," Aunt Libby urged. "Bring everything into the kitchen and have at it." Then, as Drayton and Haley trudged past them, Aunt Libby said to Theodosia, "How was the funeral? I assume you went?"

"I did," said Theodosia, "and it was sad, as are all funerals."

"But you're holding up."

"Because I'm keeping busy," said Theodosia.

"Ah," said Aunt Libby, a gleam in her eye.

While Haley quickly unpacked her coolers and began to assemble tea sandwiches, Drayton set about brewing tea.

Theodosia, nervous about seating and serving, ducked out the front door to check the arrangements. But just as Aunt Libby had promised, tables were scattered across her front lawn, which swept down to the pond like a carpet of green velvet. A separate tea table, draped in white linen, had also been set up for the staging of their outdoor tea service.

Aunt Libby had been quite right about the view. The sun-dappled pond shimmered and rippled as flocks of well-fed birds cawed their greetings and wheeled in circles across the sky. Truly a wondrous sight!

"How are the sandwiches coming?" Theodosia asked, as she popped back into the kitchen.

"Coming along great," said Haley. Her butter knife was fairly flying across the slices of bread that she'd laid out.

"How many guests are we expecting?" asked Drayton.

"There were thirty as of yesterday," said Theodosia. "But there'll probably be a few drop-ins."

"No problem," said Haley, "we've got plenty of food."

"Oh, my gosh," said Theodosia, as Haley grabbed a large bread knife and began slicing off crusts with the skill of a samurai warrior. "You're using the silver Tiffany trays?"

"That's what Aunt Libby gave us," said Haley. "She said they hadn't been used for a couple of years and were just sitting on her sideboard looking pretty but gathering dust." She paused. "Except we dusted them."

"Always nice to enjoy the good pieces," said Drayton. Even though he owned a fine, almost museum-quality collection of tea ware that included teacups by Shelley, Spode, and Royal Winton, he wasn't averse to pulling them out and using them for a simple cup of Assam.

"I see her point," said Theodosia. "If this isn't enough of a festive occasion, what is?"

"So how are we going to work this?" asked Drayton, draping an apron around his neck.

"We'll serve the walnut scones first," said Haley, "with the maple pecan butter." She quickly scooped her discarded crusts into a large silver bowl for later distribution to the birds. "Then our second course of quiche."

"Just quiche?" asked Theodosia. She had a sneaking feeling that Haley had something extra up her sleeve.

"Okay, okay," said Haley. "So I made my famous mushroom mornay sauce to drizzle on top."

"Yum," said Drayton. "And a fine sauce it is."

"After the quiche," said Haley, "we'll place three-tiered trays on each of the tables. Tea sandwiches on the top and middle tiers, of course, brownie bites on the bottom tier."

"You're always so well organized," said Theodosia.

Haley nodded, "I am in theory. But nothing ever goes off without a hitch."

But this tea did.

As her guests arrived, Aunt Libby greeted them and led them around front to the tables. After air kisses and exuberant hellos were exchanged, everyone settled in expectantly for their fancy tea luncheon.

That was when Theodosia and Drayton snapped to the business at hand. Theodosia carried out the first round of scones, passed around footed crystal dishes filled with Devonshire cream and sweet honey, made sure everyone was properly served, and then chatted with the guests, many of whom she knew through Aunt Libby. Drayton, armed with two teapots, threaded his way among the tables, pouring tea, answering questions, and doling out little tidbits of information on tea.

Aunt Libby, being Aunt Libby, kept popping up from her chair and offering to help.

"Sit," Theodosia told her. "Enjoy your guests and your event."

"But you're working so hard," she protested.

"Nonsense," said Theodosia. "This is what we do. This is what we love."

And, of course, it was.

* * *

In between the quiche and the tea sandwiches, with every-thing humming like clockwork, Theodosia found time to take a breather. She poured herself a cup of Earl Grey and ambled over to the table where Delaine was seated.

"Thanks for coming," Theodosia said, sliding into the chair across from her. "It means a lot to Aunt Libby that you're here." She paused. "It means a lot to me, too." Hopefully, last night's somewhat heated exchange had been forgotten and forgiven.

"What are friends for?" Delaine chirped. She was resplen-dent in a hot-pink bouclé suit and matching garden-party hat. As she spoke, Delaine was carefully high-grading the egg mixture from the quiche crust, obviously mindful of carbs. "Besides, this is your aunt's charity event. And you know I'm a huge believer in supporting charities. Especially one that helps poor little kitties and dogs."

"Yes, you are very supportive," said Theodosia. Delaine could be maddening, gossipy, and even a touch vulgar, but she was socially conscious and had a terrifically huge heart. Particularly when it came to animals.

"Besides," said Delaine, "I know I can count on you when I have my Clothes Horse Race."

"What is that exactly?" asked Theodosia. Delaine had been chattering about this upcoming event, but Theodosia was still unclear on the details.

"I'm doing a fund-raiser at my boutique to help buy suit-able business attire for women who are trying to reenter the job market," said Delaine. "Most of them have endured some sort of hard-luck struggle—drug rehab, a nasty divorce, domestic violence. Well, you get the picture."

"That sounds like a very worthwhile cause," said Theo-dosia.

Delaine nodded. "Oh, it is. Not everyone was born with a silver spoon in their mouth like . . . um . . . we were."

"Delaine," said Theodosia, deciding to take a small shot in the dark, "how well do you know Peaches Pafford?"

Delaine wrinkled her nose as she flicked away a wayward crumb and said, "Fairly well." Then she seemed to reconsider her words and said, "Well, Peaches has certainly been a good customer in my shop. In fact, she's developed quite a penchant for designer suits and casual silks. And, of course, I've dined at her various restaurants many, many times."

"Let me phrase it differently," said Theodosia. "What do you know about her?"

Delaine narrowed her eyes. "You mean like . . . personal information?"

Theodosia lifted a shoulder. *Yes. That might be of help.*

Delaine fiddled with her enormous moonstone ring as she considered this for a few moments, then said, "She's actually a little guarded about her personal life. But what I *can* tell you is this—Peaches is an extremely good businesswoman. Very smart, very tough."

"Tough," said Theodosia, "in what way?"

"Brutal when it comes to negotiating," said Delaine. "The lease for her newest restaurant, Ariel?" Delaine gave a sharp laugh that was almost a bark. "Peaches pounded Bell Management into the ground. She basically pulverized their leasing agent and got her lease agreement down to something like sixteen dollars a square foot. And I'm talking gross, not net!" Delaine was clearly impressed. "Yup, Peaches goes for the jugular."

Ten minutes later, the tea trays set out on the tables, Haley headed back to Charleston and Theodosia regrouped with Drayton.

"The hard part's over now," Drayton told her. "From here on we can pretty much coast to the finish line."

"So no problems at all?" said Theodosia.

"Delaine was a little demanding, but when isn't she?"

Theodosia chuckled. "She's like one of those rock stars with a ten-page rider on her contract. You know, with demands for white flowers or aromatherapy candles in their dressing room. Or bowls full of Skittles."

"Or Oxycontin," said Drayton.

Aunt Libby noticed them chatting and scurried over.

"How do you think it's going?" Aunt Libby asked.

"A huge success," Drayton proclaimed. "Very well received."

"What was the charge per person?" Theodosia asked, mindful that the event was a fund-raiser.

"We sold tickets for twenty-eight dollars," said Aunt Libby.

"And you've pulled . . . what? Thirty-four, maybe thirty-five guests?" said Theodosia. She ran a quick computation in her head. "That's almost a thousand dollars that will go into the coffers of your animal rescue group."

"Less food costs," said Aunt Libby.

Theodosia waved a hand. "Consider the food my contribution."

"Oh, you dear girl!" said Libby, clutching her arm.

"But let's not rest on our laurels," said Drayton, still anxious to please their guests.

"Refills, then," agreed Theodosia.

"Theo!" called Delaine. She raised an arm and snapped her fingers to gain Theodosia's attention. "Over here!"

Theodosia hurried to Delaine's table with a fresh-brewed pot of tea. "More strawberry Darjeeling?" she asked.

"Refills would be lovely," said Delaine. "But I really called you over so I could introduce you to Majel Carter."

"Ah," said Theodosia, instantly recognizing the name and offering a quick smile to the woman who was now seated across from Delaine. "You're the executive director of Tuesday's Child."

"Guilty as charged," said Majel, holding up her teacup. She was in her early forties, with luminous brown eyes, brown hair curled into a soft bob, and a very kind face. Basically, Majel looked like someone who would probably head a charity devoted to children.

Delaine nodded excitedly. "That's right. Majel founded Tuesday's Child, the charity you so graciously agreed to do the scavenger hunt for." She threw Theodosia a cagey look. "You *are* still participating in the scavenger hunt, aren't you?"

Is there a way to worm my way out of this? Theodosia wondered. *Hmm. Doesn't seem likely.*

"Yes, of course I am," said Theodosia.

"That's so kind of you," said Majel. She had a slightly distracted air about her and a slow, measured way of speaking. Theodosia figured it was probably because Majel dealt primarily with children. Or maybe she had a degree in psychology and was just very deliberate about choosing her words.

"And I want to apologize for not making it to your tea shop yesterday," said Majel.

"Not a problem," said Theodosia.

Majel continued to focus her gaze on Theodosia. "Anyway, when Delaine told me what was going on here today, I decided to drop by and thank you. I appreciate so much that you've agreed to be our sponsor in the scavenger hunt. We're a newer charity and not all that well known yet in the community." Her eyes crinkled. "But after all the kindness of late, I pretty much feel like Tuesday's Child has won the lottery."

"You have," Delaine said with relish.

"How so?" asked Theodosia.

"First the Gibbes Museum offered us the proceeds from this month's fishbowl," said Majel, "and now your tea shop is sponsoring us in the scavenger hunt." She reached out and clutched Theodosia's hand. "In a way you've . . . you've become a kind of guardian angel."

Majel's words and gesture touched Theodosia's heart. And she made up her mind, then and there, to throw herself into the scavenger hunt one hundred percent. She realized she'd been a little grudging about participating. But . . . enough of that.

"There are a lot of at-risk kids who are going to benefit from this," Majel assured her.

"And that's what it's all about," said Theodosia, still feeling guilty for trying to wiggle her way out.

"Oh, look," said Delaine, gesturing and giving an excited little squeal, "I think Drayton is going to do one of his recitations."

"He does so love center stage," said Theodosia. Fact was, Drayton delighted in reciting bits and pieces of tea poetry. And it would appear that one of today's guests had asked him to perform.

The chatter at the tables suddenly dropped off by several decibels and a hush spread across the crowd as all eyes focused on Drayton.

"This," Drayton said, posturing with a rose medallion teapot cupped in the crook of his arm, "is from a Chinese poem penned by Tso Ssu back in the second century." He gave a quick smile. "And I think it's rather appropriate considering our lovely locale."

Then Drayton began to recite in his best oratorical voice:

> *The wild duck soars then hovers*
> *Over my garden orchard.*
> *The fruit has fallen, fresh, and*
> *Ready to pick.*
> *I long for flowers that bend with*

> *The wind and rain.*
> *In my mind I write a play about Tea.*
> *The wind breathes and sighs among*
> *The tripods and cauldrons.*

Applause broke out and Drayton bowed deeply. "Thank you, thank you so much." He spread his arms out and said, "Some of you also had questions? About tea, that is."

A woman in a bright yellow suit raised her hand.

"Yes," said Drayton, pleased.

"A friend told me that the teatime ritual was invented by the Chinese," said the woman. "But I thought the Queen of England came up with it. Which of us is right?"

"Actually," said Drayton, "teatime was invented by the Duchess of Bedford around 1841, to help counteract her afternoon slump." He paused, a twinkle in his eye. "Of course, we don't know what the *Duke* of Bedford was up to."

Laughter ensued.

"Another question?" said Drayton, enjoying himself.

There *was* another question. A woman asked, "When was the first tea brought over from China?"

"The clipper ships first brought their tea cargo to England in the early sixteen hundreds," said Drayton.

"So it took a while," the woman mused.

"Oolong time," Drayton laughed. Then he glanced around, found Aunt Libby in the crowd, and waved for her to come up.

Aunt Libby shook her head, reluctant to be front and center.

But Drayton wasn't having it. "No," he called out to Aunt Libby, "you have to do this. After all, you're the one all these delightful ladies came to support. You and your charity."

"Madison's Home," said Aunt Libby. Now she stood up and made her way to the front of the group. With each step her confidence seemed to grow by leaps and bounds. She let

Drayton give her a kiss, then turned to face her audience. "Thank you all so much for coming," said Aunt Libby. "I guess it's no secret that I'm a huge animal lover. You can pretty much tell by all the birdhouses and feeding stations I have here at Cane Ridge."

There was laughter and nods among the ladies.

Aunt Libby grinned. "I'm also keenly committed to helping stray dogs and cats find a safe, loving home. And that's why the proceeds from today's tea will be going to a wonderful shelter called Madison's Home. It's a no-kill shelter here in Colleton County that's run by a group of very dedicated volunteers. But they can't go it alone, and that's where all of you come in." She hesitated. "The support you've given us here today will make it possible to feed and house many more lovely little creatures for several months."

Applause rang out and Drayton, who'd moved over to stand next to Theodosia, remarked, "Not a dry eye in the house."

"Charity must run in the family," said Majel, smiling at Theodosia.

Slightly embarrassed, Theodosia said, "I like to help out where I can."

"I so appreciate that," said Majel, "especially since the City Charities scavenger hunt starts tomorrow night."

"That's right," said Theodosia.

"And Delaine explained to you how this particular scavenger hunt works?"

Theodosia glanced at Delaine, who was now wandering from table to table, glad-handing people like crazy. Delaine had strong-armed her into participating in the scavenger hunt, but Theodosia had no clue about her actual role. Was she supposed to hunt things down? Was she supposed to field a team?

"Delaine gave me some rudimentary information," Theodosia said, hedging, "but if you could run the basic rules and regulations past me, I'd really appreciate it."

"Well, this scavenger hunt is very fun and techy," said Majel. "Instead of going out and actually *collecting* items, you locate the items or places, take a photo, then send it back to our website."

"Right," said Theodosia. She was greatly relieved she didn't have to drive to hell and gone, then load up her Jeep with a ton of useless, bizarre junk.

"You'll receive your official list tomorrow," said Majel. "Then, after you've hunted down your items, and if the judges deem your list to be complete, you'll move into the finals."

"That's it?" said Theodosia, sounding relieved. She'd thought it'd be more complicated than that.

"That's it," said Majel. She smiled as Aunt Libby came up to their table. "Hello there. I'm the party crasher."

Theodosia made quick introductions between Aunt Libby and Majel, then said, "You think it was a success?"

"Oh, goodness me," said Aunt Libby, "it's a rousing success." She put a hand on Theodosia's shoulder. "And our guests have been raving about your scones. As well as the cream honey."

"That reminds me," said Theodosia. "I'm driving down to Dubose Bees on Friday to check out a new product. How would you like to come along? I could swing by and pick you up."

Aunt Libby grinned. "I'd love to, you know I would."

"Then it's settled," said Theodosia. "We have a date for Friday afternoon."

"Don't let me forget," said Aunt Libby. "Before you leave today, I've got some lovely plantings for you to take back with you. Some dwarf iris, herbs, and wild violets for you to plant in your backyard garden."

"And I've got a check for you," said Drayton, swooping in.

"What?" said Aunt Libby.

"For your charity." He dropped a personal check into her hands and smiled as he saw tears spring to her eyes.

"Why, Drayton," said Theodosia, "I had no idea you had such a soft spot in your heart for dogs and cats."

"Please," he said, stiffening, "tell no one."

14

❧

It was late afternoon by the time Theodosia and Drayton made it back to the Indigo Tea Shop. The place was locked up tight, with no sign of Haley. Probably, Theodosia decided, she was upstairs, soaking in the bathtub with some of the Indigo Tea Shop's own Lazy Lavender Bath Tea. Haley had gotten up at five this morning just to prep and prepare all the food, so she certainly deserved to kick back. Especially since Haley had promised to drop by later tonight and pick up the boxes for the Coffee & Tea Expo. Long day for Haley. Long day for everyone.

"You think we can just stash this stuff in your office?" Drayton asked, as he muscled one of the coolers out of the car. "Deal with it tomorrow?" He didn't just sound tired, his shoulders drooped and his walk was more of a shuffle.

"Works for me," said Theodosia. There weren't any leftovers—what little that remained had been given to Aunt Libby—so it shouldn't be a problem. As far as the plants Aunt Libby had given her, well, those were going to stay here, too. She'd sort out how she was going to deal with them tomorrow.

"Then I'm going directly home," said Drayton. "To slouch in my leather chair and lose myself in a good book. And perhaps contemplate an opera. *Turandot* or *Don Giovanni.*"

"No TV?" Theodosia asked. "No surfing the Net?" It was her little joke. Drayton was a confirmed Luddite who despised any sort of newfangled technology and still prized his collection of vinyl records. There'd be no iPod with earbuds for him.

"I suppose I'm just an old-fashioned fellow," said Drayton. "Who's set in his ways."

"You have convictions," said Theodosia. "Nothing wrong with that."

After dropping Drayton at his home in the historic district, Theodosia was happy to finally pull into her driveway. She knew Earl Grey was okay, since Mrs. Berry, a retired schoolteacher from down the block, picked him up every afternoon and took him for a nice long walk. Probably was clandestinely teaching him his ABCs, too. And how to add and subtract. Or do quantum physics.

"Oh, hey," Theodosia said, as she ducked around the little fishpond that was rimmed in rocks and approached her back door. "What's this?"

A brown cardboard box sat on her back stoop. A delivery.

Scooping it up, Theodosia noted the return address. "It's here," she said aloud, feeling a little tug of joy.

A muffled woof from inside the house greeted her.

Theodosia juggled the box, stuck her key in the lock, and pushed open the door. "I'm home, dear," she announced.

Earl Grey immediately stuck his furry muzzle into her cupped hand. It was a welcome-home ritual they'd repeated for several years.

"Hey, guy," she said. She felt hot doggy breath on her hand and was instantly comforted. "How you doin'?"

"Rrrow." *Good. And you?*

Theodosia set the box on the kitchen table. "Look here. My teapot finally arrived. That was the thump you probably heard at the back door."

Earl Grey cocked his head, then watched as Theodosia grabbed a sharp knife, carefully cut the packing tape, and opened the box.

"Plastic beans," she said, making a face. "Awful."

She swished the little nasties aside, even as they stuck maddeningly to her fingers, and pulled out her teapot. It had a blue-and-purple pansy motif against a swirl background. Manufactured by Arthur Wood & Son in Staffordshire, England.

Earl Grey nosed closer, the better to see and share the moment, as most dogs are wont to do.

She held the teapot lower so he could sniff. Earl Grey did so and was politely positive. Still, he wasn't quite as thrilled as Theodosia.

Once Theodosia had taken a quick turn around the block with Earl Grey, she called Shelby.

"Shelby," she said, "this is Theodosia."

"Oh . . . hi." Shelby sounded distracted. And lots more distant than she'd been this morning after the service.

"We need to get together," said Theodosia.

"Mmm," said Shelby, hedging, "I'm kind of busy right now."

"Right now this minute or right now this evening?" asked Theodosia. She wasn't about to let Shelby off the hook. "Because we really need to talk. So here's a plan, why don't we meet up around eight o'clock?"

There was silence on the other end of the line and then Shelby said, "I suppose. So . . . maybe meet at a coffee shop?"

She wants to meet in neutral territory, Theodosia thought. *She doesn't want to come here.*

"Sure. Which one?"

"How about the Big Grind over on Water Street?"

"See you at eight," said Theodosia.

But when quarter to eight rolled around, Theodosia was already there. She'd arrived early so she could scope the location and pick a table where they wouldn't be disturbed. Now she was waiting and thinking, preparing herself mentally to ask Shelby some hard and probing questions.

At five past eight, Shelby rolled in. Dressed in blue jeans and a mauve T-shirt, with a fringed suede bag slung across her shoulders, she gazed around blankly, then finally spotted Theodosia. She walked slowly over to the table and sat down.

"I hope you don't mind meeting at a coffee shop like this," were Shelby's opening words. She gave a sheepish grin as she set her bag down and they both watched it puddle on the table. "I hope you don't think it's akin to sleeping with the enemy."

"Not at all," said Theodosia. *Maybe just a little bit.*

"And they do serve tea," Shelby pointed out.

"Yes, they do," said Theodosia. She'd already gone to the counter and bought a glass of grapefruit juice. "It was thoughtful of you to pick a place that has tea on the menu." Theodosia knew the tea served here came in little bags instead of being fresh-brewed from tea leaves. Bags were fine in a pinch, as long as you realized they contained the dregs of tea leaves— the little bits and pieces of leaves and stems that were left behind once the really fine leaves were selectively chosen, measured out, and packaged by the better tea providers.

"You want anything?" Shelby asked.

Theodosia lifted her cup.

"Be right back," said Shelby, as she dug out her wallet and headed for the counter.

Shelby was uncomfortable and stalling, but Theodosia didn't much care. She was going to get to the heart of the matter—the will and inheritance—even if Shelby squirmed like a worm on a hook for the next thirty minutes.

When Shelby returned to the table with a cup of coffee, Theodosia didn't waste any time. "I have a few questions," she said.

"I know you do," said Shelby. She took a sip of coffee, winced, then blew on it.

"First things first," said Theodosia. "Do you know anything about the missing file?"

Shelby rolled her eyes. "Oh, jeez. You mean the one marked *Current Projects?*"

"That's the one exactly."

"I don't have it," said Shelby. "All I can tell you is that the police have been asking me about it nonstop."

"I'm sure you can see why," said Theodosia. "The contents are missing and we—that is, Detective Tidwell and I—believe they might hold pertinent business information. In fact, I'd imagine you'd want to recover it, too. After all, Parker *did* name you as his heir and insurance beneficiary."

Shelby looked unsettled. "I had no idea he was going to do that!"

"But now you do," said Theodosia. "Now you're a very rich girl."

"I don't *want* to be."

"That's beside the point," said Theodosia. "Now Solstice is your restaurant and you've been dumped right in the middle of the soup."

"The soup?" said Shelby, not understanding.

"A highly suspicious death. And the ensuing murder investigation," said Theodosia, biting off each word. "Which will grind relentlessly forward until Parker's killer is apprehended."

Shelby stared at Theodosia, and then her eyes went wide and her guarded expression suddenly crumpled. "Oh, my gosh!" she moaned. "You think I killed him, don't you?"

"Did you?" asked Theodosia. She had to ask.

"No!" Shelby wailed. "Of course not!"

"But you were at the Neptune Aquarium that night."

"I *told* you that!"

"And you could have easily led Parker onto those walkways," said Theodosia. "You could have slipped him a coy little note and he wouldn't have been one bit suspicious. In fact, he probably would have thought you had some delicious little surprise up your sleeve."

"Not *that* kind of surprise!" Shelby cried. "Believe me, I'm just as confused and upset as you are!"

Theodosia's expression was one of cool appraisal. Did she believe this girl? Or was Shelby incredibly skilled at deception? That was the big question, wasn't it?

"Please," said Shelby, looking pained. "You have to believe me. I never would've harmed Parker or conspired to set him up."

Theodosia continued to stare at her. "I want to believe you." *Do I really?*

"Then believe me!" Shelby cried. "That's not who I am. I'm not a killer!"

Theodosia took a sip of juice while Shelby pulled a Kleenex from her bag and dabbed at her eyes.

Crocodile tears? Or genuine tears?

A few seconds ticked by. "Okay, then," said Theodosia.

"You believe me?" asked Shelby, still sniffling.

"I want to," said Theodosia. "I really do."

"Then ask me anything," said Shelby. "I want Parker's killer brought to justice just as much as you do. That's why I came to you in the first place!"

"In that case," said Theodosia, "I want you to try to dredge up some answers for me."

"I've been trying!" said Shelby. "But between talking to you and the police and his family, my brain is like cobwebs! Because I don't think I really *know* anything!"

Theodosia held up a hand. "I hear what you're saying. But a few days have passed, and now you've had some time to reflect. To kind of digest everything."

"Yeah. Maybe." Shelby didn't sound convinced.

"I know I asked you this before, but what *was* going on in Parker's life?"

Shelby gave a helpless shrug. "I don't know. Probably just . . . business as usual."

"Think," said Theodosia. "Think hard. Had he been worried about anything in particular? Were there certain problems or issues that were preying on his mind?"

Shelby shook her head again.

"Anything to do with his restaurant? Perhaps something that had veered off track?"

Shelby touched her foam cup to her lips and nibbled at it. Seconds passed. She said, "You mean like the aquarium deal?"

15

Theodosia's heart did a slow-motion flip-flop. *"What* aquarium deal?"

"The one for the restaurant franchise," said Shelby. Then she shook her head, as if to quickly dismiss the idea. "No, it wouldn't have made any difference. That deal had pretty much evaporated."

Theodosia put her elbows on the table and leaned forward expectantly. "Tell me all about the restaurant franchise. And start from the very beginning."

"Oh," said Shelby, her brows puckering as she tried to construct her thoughts, "but that was all over with maybe a month ago."

"Tell me anyway," said Theodosia, trying to sound a note of encouragement.

"At one point Parker was under the impression that he was going to be awarded the restaurant franchise at the Neptune Aquarium."

"Okay," said Theodosia.

Shelby nodded. "They'd issued something called an RFT?"

"An RFP?" asked Theodosia. "A request for proposal?"

Shelby snapped her fingers. "That's it. Anyway, Parker had put together a whole pitch . . . a proposal. And a pretty neat one at that. His idea was to call the restaurant Angel Fish and serve bistro-type fare. You know, grilled fish, steaks with *pommes frites*, a couple of pasta dishes."

"And his pitch was well-received?"

"As I recall, it was at the time. Parker met with the director and was pretty much promised he'd be given the restaurant."

"Just to be clear," said Theodosia, "when you say director, we're talking about David Sedakis."

"Yes."

"So the Neptune Aquarium gave the nod and there was a contract drawn up? An agreement was put in place?"

"Mmm . . . it seemed like there was," said Shelby. "But there couldn't have been, could there? Because the deal went away." She made a little accompanying sound. *"Pfft."*

So that's why Sedakis tabled the restaurant discussion last night, thought Theodosia. *Because Parker's name would have probably come up. And there I was, sitting right there in the middle of his cozy little group!*

Theodosia pondered this new development. David Sedakis had been seemingly won over by Parker's proposal, had even told him on the down low that he was going to be awarded a contract. Then Sedakis had changed his mind and taken it away from Parker.

And then Parker was murdered. At the Neptune Aquarium.

From Theodosia's vantage point, the whole sorry mess made Sedakis look very, very suspicious.

Theodosia straightened up in her chair. "Who did get the franchise?" she asked. The restaurant hadn't opened yet, wouldn't for several more weeks, so it was anybody's guess.

Shelby shrugged. "No idea."

"But it was someone other than Parker?"

"I suppose."

Could it be Peaches Pafford? Theodosia wondered.

Shelby sipped her coffee and stared at Theodosia.

"Do the police know about this?" Theodosia asked. "Did you tell Tidwell or one of his investigators that Parker had a possible deal pending with the Neptune Aquarium?"

Shelby blinked several times. "No, I didn't. You think it's important?"

"Yes, it's important." Theodosia was energized and practically shouting now. "In fact, this information could turn out to be a very big piece of the puzzle."

"Oh wow," said Shelby, looking stunned. "I had no idea."

But Theodosia had already pulled out her cell phone and was dialing Tidwell's number. It rang at the police station downtown, and then she had to do some fast talking to get past his gatekeepers. Finally she had Tidwell on the line.

"Why are you calling me at home?" Tidwell asked, sounding both impatient and grumpy.

Theodosia quickly delivered the news about the restaurant franchise at the Neptune Aquarium. "Did you know about this?" she asked. "That Parker had been awarded the restaurant deal then shut out?"

"First I've heard," said Tidwell. "Obviously, no one at the aquarium was particularly forthcoming with this information, either."

"Especially from their board of directors," said Theodosia. "Unless nobody knew about this except Sedakis. Is that possible?"

"Possible," said Tidwell.

"Maybe," Theodosia theorized, "Sedakis dumped Parker because he was paid to?"

"You mean Sedakis accepted a bribe from someone?" said Tidwell.

"Could have happened," said Theodosia. "The aquarium

deal would be a nice fat plum for any restaurateur. Except that . . ." Theodosia was really rolling now. "Except that maybe Parker threatened to expose Sedakis's questionable business practices."

"You're making an awfully big leap," said Tidwell.

"But it could have happened that way," said Theodosia.

"Here's what I want you to do," said Tidwell. "Tell your young lady, Shelby, to go on home. Tell her I'll be sending two investigators over to her house shortly."

"Just a minute," said Theodosia. She dropped her phone and said to Shelby, "You're supposed to go home. Two investigators are going to come by and . . ."

"No!" Shelby wailed. "I've already *been* down that road."

Theodosia leaned across the table and grabbed the girl's wrist. "Listen, Shelby, this is a *good* thing! The police are going to be very kind and ask you some very basic questions about the aquarium deal." She held the phone up to her face again. "Did you hear that?" she asked Tidwell. "They *are* going to be kind and considerate, aren't they?"

"Yes," said a reluctant Tidwell.

Turning her attention back to Shelby, Theodosia said, "This is good, honey. This could be a break in the case."

Shelby still looked doubtful. "You think?"

"Yes, I do. And kudos to you for helping out."

But Shelby was still nervous. "I really hate this. I know the police are still suspicious of me."

"If you didn't do anything," said Theodosia, "then you haven't got a thing to worry about." *And if you did, then watch out!*

When Theodosia arrived home, Haley and her boyfriend were waiting in the backyard. Scrunched together among the camellias on a black wrought-iron bench, they were engaged in a little innocent canoodling.

"Sorry to keep you guys waiting," said Theodosia, as she scrambled up the walk and unlocked the back door.

"That's okay," said Haley. "We're cool."

"Well, for gosh sakes, come in," said Theodosia. She threw open the door and Earl Grey came bounding out, head high, legs churning.

"Oops," said Theodosia. She grabbed him by the collar and pulled him up short. "Not so fast, Mr. Dog. Not until we've all been introduced."

"Theodosia," said Haley, "this is Jack Dickey. My friend with the van."

"Nice to meet you, Jack," said Theodosia. "And thanks for offering to help us move all our stuff." She gave him a sideways glance. "Or did you get shanghaied?"

"Hard to say no to Haley," Jack grinned, as Earl Grey twisted and strained to get closer to him.

"Hey, boy." Jack stuck out a hand for Earl Grey to sniff. "You're a nice guy." He looked at Theodosia. "What breed?"

"Dalbrador," said Theodosia.

"I have a Sharbrador of my own," said Jack.

"Also an excellent pedigree," said Theodosia. They all trooped into her kitchen then, and she kicked at one of the boxes with her toe. "Here are the boxes. All tea and T-Bath products."

"Piece of cake," said Jack, bending to scoop up two boxes at once. "And you want these delivered to the Coliseum?"

"That's right," said Theodosia. "Right to the dock. There's supposed to be someone there until ten tonight."

The three of them bent and hoisted and grunted for a few minutes until all the boxes had been stacked in the back of Jack's van.

"Perfect," said Theodosia, giving the rear fender a little tap. "Thanks so much."

"Anytime," said Jack, as Haley beamed at him.

"You're sure I can't pay you for this?" asked Theodosia.

"Just happy to help out," said Jack.

"You be sure to drop by the tea shop," said Theodosia. "The way I see it, you've earned quite a few chits for free lunches."

"Sounds good," said Jack, smiling at Haley.

"Good night," said Haley, waving. "See you at the expo tomorrow."

Theodosia turned to go back inside, while Earl Grey lunged after Haley and Jack.

"Earl Grey?" said Theodosia. She clapped her hands together. "Come on, fella."

"I think he wants to go with us," said Jack.

Haley took up the cheer. "Hey, pup, you want to take a ride with us? Maybe stop for a burger, then sleep over at my place?"

As if he were being invited on an outing (which he was), Earl Grey threw Theodosia an eager *Can I, Mom?* look.

Theodosia was tickled by Haley's invitation. "Are you sure you want to take him? You have to be at the expo first thing tomorrow."

"No problem," said Haley. "Anyway, it'll be fun. Like a doggy pajama party." She bent down and ruffled the fur on Earl Grey's shoulder. "And you're already wearing your fleece jammies, aren't you?"

Theodosia considered this. Haley now lived in the apartment above the tea shop where she used to live. So, really, Earl Grey would be going back to his old familiar haunt.

"Well, sure, I guess so," said Theodosia. *Why not?* "Okay." She waved both hands. "*Bon soir.* See you all tomorrow."

With Earl Grey gone for the night, Theodosia had the place all to herself. She wandered upstairs, where she'd set up her own little reading room in the second-floor turret and settled into an overstuffed red-and-blue chintz chair. She grabbed a book she'd been reading—a really fine thriller—then propped it open and tried to concentrate.

But she found herself too keyed up to read. The funeral this morning, Aunt Libby's tea party this afternoon, and then her meeting with Shelby tonight had left her feeling jazzed and unsettled. And, of course, Parker's death still hung heavy over her head.

Theodosia was also half hoping and waiting for Tidwell to call back. Surely he'd call and give her a quick report, wouldn't he? After all, she'd been instrumental in uncovering what could be a rather important clue.

But by the time her old Seth Thomas mantel clock hammered out its ten o'clock chime, Tidwell still hadn't called. And Theodosia decided he probably wasn't going to call.

Typical Tidwell.

She snuggled in, determined to plow through another few chapters. Finally, her mind engaged and she tumbled down the rabbit hole to lose herself in her book.

But an hour later, when Theodosia was ready for bed, her cozy little cottage seemed like a very lonely place indeed without her beloved Earl Grey.

16

⁓❧⁓

The Coffee & Tea Expo had been the brainchild of the Eastern Seaboard Coffee Association, a loosely formed coalition of
coffee wholesalers and distributors. They'd decided to stage a
major coffee expo at the North Charleston Coliseum to
appeal to the many retailers and coffee shops who bought
and resold their products, with expectations and high hopes
that these retailers might buy and resell even more.

But the Coffee Association had been able to persuade
only three dozen or so coffee and food vendors to participate.
And three dozen booths did not an expo make.

After much scratching of heads, someone had the brilliant
idea to expand the expo to include tea wholesalers and vendors. The tea people, enthused by this invitation, had jumped
on board wholeheartedly and even pulled in several trade
councils as well as a few overseas vendors. Then they suggested that tastings, cooking demos, and a few breakout
seminars be added to the roster of events. That really kicked
the expo into high gear and boosted the number to more

than eighty exhibitors, a number that seemed to resonate happily with everyone.

And now Theodosia was making her way down the first row of exhibitors, checking her program, fairly impressed by the variety and caliber of the exhibitors. A spectacular black-and-green bamboo-themed booth housed the Chen Lung Tea Company from Taipei. They were already handing out samples of their silver jasmine tea. Down the row were two food service vendors, Chatterly Cheesecake Company and Dixie's Fine Chocolates. Plus there were umpteen booths that displayed teakettles and tea cozies, coffeepots and funky coffee mugs, as well as booths showcasing Jamaican Blue Mountain coffee and Kenyan rooibos tea.

Theodosia rambled through the expo, thoroughly enjoying herself, and finally stumbling upon the Indigo Tea Shop booth, which Haley had designed and pretty much volunteered to honcho. At least for a short time this morning.

They'd opted for the bare-bones booth, which consisted of a plain black backdrop, a six-foot table, and two chairs, then added their own touches to make the whole thing pop. Now exotic posters depicting mountainous tea gardens in China and India formed the backdrop, and a large Indigo Tea Shop banner topped the whole thing. A shelf was prominently lined with T-Bath products, and a larger, lower shelf held silver tins filled with Drayton's proprietary blends of tea. They'd debated over which of his teas to wholesale at the expo, then selected Cooper River Cranberry, Britannia Breakfast Blend, and Lemon Verbena, just because those were the ones Drayton had pushed and because those blends had proved to be perennial best sellers. As Theodosia liked to say, "Shoot the easy ones first."

Haley was perched behind the table, chatting away with two women. When she saw Theodosia elbowing her way through the already sizable morning crowd, she grinned and waved her over.

"This is the tea shop owner I was telling you about,"

Haley said to the two women who'd convened at her booth. "Theodosia Browning. She's a really smart entrepreneur and the founder of the Indigo Tea Shop."

Both women nodded politely and with interest.

"Theo," Haley burbled on, "I want you to meet Helen and Andrea. These two ladies are planning to open a tea shop in Florence." Florence was a medium-sized town some two hundred miles north of Charleston.

"Nice to meet you," said Theodosia. "And best of luck to you."

"Thank you," said Helen, who looked at her expectantly. "Haley was just pitching us on the idea of buying some of your tea blends in bulk."

"For brewing in our tea shop," added Andrea. "And, I guess, retailing, too."

Haley jumped in again. "Like I mentioned before, our tea master, Drayton Conneley, really knows his tea. He worked for a tea wholesaler in London and has even attended several of the tea auctions in Amsterdam."

"Tea auctions?" said Andrea. This was news to her.

"Oh yeah," said Haley. "Amsterdam is pretty much where all the world's tea is bought and sold. That's where the best tea leaves are bought by the pickiest tea companies. Then what's left over, the dust and dregs and things, is snapped up by the tea bag companies."

"That's how it works?" said Helen. "I had no idea."

"Tell you what," said Haley, "take one of our brochures and think about it."

"And if you're interested in retailing your own brand of tea, we can help you with private labeling," said Theodosia.

"Sounds good," said Helen.

"And call if you have questions," Theodosia added. "We're always happy to help out fellow tea shop owners."

"Hey," Haley said to Theodosia, as the two women wandered off, "what do you think of our booth?"

"Looks great," said Theodosia. "And it would appear you've been fairly busy."

"Aw, not so much," said Haley, "it's only the first day. I think tomorrow will be the biggie." She pushed her stick-straight hair behind her ears. "I didn't think you'd show up quite this early."

"I thought you might be anxious to head back to the Indigo Tea Shop," said Theodosia.

"I am," said Haley, "since we've got the Broad Street Garden Club coming in at noon."

Theodosia glanced at her watch. "What time is Jenny supposed to take over?" Jenny Hartley was a friend of Haley's who was going to man the tea booth until Haley could come back in midafternoon.

"She should be here around ten, ten thirty," said Haley. "Think you can hold out until then?"

"I'll do my best," said Theodosia.

"Oh, hey," said Haley, "I already wrote up a couple of orders for our Vanilla Honey Blend." Vanilla Honey Blend was one of Drayton's house blends that combined white tea from China's Fujian province with hints of vanilla and honey. "Isn't it neat," Haley continued, "how giving out free samples really helps?"

"Yes, it does help," said Theodosia, who'd logged several years as a marketing executive before she'd left that hurly-burly 24/7 world to run a tea shop.

Theodosia slipped behind the table then and took over the booth. She handed out samples, greeted a few tea vendors she knew, and tried to look friendly and approachable as retailers streamed past. She wasn't sure how beneficial this booth would prove to be, but she was anxious to test the results. After all, tea drinking was still growing by leaps and bounds and she had almost two dozen house blends she could retail. To say nothing of her T-Bath products. In this tight economy, every little bit helped when it came to fluffing up the bottom line.

"Well, Theo-*do*-sia," brayed Peaches Pafford. She sidled

up to the booth and gazed around. "I didn't expect to find *you* here. And manning your own little booth at that." Peaches's laugh was almost a snicker. "Aren't you just the eager beaver little entrepreneur."

Theodosia, who'd been explaining the difference between first-flush and second-flush Darjeeling to a potential customer, stopped what she was doing and took a long, hard look at Peaches. *What is she doing here? Besides interrupting me?*

Peaches, meanwhile, jabbed an index finger at a tin of Indian spice tea. "Indian spice," she said loudly, "does that mean it's genuinely spicy or just fruity?"

"Excuse me," Theodosia said to her customer, then turned to deal with the disruptive Peaches. "Peaches? Is there something I can help you with?" Her tone was cool and the subtext of her question was, *Why are you being so rude?*

As if Peaches knew what Theodosia was really asking, she said, "And do you have chocolate tea also?"

Theodosia sighed inwardly as she stared at Peaches. Today Peaches was wearing a pink pantsuit with her slightly pinkish hair lacquered into a lazy swirl. Somewhere, in the back of Theodosia's brain, was a fuzzy memory of a character named Strawberry Shortcake.

"Chocolate tea?" Peaches said again.

"Um, you're planning to serve chocolate tea at one of your four-star restaurants?" It was all Theodosia could come up with at the moment.

Peaches let loose a throaty laugh. "No, silly. I'm thinking seriously about expanding my company and opening a patisserie." She hesitated. "Among other things."

"Really," said Theodosia. *Now what does she have up her proverbial sleeve?*

Peaches assumed a pussycat grin. "I was thinking of calling my patisserie Bittersweet." She tapped a tin of tea with a manicured forefinger. "You like that name?"

"Sure," said Theodosia, with just enough enthusiasm to remain polite. "It's a great name."

Peaches rattled on. "Like I said, it would be a strictly Parisian-style patisserie. And with a name like Bittersweet, we'd no doubt serve indulgences like chocolate walnut bread, chocolate velvet brownies, chocolate latte scones, and even chocolate biscotti." She paused. "Who knows? If I get Bittersweet off the ground we might even have to enter the chocolatier contest."

"Which Haley recently won," said Theodosia.

"Oh, did she?" said Peaches, making a big show of not knowing. But, of course, she really did know.

"Anything I can do to help," said Theodosia, moving away from Peaches, "be sure to let me know."

Peaches waggled her fingers. "Oh, I will, dear. I will."

Thirty minutes later, Jenny showed up and Theodosia was quite happy to relinquish her apron as well as her booth duties.

"You'll be okay?" Theodosia asked Jenny. "Haley briefed you?"

"She did," said Jenny. "But I'm pretty much an old hand at this. I worked the exotic food show at Johnson and Wales last year."

"Then you know your stuff," said Theodosia.

"To be honest," said Jenny, "I was the one who kind of coached Haley on how to handle this booth."

"Blessings on your head, then," said Theodosia, happy to be free, "because you know what you're doing." She ducked down another row of booths, hoping for a final quick look before she headed back to the tea shop.

But rounding the corner by the India Tea Producers booth, she hit a wall of people who seemed to be going nowhere fast. And from the steamy, malty aroma permeating the air, Theodosia figured they were lined up for a taste of Assam. So Theodosia jigged left and, as if things weren't weird enough in her life, ran smack-dab into Lyle Manship.

"You!" she cried, rearing back. Manship was pretty much the last person she expected to see here.

It took Manship a few seconds to recognize her. Then he said, "And you. Tea lady. We meet again."

"I didn't know you were a coffee and tea aficionado," she said.

"I'm not," he told her. "Truth be told, I'd rather hoist a good glass of Bordeaux or a tumbler of Jameson. But my café, Violet's, has definitely moved in the direction of gourmet coffees and teas, so I have to stay on top of things." He shrugged. "It's what the market is asking for."

"Yes," said Theodosia. "The market."

Manship squinted at her, as if he were sizing her up for something, then said, "You know a lot about tea, huh?"

"A fair amount," she said. "Although there are endless varieties and blends, so it seems I'm constantly learning something new."

"Then I might have an interesting proposition for you," said Manship.

Theodosia looked askance. "What's that?"

"Would you ever consider leading a tea cruise?" Manship asked. He held up his hand and said, "Before you answer that, let me explain a little bit."

"Okay."

"I have a friend who runs a small cruise ship line out of Miami. Insignia Cruises? Maybe you've heard of them?"

"Not really," said Theodosia. The only time she ever paid attention to cruise ships was when one of them made national news. When all the passengers came down with some weird influenza or when someone, often a newlywed for some odd reason, took a dive over the railing never to be heard from again.

"Insignia Cruises," Manship explained, "has smaller-capacity ships and actually *themes* its various voyages. You know, shopping cruises, bridge tournament cruises . . ."

"And tea cruises," said Theodosia.

"That's it," said Manship. "Their ports of call tend to be places like George Town in Grand Cayman or Nassau in the Bahamas. Major shopping ports especially geared toward the ladies, who tend to go a little gaga over all that duty-free shopping."

"Isn't Grand Cayman big with offshore banking?" Theodosia asked him.

Manship shrugged. "There's that, too." He rocked back on his heels and studied her. "So. Are you interested?"

Theodosia shook her head. *Work for this sleazeball? Not on your life.* "No," she said. "No, I'm really not."

17

Haley and Miss Dimple were working toe to toe in the kitchen when Theodosia returned.

"Hey," said Haley, looking up from the pan of sweet potato butter she was stirring. "I take it Jenny showed up as promised?"

"She sure did," said Theodosia. "Precisely when she said she would."

"Don't you love people who keep their promises?" asked Haley. "Don't you wish more people would honor their word about things?"

"It would certainly make life easier," said Theodosia. She grabbed a clean spoon, dipped it into a bowl filled with lemon curd, and took a taste. Delicious!

"We're talking about reliable folks like you, Miss Dimple," said Haley, sidling over and giving her diminutive assistant a shoulder nudge. "We know we can always count on you."

"Like yesterday," said Theodosia. "We can't thank you enough. Your brother, too."

"Oh, I think he had fun," said Miss Dimple. "Gave him a chance to mix with people and be pedantic."

"You guys were real troopers," Haley told Miss Dimple.

Miss Dimple grinned from ear to ear and ducked her head. "You're all such loves," she cooed. "Which is why it's always so much fun to work here."

"You hear that?" Haley chortled, "she thinks it's *fun*. It's not just a job, it's an adventure."

"Excuse me," said Drayton, as he pushed his way into the kitchen to join them. "Is someone all gung ho and planning to enlist? Looking for adventure, et al.?"

"That's right, Drayton," said Haley, as she pulled a baking sheet of biscuits from the oven. "I've developed a sudden hankering to tap my inner machismo and jump out of helicopters. Or helos, as the guys call them nowadays."

"Then you should join the National Guard," said Miss Dimple. "I have a friend whose granddaughter joined the Guard and she's just crazy about driving Humvees all over the place."

"Humvees?" said Haley, her eyes lighting up. "Now that's what I call fun!"

"You need help in the tea room?" Theodosia asked Drayton.

"Not quite yet," said Drayton. "Miss Dimple's been running orders in and out and doing a superb job."

"Oh, Drayton," Miss Dimple said, turning a primrose pink. "How you do go on."

"But in twenty minutes or so when our garden club guests arrive," said Drayton, "then I shall need you, my dear Theo, to play genial hostess and chat everyone up."

"Chatting's my thing," said Theodosia.

"So how was the expo?" asked Drayton.

"Very impressive," said Theodosia. "And much larger than I thought it would be. Lots of vendors."

"That's good," said Drayton. "How about attendance? Haley seemed to think it was busy enough."

"It seems to be drawing a good crowd," said Theodosia.

"Are you worried about your lecture this afternoon?" Haley asked. "Not enough people in the audience?"

"That's really the last thing on my mind," said Drayton. He shifted his attention back to Theodosia. "Did you see the enormous bouquet of flowers that arrived?"

"Pink roses and peach hydrangeas," said Miss Dimple. "A spectacular arrangement with an aroma to die for. It practically overpowers all of Drayton's teas."

"Let me guess," said Theodosia. "The garden club sent the bouquet over? To grace their luncheon table?"

"Exactly," said Drayton. "Which Miss Dimple and I have set with Jason English bone china and Reed and Barton flatware."

"Huh," said Haley. "The fancy stuff."

"That's because they're fancy ladies," said Miss Dimple. "They all have big homes and big gardens."

"And big money," Haley added.

"Wait until you see what's on the other tables," Drayton said to Theodosia.

"What?" she said.

Drayton smiled. "Our dear Miss Dimple took all those plants Aunt Libby sent home with you yesterday and planted them in those chipped teacups you were going to toss."

"Seriously?" said Theodosia.

"You should see them," chimed in Haley. "Adorable. With all the leaves and stuff you can't even see the chipped rims."

"Those plants were beginning to wilt and the teacups seemed too nice to throw in the garbage," said Miss Dimple.

"You're an angel," Theodosia told Miss Dimple, who blushed furiously at her words.

"But now to work," said Drayton, doing a quick check of Haley's prep table. "Kindly remind me, Haley, our first course today shall be chilled soup?"

"Righto," said Haley. "Summer gazpacho with Parmesan crisps."

"Mmm," said Miss Dimple, wrinkling her nose. "And are those Parmesan crisps ever good. Easy to make, too. Haley just mounded little bits of cheese on a baking sheet and a few minutes later, poof! Thin little puddles of cheesy delight."

"Moving to a summer menu puts me in the mood to brew a pot of my cinnamon summer blend," said Drayton.

"Then why don't you?" said Theodosia. "It would be especially lovely with our main course of chicken divan and hot biscuits."

"Yes, it would," said Drayton, looking pleased.

Everyone put their noses to the grindstone then, while Theodosia ducked back into her office. There was a pile of invoices stacked on top of her desk and if she didn't sift through it and mark exactly which ones should be paid, nobody would receive their check.

So that was what she did for fifteen minutes, working quickly, approving most, putting a couple on the back burner because of incomplete deliveries. But all the while, in the back of Theodosia's mind, was a low-level rumble about Parker. A feeling that she should have figured out more than she did. That she should be working dutifully on finding a suspect.

Finally, Theodosia put down her pen, scrunched around in her chair until she found a comfy pose, and stared at the wall across from her desk. Tried to zone out and let random ideas come floating into her mind.

Because, for some strange reason, like a cluster of auspicious planetary aspects in the western sky, a number of suspects seemed to have lined up nice and neatly. Peaches Pafford was one, simply because she'd been trying to wrest control of Solstice from Parker.

Then there was Lyle Manship, slightly shady and a touch

aggressive, who had also been working on a deal with Parker. A deal that had recently fallen through.

David Sedakis seemed like a reasonable suspect, too. Mostly because he'd jilted Parker businesswise and then the murder had happened right under his nose at the aquarium he headed. So Sedakis had *access*.

Of course, Shelby was still rattling around in the mix, and so was Joe Beaudry, the lawyer who'd been an almost-partner.

And there was something else, too. Something pinging around inside Theodosia's brain that she couldn't quite access. Was it something she'd seen? Something she'd heard? Theodosia tried to dredge it up and couldn't.

Hmm. Maybe later. Maybe my mind will cough it up.

So, when all was said and done, what exactly was she left with? Theodosia slipped out of her ballet flats, wiggled her toes, and let them sink into the Persian carpet. What indeed? There were suspects with motives, motives that were a little foggy, and no proof to convict—or at least arrest—anyone at all.

And, strangely enough, everyone seemed to keep circling around Solstice and around her. What was that tried-and-true maxim? The killer always returns to the scene of the crime?

So . . . had anyone returned?

Theodosia tapped a finger against her desk and frowned. *Actually, they never really left.*

Theodosia's friend Sarah Stillwell was no longer president of the Broad Street Garden Club, but a friendly, bubbly social-ite by the name of Charlotte Webster had taken her place. Charlotte was a dynamo in a pale-peach suit and cream-colored straw hat who ushered in eight expectant garden club members, then carefully orchestrated their seats around the large circular table. Their flowers sat center stage while tiny flames from tall, pink tapers danced and flickered, causing the dishes, crystal, and flatware to sparkle.

"Perfection!" Charlotte declared, then immediately grabbed Theodosia by the arm and introduced herself. "I'm *so* happy to meet you," she gushed. "And so delighted you could accommodate our little group with just a few days' notice."

"We're delighted to have you," said Theodosia. It was always fun to host a larger group. Let the Indigo Tea Shop show its stuff, so to speak. She glanced around the table, smiling at each guest, then said, "We have a four-course menu for you today, beginning with our famous cranberry oat scones served with generous dollops of lemon curd. The second course consists of a summer gazpacho, made with fresh-picked tomatoes, sweet onions, and home-grown cucumbers."

There was a spatter of applause.

For your luncheon entrée," Theodosia continued, "we'll be serving chicken divan accompanied by baby spring peas and hot biscuits. And, last but not least, we shall try to enchant you with our famous three-tiered trays filled with chocolate bars, Charleston pecan brownie bars, and miniature cheesecakes."

"For your tea-drinking enjoyment," said Drayton, "I've brewed pots of full-bodied Lapsang souchong as well as my proprietary cinnamon summer blend. And, please, if one or the other isn't quite to your liking, be sure to let me know your preference. We have more than three hundred varieties of loose-leaf tea in stock here at the Indigo Tea Shop, so I'm sure I can find one exactly right for you."

Miss Dimple carried out a tray piled with scones, and Theodosia, using her silver serving tongs, gently placed one on everyone's plate. The scones were followed by individual footed glass dishes filled with lemon curd.

Some fifteen minutes later, after receiving oohs and ahhs and doing refills on tea, they served the gazpacho garnished with Parmesan crisps. And once soup spoons began to delicately clink, Theodosia pulled herself away for a short breather.

Or thought she was, because just as customers vacated two of their smaller tables, Delaine and Majel came spilling in.

"Oh, you're frightfully busy!" exclaimed Delaine, glancing around. She seemed keenly disappointed that Theodosia was doing so well. "And with the garden club yet. Hello, ladies!" she cooed and got friendly hellos back in return. Delaine had once served as vice president but had stepped down to pay more attention to her retail shop. Now she turned an unhappy gaze on Theodosia. "You're practically filled!"

"Not to worry," said Theodosia. "Space may be at a premium, but I'll always find room for the two of you."

"Glad to hear it," Delaine chirped. "Since I've pretty much become a regular here!"

"You certainly are," Theodosia agreed. She grabbed two tea menus, then ushered Delaine and Majel to a table that Miss Dimple had hastily cleared and set.

"Seems to me," said Delaine, looking rather self-important, "there should be some sort of polite acknowledgment of my patronage." Her eyes lit up. "Perhaps a small brass plaque on one of the tables?"

"Let me think about that," Theodosia told her. *For about two seconds.*

"Or are you too busy *investigating*?" asked Delaine. She smirked and rolled her eyes.

Majel, bless her soul, defused the moment. "This is such a treat!" she exclaimed. "To be able to enjoy a proper tea two days running."

"It does kind of get in your blood," Delaine confided.

"I'm glad you were able to make it to Aunt Libby's place yesterday," Theodosia told Majel.

"Oh, my goodness," said Majel. "It wasn't only just a marvelous event, it was also an eye-opener. Everything about the tea service was so elegant and perfect." She hunched forward in her chair, and a look of hopefulness crossed her face. "Theodosia, I know this is probably a *huge* imposition—I mean, you're already doing so much for us with your participation in the scavenger hunt. But I'd be thrilled if you came out to Angel's Rest sometime and gave an etiquette lesson to our girls."

Delaine smiled a knowing smile. "Angel's Rest is the summer camp that Tuesday's Child owns and operates." She rolled her eyes for added emphasis. "*Very* worthwhile. I'm planning to host a major fund-raiser myself."

"Where's your camp located?" Theodosia asked.

"Over near Early Branch," Majel explained. "Close to the Salkahartchie River."

"Where it's all pretty and woodsy," said Delaine.

"I'd like very much to come visit," said Theodosia. "In fact, I'd be honored." She could think of nothing nicer than teaching a group of at-risk girls the fine art of tea. Anytime you could impart a tiny bit of gentility in someone's life, it helped nurture the soul.

Theodosia was just starting to clear dishes when she happened to overhear a shocking bit of gossip.

"You know that young woman who inherited the restaurant?" said Charlotte.

The two women to either side of her nodded. One of them said, "Solstice?"

"That's right," said Charlotte. "Anyway, I just heard that she struck a deal to sell the place."

Theodosia practically dropped the tray she was balancing. What? Shelby was selling Solstice? Two days after inheriting it? What on earth was going on?

Theodosia did a little more eavesdropping.

"I just heard about it this morning," Charlotte continued. "When I dropped by the City Charities office on my way here. Apparently Peaches Pafford struck a deal with the young woman to buy the place."

"The girl is probably happy to be rid of it," said Charlotte's companion. "And darned lucky that a businesswoman of Peaches's caliber would take it off her hands."

Theodosia set her tray down on a nearby empty table and took a step backward. The blood seemed to have drained from her face; her legs felt heavy and wooden as she staggered over to the front counter.

How could this happen? Theodosia wondered. For goodness' sake, she'd just *seen* Shelby last night and the girl hadn't uttered a peep about selling Solstice! Not only that, she'd talked to Peaches a couple of hours ago and the woman hadn't let on a thing. What was going on?

"I have to talk to her," Theodosia muttered to no one, then fled to her office.

But a quick phone call to Shelby's cell phone got her nowhere. And trying to reach her at Solstice proved impossible. René answered, but he didn't know where she was.

"But you know about the sale?" asked Theodosia. "That Shelby is selling Solstice to Peaches Pafford?"

"Are you kidding?" said René. "We just heard!"

"Are you in shock?"

"More like we're in mourning," said René. "I guess we'll all have to pump up our résumés and make some calls."

"You wouldn't want to work for Peaches?" asked Theodosia.

"Are you kidding?" said René. "With her reputation?"

"Oh, my goodness," said Theodosia, hanging up the phone. "What *is* going on?"

Tilting her head forward, she dropped it into her hands

and massaged the base of her neck, then moved up to the really sore spots along her occipital ridge. Had Shelby been working in concert with Peaches all along? Had everything been a big setup?

Or had Shelby engineered this on her own? Was it possible Shelby had seen that Parker was vulnerable? That she had led him on like crazy? Then somehow persuaded Parker to name her as heir and beneficiary so she could profit?

Is Shelby that much of a weasel?

Okay, she could definitely see Shelby worming her way into Parker's life. But Shelby didn't strike her as any kind of mastermind. So was someone else in the background pulling the strings?

Who would that be?

Theodosia's mind continued to churn. She stood up, walked a few feet, spun around, and collapsed back into her chair. *Have to figure this out*, she told herself. Have to try to get past the shock and emotion and think logically about all this.

She sat quietly for a few minutes, exploring various theories, running permutations through her overwrought brain. And then, like a tar bubble finally oozing its way up and escaping to the earth's surface, she thought, *Joe Beaudry?*

He was sneaky enough, smarmy enough, and knew the financials firsthand. Had he somehow set this up? Had Beaudry been working behind the scenes in collusion with Peaches? Had Joe Beaudry completely duped Parker?

And then killed him?

The idea was just too horrible to contemplate.

When the ladies from the garden club finally finished their luncheon and began exploring the tea shop and gift corner, Theodosia decided it was high time to corner Charlotte.

She found her admiring a shelf of antique teacups and the wreaths that hung on the wall.

"Your grapevine wreaths are adorable," said Charlotte. "And I love that you decorated them with tiny teacups." She lifted an index finger and gently touched one.

"Charlotte," said Theodosia, "I couldn't help overhear your conversation about Solstice being sold to Peaches Pafford."

Charlotte's eyes went suddenly wide, and she put a hand to her face. "Oh dear, me and my big mouth. Did I just make a boo-boo?"

"No, it's okay," said Theodosia. "Really."

But Charlotte looked wary. "Really, Theodosia, it completely slipped my mind that you used to date Parker Scully."

"That's okay," said Theodosia. "Truly, you didn't offend me. But what I want to know is . . . how exactly did you hear about this?"

"I got the news straight from Bob Coy," said Charlotte. "The catering manager at the Charleston Hotel. He was just coming into the City Charities office as I was leaving. We said hi and started talking and one thing led to another."

"You're sure about this deal?" asked Theodosia. After all, Charleston was a city that thrived on gossip. Old families and old rivalries, big money and big problems. In many ways it was not unlike a long-running soap opera.

"Pretty sure," said Charlotte.

"Wow," said Theodosia, looking discombobulated.

"You want me to call Bob again?" asked Charlotte. "Try to track down the rumor?"

"No, no, that's not necessary," said Theodosia. "The news just kind of stunned me, I guess."

"You look stunned," said Charlotte.

"Sorry if I seem overly gossipy about this," said Theodosia.

"That's okay," said Charlotte. "I can see where you'd be upset. Especially in light of that awful . . . drowning."

* * *

Back in her office, Theodosia placed a hurried phone call.

"Joe Beaudry, please," said Theodosia when the reception-ist, Betty, came on the line.

"I'm sorry," said Betty, "he's out at the moment. May I take a message?"

"No, I . . . well, maybe you can help me," said Theodosia.

"I'll certainly try," said Betty.

"This is Theodosia Browning. I was in the other day talk-ing to Joe?"

"Yes, of course," said Betty.

"Anyway," said Theodosia, "I wanted to chat with Joe about the Solstice deal." She hesitated. "The restaurant that he's . . . um . . . brokering?"

"Yes?" said Betty. "I can surely check his calendar and fit you in."

"Um . . . he is brokering that deal, am I correct?"

"That's right," said Betty. "May I have him call you when he returns?"

"No," said Theodosia. "That's okay. I'll get ahold of him later."

But in her mind she knew it wasn't okay. It wasn't okay at all.

Theodosia tried to get Tidwell on the line then, but he was out. So she hung up the phone, trying to puzzle through this new piece of information.

"Knock knock." Drayton stood in the doorway, a worried look on his face. "I just heard a nasty rumor," he said.

"About Peaches buying Solstice?"

Drayton nodded.

"It's more than a rumor," said Theodosia.

"Bizarre," said Drayton.

"Hold on, it gets worse. Joe Beaudry is brokering the deal."

"The sleazy lawyer?"

"Bingo," said Theodosia. "And, I might add, the sleazy lawyer that led Parker on with promises of financing." She pushed a mass of auburn hair off her forehead. "Don't you have to take off for your lecture?"

"In about five minutes, yes," said Drayton. He sat down in the chair across from her desk and said, "I don't care about who owns what restaurant. What I care about is who murdered Parker."

"I hear you," said Theodosia. "With all these people who are sort of intertwined in business deals, it's easy to forget what's really at the heart of the matter."

"Murder," said Drayton, stretching the word out for emphasis. He was quiet for a long moment, then added, "You look like you're at sixes and sevens."

"I'm spinning," Theodosia agreed. "I don't know if Shelby was in league with Peaches all along, if Joe Beaudry is a killer who's playing everybody for a fool, or if Lyle Manship is the dark horse in all of this."

"Very confusing," agreed Drayton.

"Yes, it is," said Theodosia. "And, as you pointed out, the awful thing is that even though Parker was laid to rest yesterday morning, everything else about his death remains totally up in the air." Theodosia let loose a deep sigh. "And the *really* awful thing is that I can't figure out which avenue to pursue or where to turn."

"Much like a stalemate in a chess game?" said Drayton.

Theodosia nodded. "Something like that."

Drayton laid a forefinger against his cheek and looked thoughtful. Then he said, "The great chess master Bobby Fischer always said, 'I don't believe in psychology, I believe in good moves.'" Drayton paused and gazed solemnly at Theodosia. "So, you have to decide . . . what's *your* next move?"

18

❧

Theodosia was on her hands and knees, stacking T-Bath products onto the lower shelves of a pine cupboard, when Detective Tidwell wandered in. From her downwardly challenged viewpoint she saw his polished Thom McAns, billowing slacks, and baggy knees as she watched him lumber to a table. About five seconds later, Haley hustled over, all prim and proper, to take his order.

Groaning inwardly, Theodosia popped her final bottles of Sweet Tea Feet Treat and Chamomile Calming Cream onto the shelf, then pulled herself up and headed over to join them.

Haley had just placed today's laser-printed menu in Tidwell's big paws when Theodosia plopped down at his table.

"I have news," she told Tidwell. "Huge news. Crazy news." She was slightly breathless and anxious to talk.

Tidwell didn't react. He continued to scan the luncheon menu, then rolled his baleful eyes upward and said to Haley, "Scone and a cup of gazpacho as well as a small pot of Formosan oolong."

"Excellent choice," said Haley, snapping the menu out of Tidwell's hands. "Although I must say I prefer the oolong from Anxi. Slightly more oxidized."

Theodosia cleared her throat. "Um, *excuse* me?" She wasn't pleased that Tidwell seemed to be ignoring her.

Finally Tidwell focused his attention on her. "Yes," he rumbled, his belly rising and falling like a restless sea behind his straining vest.

"Shelby is selling Solstice to Peaches Pafford," Theodosia told him in a rush. "And Joe Beaudry is brokering the deal."

"I know," said Tidwell.

Stunned, Theodosia sat back in her chair. "You know about this? Already?" How was that possible? "How do you know?"

Tidwell offered a curl of his lip. "I have my ways."

"You mean like . . . informants?"

His chubby fingers spread out and rose off the table a few inches.

"Really," said Theodosia. She was impressed. Then again, Tidwell might resemble a slumbering bear, but he was really a wolverine. Canny, ferocious, always ready to pounce. Half the time—no, most of the time—his somnolent manner was merely a clever ruse.

"Still," allowed Tidwell, "an interesting turn of events."

"I find it bizarre," said Theodosia.

"But not so unusual that attorney Beaudry is involved," said Tidwell. "After all, he'd already had initial dealings with Mr. Scully and had crunched the numbers, so to speak. So Beaudry knew the situation with Solstice and was patently familiar with the books."

"But for a sale to happen that quick?" said Theodosia. "It seems very strange."

"The sale hasn't happened," Tidwell pointed out. "An offer was made and accepted. Nothing exists on paper yet."

Haley showed up at the table with Tidwell's scone, a cup of soup, and a small teapot tucked inside a calico tea cozy.

"You'll want to let that steep one additional minute," she admonished, then slipped away.

Tidwell picked up his soup spoon, dipped it gingerly, and took a quick taste.

"Good?" said Theodosia.

"Very good," said Tidwell. He took another taste, then said, "I, too, have news."

"About . . . ?"

"The restaurant franchise at the aquarium," said Tidwell. "The one you were so distressed about last evening?"

"Please don't tell me," said Theodosia, "that Peaches Pafford is involved in that deal, too. That she made some under-the-table deal to get the franchise."

Tidwell's jowls sloshed as he shook his head. "Not at all. That plum franchise was awarded to Lyle Manship."

Theodosia gaped at him. "No kidding?"

Tidwell stared back at her. "Something tells me you two have crossed paths."

Theodosia decided not to tell Tidwell about her little jaunt down to Savannah. Instead she said, "Manship accosted me this morning at the Coffee & Tea Expo."

Tidwell looked mildly amused. "Really, Miss Browning. You were accosted?"

"Okay, he was pushy," said Theodosia. "He asked if I wanted to lead a tea tour."

"Locally?"

"No," said Theodosia. "On some cruise ship line."

"And did you accept?" Tidwell seemed to be playing with her now. One of his cat-and-mouse games.

"Hardly," said Theodosia. "I have far better things to do than get involved with the likes of him."

"*Better things* meaning you're going to continue to investigate?" Tidwell's tone was chiding.

"How can I not?" said Theodosia. "When everything keeps happening all around me?"

"You're a virtual vortex," responded Tidwell.

"Seriously," said Theodosia, "that's exactly what it feels like." She slumped in her chair, then said, "I still can't get past Shelby inheriting Solstice and Joe Beaudry brokering the sale. Doesn't it all seem just a little too speedy? A little too cozy?"

"Cozy, yes," said Tidwell. "I'll even give you unseemly and suspicious. But, as far as I know, not illegal."

"But just too convenient for words," said Theodosia.

Tidwell sliced his scone in half, slathered it with about eight pats of butter, added a large glop of strawberry jam, then popped a huge bite into his mouth. He chewed thoughtfully, swallowed, then said, "I should probably tell you about the file."

"File?" said Theodosia, pouncing on his words. "Are you talking about the *missing* file?"

"Ah," said Tidwell, holding up an index finger, "but now it's no longer missing."

"What? The information's been recovered?" This was seriously big news! "From where?" Theodosia asked. "I mean . . . who had it?"

"Interestingly enough," said Tidwell, "the file was discovered in Parker's car."

"Huh?" said Theodosia. "In his car? But . . . what?"

"Parker's brother called," Tidwell told her. "Charles. He was at Parker's apartment and happened to look in his car. There it was, just sitting on the backseat."

"A file," said Theodosia.

"Right," said Tidwell. "A file marked *Properties.*"

"A green file folder just like all the others?"

"Correct," said Tidwell. "And it was full. A nice fat compendium of paperwork."

"Full of . . ." She waggled her fingers to prompt him.

"Contracts, commercial real estate listings, a prospectus here and there, a couple of pitches. All dealing with restaurants or properties Mr. Scully was looking at. And financing proposals."

"So all the deals," Theodosia said slowly. She was having trouble processing this information. "Are you telling me the business information that we *thought* had been stolen really wasn't missing after all?"

"That's about the size of it," said Tidwell. "The paperwork for all Mr. Scully's potential projects and deals is now accounted for."

"Even the deal with the Neptune Aquarium?"

"There was a copy of Parker Scully's pitch to them, yes," said Tidwell.

Theodosia drummed her fingers on the table. Something still didn't make sense. The file that had been found in Parker's car was still not the file with the missing contents. "Then what was in the file marked *Current Projects?*" she asked.

Tidwell's shook his head in a dismissive gesture. "Probably nothing important."

"No," said Theodosia, "it had to be something important. The contents were missing from Parker's office. Presumably stolen."

But Tidwell didn't see it that way. "Highly doubtful. I'm of a mind that the contents had merely been tossed out. Perhaps they were old invoices. Or orders for restaurant supplies. Mundane items," said Tidwell. "Or simply worthless."

"Maybe," said Theodosia. But, somehow, she wasn't completely convinced.

Theodosia rinsed out a dozen or so teapots, wiped them carefully, then arranged them on the shelf just below their rows and rows of tea tins. When everything was tidy and neat, according to Drayton's standards anyway, she set about sweeping the floor. Because she wanted the Indigo Tea Shop to be a sparkling little jewel box, she strived to keep it absolutely pristine at all times. However, since the place had functioned as a small stable in its long-ago previous life, dust seemed to have an insidious way of seeping in. Maybe it was just because of daily wear and tear; maybe it found its way up through the pegged wood floorboards?

"Theo," said Drayton. He stood with his watch in one hand and a cup of tea in the other. "We should talk about the tea ceremony tomorrow night. At the Heritage Society."

Theodosia straightened up. "I didn't know you were back. So how'd your lecture go?"

"Quite well," said Drayton. "Practically a packed house."

"And you talked about . . ."

"The legend of tea going back to the Qin dynasty in two hundred B.C.," said Drayton. "Then I talked about how the tea gardens spread from the Sichuan hills down into the Yangtze Valley . . ."

"And quoted some tea poetry," said Theodosia.

Drayton smiled. "Sung dynasty, to be exact. And wound up talking about tea production today."

"This expo is proving to be a good thing," said Theodosia. "For the tea community, anyway."

"Many of whom will be attending the big finale tomorrow night."

"I take it you made a special point of inviting your audience to our Japanese tea ceremony."

"How could I not?" said Drayton.

"And your plans remain pretty much the same? Haley and I will serve tea on the patio while you give a short demonstration on *chado*." *Chado* was the Japanese word for "the way of tea."

"Yes, but I always like to run things past you," smiled Drayton.

"Why?"

"Because I do," Drayton said patiently. Then added, "Perhaps because I have a touch of the obsessive-compulsive?"

"No," said Theodosia, "that's Haley. She's the one who's

slightly OCD. Do you know she actually *identified* with the wacko guy in *Sleeping with the Enemy*? The one who kept straightening the towels."

"What are you saying about me?" asked Haley, as she popped out from behind the velvet curtain.

"We're marveling over your prodigious baking skills," said Drayton.

"Yeah?" said Haley, as her sharp eyes scoured the floor. "You missed a spot." She pointed at a minuscule speck.

"See what I mean?" said Theodosia.

"I know you guys were talking about me," said Haley. She crossed her arms, gave them a suspicious glance, and all but tapped a foot.

"Actually," said Drayton, "we were going to quickly go over the plans for the tea ceremony we're presenting tomorrow evening. Care to join us?"

Haley plopped herself down in a captain's chair. "Oh goody. Let's do that. I always feel more confident when we run through our plans."

"The tea we'll serve," said Drayton, "will obviously be Japanese Gyokuro." This was the finest Japanese green tea, bright in color with a deep vegetal flavor.

"The good stuff," said Haley. Gyokuro retailed for ten dollars an ounce, versus the everyday Sencha that sold for something like two dollars an ounce.

"Of course," said Drayton. "To serve anything less to our guests from the Coffee & Tea Expo would be heresy."

"And for the food?" said Theodosia, glancing at Haley.

"Chicken kushiyaki, shrimp tempura, and rice balls wrapped in nori," said Haley. "I'll prep everything here, but cook the tempura in the Heritage Society's kitchen. That stuff's only good if it's crisp and hot from the deep fryer!"

"A lot of work," said Drayton, impressed.

Haley gave him a baleful look. "Theo wanted a whizbang finale for the Coffee & Tea Expo."

"But I don't want you to burn out," said Theodosia, concerned now. "You've been working double-duty all week."

Haley yawned. "I am a little tired."

"You just need a strong cup of tea," said Drayton, heading for the front counter.

"Oh man," said Haley, yawning again. "And we're supposed to do that scavenger hunt tonight."

"I think you'd better stay home and get some rest," said Theodosia.

"You think?" said Haley.

"Yes, I do," said Theodosia. "But I have one favor to ask."

"Shoot," said Haley.

"Can you keep Earl Grey until later tonight?"

A grin creased Haley's face. "Sure. No problem. As long as we've got his . . ."

"There's dry kibble and a can of dog food in my office," said Theodosia.

"So I don't have to make him scrambled eggs?"

"Not unless he rings for room service," laughed Theodosia.

"Then who's going to . . ." began Haley.

"Oh, Drayton," Theodosia called in a singsong voice.

Drayton whirled about, a blue-and-white Chinese teapot clutched in one hand. "Yes?"

"I have a favor to ask."

"Hmm," he said, "last time you asked for a favor it was to go hunting for wild herbs. Purslane and winter cress, if I recall."

"And you came back with tiny green burrs stuck all over your pants legs," laughed Haley.

"This is a lot easier," said Theodosia. "It has to do with the scavenger hunt."

Drayton visibly grimaced. "Don't you think I'm a little *old* for scavenger hunts?"

"You're not old," said Theodosia, "and you're especially not old for what this one entails. All you have to do is ride shot-gun with me and snap a few photos."

This time Drayton winced. "You want me to take photos?"

"That's right." Theodosia held up her cell phone in a kind of show-and-tell gesture. "I drive and you snap the pictures."

"I see," said Drayton, tilting his head to one side. Which meant he really didn't see at all.

"We drive around with our list," Theodosia explained patiently. "And photograph everything that's on it. Once that's done, the photos get e-mailed to the City Charities people."

Drayton looked baffled. "I'm supposed to take pictures with a cell phone and e-mail them?"

"Just pretend it's a Brownie Starflash," Haley said. She'd been sitting back, enjoying the exchange. "Or, better yet, one of those old-fashioned Rolleiflex cameras."

"You're not helping," Theodosia said to Haley.

"Just don't get so hung up on technology," Haley said to Drayton. "It's not like you're being asked to write code or debug a program."

Drayton still seemed unnerved.

"The thing is," said Theodosia, trying to defuse the situation, "the camera's built in. It's what they call a smart phone."

"Obviously," said Drayton, "far smarter than I."

19

Dark clouds galloped across the night sky, harboring a threat of rain, as Theodosia rolled down a narrow back alley that wound behind the Charleston Library Association. They were on their third landmark and, so far, it was slowgoing.

"It would have been much easier to do this in daylight," said Drayton.

"Agreed," said Theodosia, "but we didn't exactly have two spare minutes to put together today." She took her foot off the gas and coasted to a stop. "Will this work? Does it give you a decent enough angle?"

"I think so," said Drayton. He held up the cell phone and aimed. "I think I'm getting the hang of this." Holding his breath, he snapped the photo, then immediately handed the cell phone over to Theodosia. "What do you think?"

Theodosia looked at his shot of the dark stone building. It was moody and ominous, but it was for sure recognizable. "Perfect," she declared. "What's next?"

Drayton studied the pages that lay in his lap. "So far we've photographed the French Huguenot Church, the Aiken-Rhett House, and the Library Association. We should also hit the Altman Art Gallery and the yacht club while we're in the vicinity."

Theodosia eased her way out of the alley, mindful of the hedges on either side and the Spanish moss that hung down and swished against the top of her Jeep. "Okay. So I'll swing over to Murray and we'll hit the yacht club. Is there something specific there we need to shoot?"

Drayton consulted his list again. "Catamaran."

"Catamaran," said Theodosia. "That should be easy enough."

"For me, yes. Because *you're* going to be the one who ventures out on those narrow docks."

"No problem," said Theodosia. She'd been skipping across docks and lugging heavy sails onto boats since she was a kid.

"I have to say," said Drayton, "this photography scavenger hunt is a fairly ingenious concept."

"Isn't it?" said Theodosia.

"It certainly beats scrounging around for strange and useless items," said Drayton. "Trying to find a truck tire or stealing someone's poor garden gnome."

Theodosia chuckled. "And then hauling it all back with us. I agree, a *virtual* hunt is a whole lot easier."

"But I'm still unclear as to how this all tallies up," said Drayton. "I mean, how do we go about beating the other teams? How do we actually *win*?" He'd never admit it, but Drayton had a competitive streak a mile wide.

"Today is round one," Theodosia explained. "So once we find and photograph all the items on our list, we submit everything to the judges. If it all checks out tomorrow and we get the thumbs-up, we advance into round two, the finals."

"Then what happens?" asked Drayton.

"More of the same on Saturday," said Theodosia, as she

braked and swung into a tight turn down a cobblestone lane. "Except we get a brand-new list of stuff to find and photograph."

"And the items gets trickier?"

"I would assume so," said Theodosia.

"Actually," said Drayton, his forehead crinkling as he studied the list, "it's going to get tricky tonight. Once we capture images of everything that's near and around the historic district, we have a fair piece of driving to do."

"Angel Oak out on Johns Island?"

"That's on the list and some place called the Hot Fish Clam Shack north of here on Highway 17."

"Good grief," said Theodosia, as she pulled into the yacht club parking lot, her tires crunching across gravel. "We're going to be doing some serious backtracking. This could take all night."

"Exactly my point."

"Okay," she said, taking the cell phone from Drayton. "You sit tight. I'll be back in two shakes." Theodosia hopped out of the Jeep and hustled across the lot, where a lone pickup truck was parked. She walked down a sloping, narrow path defined by white chains on either side, past the yellow wooden clubhouse festooned with flags and white trim, and, finally, out onto the dock of the Charleston Yacht Club.

Head down, Theodosia hunched forward as she stepped along the wooden planks. They beat a hollow cadence beneath her feet and she could hear the lap of waves underneath. It was also decidedly cooler and windier out here. The warmth of the spring day had pretty much evaporated and the cool mist of the Atlantic had stolen in. There was a reason halyards clanked loudly against aluminum masts and boats rocked to and fro, tugging antagonistically at their moorings. Probably, Theodosia decided, the wind was blowing in at a good ten knots.

It took one wrong turn and a little backtracking before

Theodosia found a catamaran moored off one of the multiple arms of the dock. But it was a nice Hobie Cat, a Wild Cat to be precise, that would work just fine for the scavenger hunt.

She snapped a picture, checked it, then took two more for safety's sake. She didn't want to risk being knocked out of the competition on account of one fuzzy photo.

As the dock rocked and dipped gently with the waves, Theodosia stared out across open water. She saw the twinkle of lights at Patriot's Point, usually a warm and welcoming sign. Only tonight, for some reason, the lights looked lonely and forlorn. Probably because they appeared so far away?

Or had she just fallen prey to her emotions?

Was she feeling guilt-ridden and anxious because nothing had been resolved in Parker's murder?

Anxious? Yes. Guilt-ridden? Perhaps.

Theodosia hurried back to her car, jumped in, and cranked up the heater. "Getting cool out there," she told Drayton.

He gazed at her, trying to pick up on her mood. Finally, he said, "Are you feeling all right?"

"Yes, of course." Theodosia put her Jeep into reverse and backed out of her parking space. "What's next?"

Drayton smoothed his list. "I think we should snap a picture of the Altman Gallery, then hit Angel Oak, then head north and try to find that oyster shack," he told her.

Some forty minutes later, they were zipping their way north on Highway 17.

"Starting to rain," Drayton observed, as light drops spattered down on the windshield, suddenly giving everything a muddled, soft-focus look.

"Just our luck," said Theodosia, turning on the wipers.

"You've been awfully quiet ever since we stopped at the marina," Drayton observed. "Did something get you thinking about Parker?"

"About him and about how I seem to keep spinning my wheels," said Theodosia.

"You're doing nothing of the sort," said Drayton.

"I appreciate the fact that you're always one of my staunchest allies," said Theodosia. "But every time I think I'm making an inroad or picking up a valuable piece of information, it pretty much dead-ends."

"You're doing your best. That's what counts."

"Still," said Theodosia, "there doesn't seem to be any payoff."

"You're a results-oriented person."

She gripped the steering wheel tighter. "Well . . . isn't everyone?"

Drayton's mouth ticked up at the corners in a rueful smile. "My dear Theodosia . . . no. No they are not."

The windshield wipers beat a syncopated rhythm as they continued up Highway 17. Rain sluiced down in earnest, forcing Theodosia to ease back to a more socially acceptable fifty-five miles per hour.

"Hard to see," said Drayton, as dark trees whipped by, lending a film noir feeling to the mostly wooded landscape. They'd been driving for a good twenty minutes, and familiar landmarks were few and far between.

"I think we have to make a turn up ahead," said Theodosia. "Or maybe we missed it. I think the clam shack's supposed to be down a side road."

"Don't you have one of those handy-dandy automatic navigation things?"

"My navigation guide is low-tech. It's folded up and stuck in the glove box."

"Ah," said Drayton.

"I've got a navigation thing on my phone," said Theodosia, "but I'm not confident about getting directions, taking pictures, and making calls all at the same time."

"Sounds like three-dimensional chess," said Drayton.

"Really."

Drayton suddenly jerked upright in his seat. "There. Up ahead. You see that green signpost?"

Theodosia braked sharply, then cranked the steering wheel hard to the right.

"Easy, easy," breathed Drayton, as they spun through the turn.

"But is this the right road?" she asked.

"Hope so," said Drayton. "Since we've already committed."

"I didn't really get a good look at the sign," said Theodosia, as she eased down the one-lane blacktopped road. Along with the rain, fog was starting to creep in.

"Pretty out here," said Drayton.

"How can you tell?" asked Theodosia. Just then a huge bolt of lightning ripped across the sky, illuminating the road ahead as well as the surrounding countryside of pines and tamarack. "Oh, yeah," Theodosia chuckled. "*Now* I see. But the question remains, is this the way to the Hot Fish Clam Shack?"

Turned out, it wasn't.

Because after they'd driven another mile or so, the road ended in a dirt parking lot at a place called Moore's Landing.

"Now that's what I call a very large pier," said Drayton. A large wooden wharf stretched from the sandy shore out into the surging Atlantic. A stiltlike arrangement of graying timbers.

"I think there's a public ferry boat that pulls in here on weekends."

Drayton glanced out the window. "Certainly no public around right now."

"No ferry boat, either," said Theodosia.

"Wrong turn," said Drayton.

"Mmm. Looks like it." Theodosia peered through the windshield, where the wipers continued to slosh. "There's a sign over there. What's it say? Can you read it?"

Drayton rolled down his window and leaned out. "I

think," he said, above the roar of wind and waves, "it's something about the Cape Romain Wildlife Refuge."

"Okay, then," said Theodosia. "We really did hook a wrong turn."

Drayton rolled up the window, then pulled out his hanky and mopped the dampness from his face. "We probably just turned too soon."

"Pretty place, though," said Theodosia. "When it's not raining cats and dogs."

"With all the building that's going on," said Drayton, "all the encroachment of civilization, it's nice to think there's a wildlife refuge so close."

"You think these waterways are protected, too?" Theodosia wondered.

"I hope so," said Drayton. "We can't just keep fishing everything to extinction. There have to be some regulations."

"Remember the whole Chilean sea bass craze?" asked Theodosia.

"It became so popular in restaurants," said Drayton, "that now there are hardly any authentic Chilean sea bass left."

"Just like the sardines in Monterey Bay," said Theodosia. "Back in the late forties."

"Steinbeck's *Cannery Row* certainly touched on that," said Drayton. "The fisheries all believed there was an endless supply. And then one day they were gone. Just totally depleted."

"I guess nothing's endless," said Theodosia.

"Except this scavenger hunt," said Drayton.

That caused Theodosia a little chuckle. "So we try again." She revved her engine, reversed her tracks, and headed back the way they'd come.

"I hope Tuesday's Child knows how hard we're working for them," said Drayton.

"Majel, their director, seems like a very dedicated woman," said Theodosia. "Who I'm positive will be most appreciative."

When they hit Highway 17 again, Theodosia turned right and headed north. "Can't be too far," she said.

"Hopefully," said Drayton, although he didn't sound hopeful at all.

They crept along at a decorous forty-five miles an hour now, eyes straining for some sign of the elusive clam shack.

"Whoa, whoa!" Drayton called out suddenly. "I think we just passed it!"

Theodosia took her foot off the gas and coasted to the side of the road. "I didn't see a thing."

"That's because the place is locked up tight. The signs aren't even lit."

"Holy moly," Theodosia breathed, as she shifted into reverse and backed down the dark highway.

"Easy," said Drayton. "Keep it straight, keep it straight."

"Hard to see where the driveway turns in," Theodosia complained.

"Ten, maybe fifteen more feet. Okay, *turn*!" said Drayton.

Theodosia did and ended up in the parking lot of the Hot Fish Clam Shack. It was a dilapidated little place that had probably once been painted white, but the encroachment of wind, water, and sea air had sandpapered it to a weather-beaten gray. Still, it looked like a welcoming little café with its funky wooden cutout of a smiling big-eyed fish leaping into a fry pan with the words HOT FISH CLAM SHACK lettered in red and yellow. And there were big, black cauldrons planted with daisies on either side of the battered front door.

"Too bad it's closed," said Drayton, gazing at the shuttered windows. "We could have had ourselves a tasty little snack."

"You'd eat here?" asked Theodosia.

"Of course."

"I doubt they have white linen tablecloths."

"I realize that."

"Red plastic baskets instead of plates."

"You seem to think I'm some kind of food snob," said Drayton, "when I'm not."

"But would you drink a longneck beer?"

Drayton smiled. "No, but I'd take a sweet tea." He held up the camera. "You or me? The rain seems to be letting up, but . . ."

Theodosia grabbed the camera. "Me. I'm feeling decidedly guilty. I think I've put you through enough tonight."

"You have," Drayton said, with a mousy grin.

Theodosia tugged her sweater around her and hopped from the car. Hopefully, she could get a good shot and they could head back to Charleston. Try to button down the last couple of scavenger hunt landmarks.

She crunched across the parking lot, a few raindrops still splotching down. She knew if her hair got too damp, it would lift and billow like a spinnaker catching the wind. And then if it dried too fast, the dreaded frizzies might follow. Most women would kill to have Theodosia's abundance of luxurious hair, but she found it a constant challenge. Especially in hot, humid Charleston.

Stepping up to the front of the building, Theodosia took a shot of the Hot Fish logo that was painted on the door. Then she stepped back, looked at the sign on the roof, and moved back some more. She found that moving off to the side of the building gave her a nice angle on the cutout fish. And, as a kind of lucky-strike extra, because they certainly needed one tonight, the fog seemed to have lifted and the rain had dwindled to a fine mist. Still not good for her hair, but excellent for hydrating the complexion.

Moving off to the side of the building also put her directly in the path of the breeze blowing in from the Atlantic. Though there were barrier islands farther out, the wind whipped between them as if through a venturi tube, gathering strength, buffeting everything in its path.

Theodosia gazed out to sea, really the Intercoastal Waterway, and was surprised to see two boats floating offshore. She stared at them, watching their yellow lights bob and dip. They seemed to hold their position, so they were probably commercial fishing boats. Certainly couldn't be that ferry boat that docked at Moore's Landing.

She watched the boats for another couple of minutes, slightly enchanted, wondering about the dedicated men who still worked this kind of difficult job. She also wondered if her little camera would be able to capture a shot of them. Better yet, if she positioned the clam shack in the foreground and the boats in the background, she might get a nice moody, sexy shot.

She took a few pictures, moving around, experimenting with different angles. When she was satisfied, she hurried back to her Jeep.

"You certainly took your time," Drayton observed, as she pulled open the driver's-side door. "So it must be a wonderful composition."

Theodosia was about to respond when a pickup truck rolled in behind them and stopped. She gazed over at it, seeing only smoked windows and hearing muffled music coming from within its dark interior. Creedence Clearwater Revival, she thought. Maybe "Run Through the Jungle" or "Up Around the Bend." After a few short moments, the truck reversed, then headed back down the main highway.

"Another hungry customer," said Drayton. "Disappointed the clam shack is closed."

"Probably," said Theodosia, just as her phone rang. She half closed the car door and stood in the parking lot to take her call. "Hello?"

It was Max.

"Hey, sweetheart, it's me!" came Max's exuberant voice.

Theodosia was suddenly grinning ear to ear. She couldn't help herself. "It's so great to hear your voice," she told him.

"How are you doing?" asked Max.

"I'm good. I'm on a scavenger hunt right now! With Drayton."

"Uh-oh," said Max. "Does that mean you two are sneaking around the historic district trying to find finials and lampposts to rip off?"

"No, this scavenger hunt's actually kind of unique," said Theodosia. "Rather than go door to door, we drive around and take photos of things. You know, like landmarks and such."

"That sounds a whole lot easier," said Max.

"And it's for charity," said Theodosia.

"I should have guessed," said Max. "You have such a good heart, always thinking of others."

"Our team is actually working for a great cause," said Theodosia. "At-risk youth. In fact, it's the same group that's getting the proceeds from your fishbowl."

"Of course," said Max. "Tuesday's Child."

"So," said Theodosia. "Are you guys coming home with an Impressionist painting?"

"Nah," said Max. "It wasn't in the cards. We had our eye on a landscape by Sisley, but basically got outbid by the Freer Gallery."

"Bigger budget," said Theodosia.

"Bigger donors," said Max. "Humongous, in fact."

"So when are you coming back?" It couldn't be soon enough for Theodosia.

"Tomorrow night," said Max.

"Eeh," said Theodosia. "Tomorrow night we're hosting the closing event for the Coffee & Tea Expo. It's a kind of Japanese tea ceremony at the Heritage Society."

"Then I'll drop by and find you," said Max.

"Really? You'll come?"

"Of course," said Max, "I might even write a haiku."

* * *

"Max said he was going to write a haiku," Theodosia told Drayton as she climbed into the car——haiku being a Japanese poem that was simple in form, yet conveyed elegant imagery and, oftentimes, a seasonal reference.

"Seventeen syllables to capture a bit of joy and a philosophical truth," said Drayton. "Never easy to do."

"You've written a few haiku yourself," said Theodosia. "There was one in particular that you recited when we hosted that Japanese tea out at Magnolia Plantation last spring." She chuckled. "When we all kind of pretended the azaleas were really cherry blossoms."

"Hah," said Drayton.

"You remember the poem?" she asked.

"As if it were yesterday," Drayton smiled. He paused, then said, "Floating on spring breezes, cherry blossoms burst with joy. So does my heart."

"Wonderful," said Theodosia. "You really should write one for tomorrow night."

"You think?" said Drayton.

"With your Japanese bonsai on display and our Japanese tea and food, it would be a perfect tie-in."

"Something to consider," said Drayton.

"Please do," said Theodosia.

20

≈✦≈

Just as Haley had predicted, the second day of the Coffee &
Tea Expo was the bigger day. Crowds thronged the floor of
the coliseum as coffee perked, tea brewed, and sales reps
repped. The air was filled with the mingled aromas of fresh-
ground beans, aromatic teas, and cinnamon.

"How's it going?" Theodosia asked Haley. She was passing
out mini bags of Drayton's Raspberry Mojo tea, a proprietary
blend of Chinese black tea flavored with raspberry and spiked
with ginseng.

"Great," said Haley, swishing back her long hair, "but I
can't wait to get out of here. I just talked to Drayton and
we've got beaucoup reservations. Looks like today's gonna be
like. . . a luncheon marathon."

"But Jenny's coming in again?"

Haley consulted her watch. "She should be here in ten
minutes."

"In the meantime . . ." said Theodosia. She looked around
and found that their booth was suddenly inundated with

customers. "You keep up the sampling," she told Haley, "while I write up orders."

They worked in tandem for another ten minutes, Haley handing out samples and, when the flow of customers suddenly slowed, doing a bang-up job of enticing even more passersby to stop at their booth.

Theodosia, meanwhile, was indeed writing up orders. A new tea shop in Savannah, Muffy's Cuppa, had heard good things about their proprietary blends, so Theodosia gave a quick sales presentation on their Lemon Verbena, Flower Song Breakfast, and Gunpowder Black teas. Which, she was happy to find, resulted in a rather sizable order.

Haley had brought in a small selection of teapots, too, and Theodosia found herself talking up the Hsi-Shing teapots in particular. Most of those purple-brown clay teapots were small and compact, ideal for retailing in a tea shop and uniquely suited for brewing a single cup of tea. Then, when she got inquiries about Devonshire cream, she found herself not only passing along the names of two good vendors, but writing out her favorite recipe, too.

By the time Theodosia came up for air, Haley was deep in conversation with . . . *Oh no, Peaches Pafford again?*

Peaches was talking earnestly, bending Haley's ear about something.

Theodosia angled closer to them and realized Peaches was talking to Haley about Bittersweet. Sharing her plans with her.

"It's a kind of coffee and tea bar but with light lunches," Peaches told her. "Served sit-down style."

"I see you're still making plans to open your little patisserie," Theodosia said.

Peaches gave a self-satisfied smile. "Yes. Absolutely I am. I've collected some marvelous recipes for cakes and cookies and breads and can't wait to get started."

"But you have something bigger going on," said Theodosia. "A big fat surprise you just sprang on all of us."

Peaches managed a quizzical look. "I did?"

"Your purchase of Solstice," said Theodosia. "That pretty much came zooming out of left field."

Peaches tried to downplay her acquisition. "Not really. It's no secret I'd been interested in the place."

"Yes, but Parker wasn't interested in selling to you," said Theodosia. She knew she was spitting a little venom along with her words, but she didn't much care. "But now, of course, Parker's not around to say no thanks to your purchase offer. Or stand in your way. Now you have everything you wanted."

Peaches's mouth twisted into a grimace. "No, dear, not quite everything."

"Tell me," said Theodosia, taking a step closer, pretty much invading Peaches's personal space. "Did you have to twist Shelby's arm?"

Peaches's eyes narrowed. "I did no such thing."

"Yes, I think you probably did," said Theodosia.

"I merely made the girl a fair and reasonable offer," said Peaches, standing her ground. "There's nothing nefarious going on, Theodosia. It was a legitimate business offer."

"But so very convenient," said Theodosia, "to have Parker out of the way."

Now Peaches tossed back a little venom of her own. "Exactly what are you implying?" She reared back and snarled, "Are you saying that *I* had something to do with the man's death?"

"Did you?" asked Haley. She'd remained quiet as the exchange between Theodosia and Peaches had grown more heated.

"Of course not!" said Peaches. "And shame on you for thinking that!" She gritted her teeth and looked like she was about to spit forth something else. Then she seemed to think better of it and flounced away in anger.

"You sure got her undies in a twist," remarked Haley.

"How long had she been talking to you?" Theodosia asked.

"You mean before you joined the conversation?"

"Well . . . yes," said Theodosia. She wasn't sure if Haley was being coy or if the argument had made her nervous.

Haley shrugged. "Not long. Couple of minutes at most."

"And Peaches was telling you about her idea for a patisserie?"

"Yeah. She wants to call it Bittersweet."

Theodosia felt an unwelcome heaviness lodge in the pit of her stomach. "Haley, did she . . . did Peaches offer you a job?" It would be just like Peaches to try to poach a valued employee.

Haley nodded. "She kind of danced around it. But . . . yeah, she pretty much did."

Theodosia's voice grew deathly quiet. "Are you considering it?"

Haley gave a lopsided grin. "What do you think?"

Theodosia swallowed hard, then said, "I think you're a self-actuated person who will do what's best for yourself careerwise."

"Excuse me," said Haley, frowning slightly and placing her hands on her hips, "but that's no way to get me to stay. It sounded more like a bunch of career aspiration mumbo-jumbo."

"Then how about this. *Please* stay. We love you."

"Theodosia," said Haley, "leaving you, Drayton, and the Indigo Tea Shop never once crossed my mind."

"Really?"

"Really. I love you guys, too, and I intend to stay as long as you'll have me." Haley held up her right hand and crooked her pinkie finger. "And I'll even pinkie-swear on that."

And so they did.

Back at the tea shop, Drayton's casual invitation hadn't only been noted, it had been acted upon—by about twenty of the coffee and tea people who'd attended his lecture. Add in the Indigo Tea Shop's regular customers, as well as a flock of tourists who'd just hopped off one of the red-and-yellow horse-drawn jitneys, and, by eleven thirty, they were slammed.

"Toss four spoonfuls of Sessa Estate Assam into that Brown Betty teapot, will you?" asked Drayton. Theodosia and Drayton were working feverishly behind the counter, brewing tea and setting up tea trays arrayed with sugar cubes, lemon slices, Devonshire cream, and jam.

Theodosia tossed in the tea, popped on a tea cozy made to resemble an orange-and-white calico cat, and said, "Which table?"

"Table five," said Drayton. "And double-check to see if they want teriyaki salmon on their garden salads or lemon chicken. I forgot to write it down and now I can't remember."

"You're all atwitter," said Theodosia.

Drayton nodded. "Poor me. My prefrontal cortex has turned to mush."

Theodosia delivered the tea, clarified the salad orders for Drayton, and quickly brewed up pots of Pouchong, cinnamon spice, and oolong tea. Then there were more deliveries to the tables and a quick visit with Haley in the kitchen.

"Whew," said Haley. She was hunched over her industrial stove, stirring a pot of seafood chowder, tasting it, judiciously adding a pinch of white pepper. "Are we as busy out there as I think we are?"

"Busier," said Theodosia. "Maybe we should have asked Miss Dimple to come in today."

"Nah, we can handle it," said Haley. "You have to do a full-court press once in a while."

"Yes, but you've been doing it all week," said Theodosia.

"Haley glanced up, a little startled. "Have I? Is that why I feel like I've been run over by a steamroller?"

"We can always get you some help. I've made that offer before, you know."

Haley shook her head. "I can't stand the idea of somebody coming into my kitchen and messing things up."

"They wouldn't mess things up," said Theodosia. "They'd be there to lend assistance. To function as a kind of assistant or sous chef."

"What about my receipts?" Haley's voice rose. "My recipes?"

"What about them?" said Theodosia.

"Whoever you hire might *steal* them!" Haley stopped herself and held up a hand. "I know, we've been over this before. And you say it won't happen. But, at the very least, those recipes might be leaked to customers. And you know those are my proprietary receipts. Handed down from my granny."

"Haley," said Theodosia, "with that kind of mind-set, how are you ever going to author a cookbook?"

"That's a problem," Haley admitted. "I mean, I *want* to do one, I've even had offers. But it still grieves me to think my recipes would be out there, just swirling around the universe." She thought for a moment. "I need to do, like, a secret cookbook."

"An unusual concept," said Theodosia, trying hard not to smile.

"How could we do that?" asked Haley.

"I don't know," said Theodosia. "Maybe print the book using invisible ink? Of course, then your recipe insiders would have to hold each page up to a candle in order to read it."

"I *like* that!" said Haley.

Theodosia grabbed a tray of salads. "Somehow I knew you would."

On Theodosia's second trip through the tea room, a hand reached out to grab her. She stopped in her tracks, raised an eyebrow, and looked down.

It was Lyle Manship. Sitting at a table by himself, looking like the cat that just swallowed the canary.

"Good heavens," said Theodosia. "You again." She made a point of not sounding pleased.

"Nice to see you, too," said Manship.

"You must be in hog heaven right about now," said Theodosia. "Since you were just awarded the restaurant franchise at the new Neptune Aquarium."

"I'm thrilled," said Manship. He threw her a smarmy grin that contained little to no warmth.

"Too bad it didn't go to a local Charleston restaurateur."

"Perhaps they're not as creative as I am," said Manship, looking decidedly smug.

"Or maybe they're not as underhanded in their business dealings," Theodosia shot back. She didn't know if money had changed hands, but it wouldn't surprise her.

"That's not very nice," said Manship.

"Are you positive you didn't attend the aquarium's opening party?" Theodosia asked.

Manship's gaze was cool and steady. "I already *told* you I wasn't there."

"Just checking your story," said Theodosia.

"Aren't you the suspicious one," said Manship. "Tell me, the day you drove down to see me, were you really following up for Parker Scully's family, or were you, dare I say it, investigating his murder?"

"Does it really matter?" said Theodosia.

Manship snorted. "Probably not." Then he seemed to shift his attitude. "Say, have you thought any more about leading that tea cruise?"

"No," said Theodosia. "I really haven't."

Twenty minutes later, with all their customers finally served, Theodosia ducked into her office. She wanted to double-check the guest list Delaine had given her. But after she'd slid her index finger down the list and looked carefully, she still didn't see Manship's name. So he definitely hadn't been an invited guest.

That wasn't to say Lyle Manship hadn't been there.

Anyone who'd come strutting into the aquarium that night dressed in black tie and shiny shoes certainly would not have been asked to present an invitation. So . . . Manship could have easily slipped in. And then, after the mayhem, after the murder, he could have slipped back out again.

Had Lyle Manship committed the perfect crime?

No, probably not. If he *had* committed the murder, Theodosia doubted it had been perfect. According to most criminologists, there wasn't any such thing as the perfect crime. Sooner or later a shred of evidence, a witness, a clue, *something* would turn up.

Unfortunately, nothing had turned up yet on Parker's murder.

"*Can you believe* it?" said Drayton, "those gents at tables four and six just requested a tea tasting." He was grabbing tins of tea, balancing them in his hands as if he were contemplating the scales of justice.

"Do you even have time?" Theodosia asked.

Drayton's eyes darted to and fro, his hands moving at lightning speed. He was clearly focused and in the zone. "I'm going to *make* time."

"Then what can I do to help?"

"Grab a tin of Kandoli Garden Assam, will you? That one has such a lovely honey flavor."

"You're going to do all Indian teas?" said Theodosia.

"Yes. And I'll brew a second-flush Darjeeling because I want them to savor that slightly muscatel flavor. And I'll round things off with a nice brisk Nilgiri."

"That'll wake them up," said Theodosia. "You want me to grab a bunch of those small Chinese cups? The ones without handles?"

"Perfect," said Drayton, as his teakettles began to shriek and he was suddenly lost in a cloud of steam.

Still customers continued to pour in.

"Do you do takeout?" asked a woman, who had waited patiently at the front counter.

"We fix a lovely box lunch," said Theodosia. "A scone with a small container of jam and two tea sandwiches."

"Is one of them chicken salad?" asked the woman.

"Today it's chicken salad with slivered almonds," said Theodosia, "and the other sandwich is goat cheese with sun-dried tomatoes."

"Mmm . . . sounds delish," said the woman. "Can I get six box lunches?"

"Coming right up," said Theodosia. She hustled into the kitchen, packaged the scones and jam, wrapped the tea sandwiches in eco-friendly waxed paper, and hustled back out. She lined up six indigo-blue takeout boxes on the counter, arranged the food inside, tossed in paper napkins, and closed the lids. For good measure—and smart marketing—she stuck a crack-and-peel sticker on each one that carried the Indigo Tea Shop logo along with their phone number.

"We seem to be getting more and more take-out orders," Drayton said, as their customer left toting a white shopping bag filled with box lunches. "We should think about putting in a deli counter."

"Where?" asked Theodosia. Clearly, between the front counter, floor-to-ceiling shelves filled with tea tins, their tables and chairs, and their various sideboards and highboys stocked chockablock with gift items, there wasn't a square inch that hadn't been optimized.

"I don't know," said Drayton. "In your office?"

"Oh, great," said Theodosia. That was all she needed.

"Just kidding," said Drayton, as he dropped a teakettle to grab the ringing phone. "Indigo Tea Shop." He listened for a second, then handed it off to her. "For you."

"Hello?" said Theodosia.

"Theodosia! It's Majel!"

"Hi there," said Theodosia. She detected a note of stress in Majel's voice. Or was it excitement? "Is everything all right?" She'd e-mailed all her photos to the City Charities website late last night. So Tuesday's Child should be officially entered in the scavenger hunt.

"Are you kidding?" came Majel's reply. "I'm completely over the moon! Thanks to all your hard work, Tuesday's Child made it into round two! Or rather I should say, *you* got us in!"

"That's wonderful," said Theodosia.

"And I have to tell you, your photos are absolutely gorgeous."

"Thank you."

"If you want to see them, they're already posted. Just go to the City Charities website and click on Scavenger Hunt."

"I'll do that," said Theodosia. She glanced at her watch and saw it was time to take off. Aunt Libby would be waiting. So would Harry Dubose and his melon honey.

"It's so kind of you to do this, Theodosia," said Majel. "I was talking with Delaine earlier today and she mentioned that you have an awful lot on your plate right now."

"Okay."

"I hope I'm not betraying any confidences here, but Delaine told me you were doing sort of an amateur sleuth thing concerning the murder of your former boyfriend." Majel's voice grew more intense. "I apologize. When we were first introduced, I *never* put two and two together. I'd heard about the death at the aquarium, but had no idea the two of you were connected. Anyway, I wanted to tell you how very sorry I am. And I hope I haven't put any additional stress on you."

"Majel," said Theodosia, "you didn't. Don't worry about it.

I'm just happy Drayton and I were able to help your organization."

"Well, so am I. Delaine said you were a smart lady, and now I've pretty much seen that firsthand. So thank you. And now we're on to the finals. To round two."

"I'll do my best," Theodosia promised.

"I know you will," said Majel.

21

~❧~

"*This is so* kind of you," Aunt Libby said to Theodosia as they bumped along in her Jeep. "And for you to go out of your way . . ."

"Seeing you," said Theodosia, "is never out of my way."

Aunt Libby smiled contentedly. She was dressed in a navy-and-white spring suit with a pair of spectator shoes to match. Very snappy. "And I noticed you brought along a basket of tea and scones," she said, glancing over her shoulder at the enormous wicker basket Haley had packed.

"Honey tea and honey scones," said Theodosia. "For Harry and the folks at Dubose Bees. Although you're certainly welcome to grab a scone if you'd like."

"I think I'm still sated from two days ago." Aunt Libby tilted her head back, as if savoring the memory. "What a glorious tea party that was. Amazing food, lovely guests . . ."

"And such a good cause," said Theodosia.

"I can't tell you how thrilled the volunteers at the animal shelter were to receive our check. This economy has been particularly hard on pets. Lots of people just can't afford to keep them anymore. So . . ." Her voice cracked. "They're forced to give them up." She reached up and wiped a tear from her eye. "Hopefully, the little darlings who've been rendered homeless will eventually be adopted by someone else."

"A sad situation," Theodosia murmured. She didn't know what she'd do if she couldn't scrape together enough money to buy food for Earl Grey. Split her own rations with him, probably. Or go without. Her dog was that dear to her.

Theodosia slowed down as she made a hard left from Rutledge Road onto Hummingbird Lane. It was a blind intersection and every signpost seemed covered in kudzu, a crazy Southern varmint plant that just loved to tangle its leafy tendrils around fences, road signs, and even the occasional small building.

"This is so much fun to drive the back roads," said Libby, gazing out the window as they whooshed past thick stands of blue-black slash pines. "So lovely to breath sweet country air and catch a glimpse of tanagers or orioles."

"You can just feel yourself relaxing out here," said Theodosia. And she really could. The bayous and deep, dark forests were therapy for the mind and soul. Living in Charleston was wonderful, of course, filled as it was with great architecture, fascinating history, fabulous food, and quirky people. But the low country, with its flowering dogwood, blue bayous, and stands of cabbage and sabal palmettos, was a veritable dreamscape.

They wound around a turn and were suddenly cruising beneath a living archway. Old-growth live oaks had spread their leafy branches across the road to form a perfect bower.

Most of the land out this way consisted of forested swamps—refuge for deer, alligators, raccoons, and even the occasional diamondback rattler.

"I'm told there's a restored rice field on the old Huntington Plantation," said Aunt Libby. "Nice to think that Carolina gold is growing out here once again."

Theodosia slowed as they drove past a small pond, all sparkling and sun-dappled. "Is that a heron?" she asked, pointing toward a stalk-legged bird.

Libby turned her sharp eyes on the bird. "Wood stork," she said.

"You really know your critters," said Theodosia.

"It's my passion," Aunt Libby admitted. She smiled to herself, then said, "So tonight's your tea ceremony?"

"That's right," said Theodosia. "At the Heritage Society. Though it's really Drayton's tea ceremony. He's the one who honchoed it, and he's the one who's going to do a demonstration on the art of taking tea in Japan."

"Sounds like a rather formal presentation," said Aunt Libby.

"Tea ceremony can be formal," said Theodosia. "Especially for the Japanese." She chuckled. "I suppose for Drayton, too. He does revere ceremony."

"Nothing wrong with that," said Aunt Libby. "I imagine he'll have his bonsai on display?"

"He's bringing along a half dozen or so. He's quite proud of those little trees."

"As well he should be," said Aunt Libby. "I remember when Drayton came out to Cane Ridge several years ago and dug up a number of small tamarack trees."

"You should see them now," said Theodosia. "He made them into a forest." Drayton had planted thirteen small tamaracks in a shallow, blue-glazed ceramic tray. And, with his judicious pruning, trimming, and placement of small rocks, he had created a display that looked exactly like a miniature forest.

"A forest," Aunt Libby marveled. "How very creative."

"He even won an award for it in a local bonsai show," said Theodosia. She gave a cursory glance in her rearview mirror and noticed a truck approaching from behind. Coming up rather fast. Probably, she decided, the truck just wanted to pass her. They were on a narrow road, with little or no shoulder, so Theodosia, being a conscientious driver, eased over a bit to allow the truck to pass her.

But it didn't. Rather, the truck nosed right up to her rear bumper and stayed there.

As the highway curved around, the road dipped slightly, revealing vast shimmering stretches of swamp on either side. Theodosia tapped her accelerator. Maybe her mistake had been to slow down. Better to just maintain a normal speed and not worry about another driver.

Except for one thing. The truck eased up ever closer, then tapped her bumper. Not enough to jar her, but enough to be noticed.

"What the . . . !" Theodosia exclaimed.

"What's going on?" Aunt Libby asked. She'd seen Theodosia glance into the rearview mirror and picked up on her tension. Had she felt the tap? Maybe.

"I don't know. That joker behind me keeps . . ."

Another tap, this time a little harder.

"Is he trying to force us off the road?" Aunt Libby asked in alarm.

"I don't know," Theodosia said again. Swamp and wetlands still stretched out on both sides of the road, so there was no convenient place to pull over and get out of the way of this rude driver. Even though there was probably no need for panic, Theodosia felt a rising tide of fear in her chest.

Glancing in her side mirror, Theodosia saw that the truck, a shiny black vehicle, was cruising along, about fifteen feet back from her now. Good. At least he'd settled down.

But it was not to last.

Suddenly, the truck accelerated like crazy! It roared toward her, jammed hard against the back of her Jeep, and then revved so hard it was practically propelling her down the road.

"Oh, dear Lord!" cried Libby. "What's happening?"

"Hang on!" said Theodosia. She could only focus her energy on one thing right now. And that most important thing was trying to maintain a straight line down the road!

For a second time, the truck dropped back. But Theodosia didn't let down her guard.

Good thing.

Because fifteen seconds later, the truck roared up from behind and punched her hard again!

This time her Jeep was smacked hard on the left rear bumper. Metal crunched loudly and her vehicle groaned in protest. Theodosia fought hard to keep her line down the middle of the road, but just when she thought she'd gained control, her rear wheels skidded and she went into a sort of controlled fishtail.

Theodosia tried to steer her way out of the fishtail—and almost made it. But then her right front tire caught the edge of the blacktop and that was all it took. She braked, tap-tap-tapping her foot against the brake pedal, and fought hard to recover and straighten out her wheels again. But they were suddenly catapulted down a slight ditch and into the swamp!

Oh crap, we're going in the drink!

Brackish water splashed across the windshield, blotting everything out. Aunt Libby let loose a frightened scream.

Theodosia continued to fight for control, but a million worries flashed through her brain. Were they going to flip over? Would the air bag deploy and smash Aunt Libby in the face? Would they sink into the bog? Was there quicksand?

None of these things came to pass, of course. They were all crazy, worst-case-scenario thoughts.

Instead, they endured a rather soft, squishy landing in about two feet of watery muck. Theodosia glanced out her window in shock as the offending black truck swept past them, oblivious of their plight. Two seconds later, it had disappeared from sight.

"Are you okay?" Theodosia screamed at Aunt Libby. "Oh, my gosh, are you . . . ?"

"I'm fine," Aunt Libby said in a small voice. "But you . . . it seemed like you bumped your head."

"Did I?" Theodosia couldn't remember. All she could recall were quick flashes, like stop-action scenes from a herky-jerky movie. Then they'd hit the water with a tremendous splash. Theodosia gazed through her windshield and saw bald cypress and tupelo standing like sentinels. Her brain flashed a final message that said, *Yup, we landed in the swamp.* Then she touched a hand to her forehead and rubbed. It *did* feel like she might have sustained a bump. "No, I'm okay," she lied.

Aunt Libby squirmed about in the passenger seat, searching for something.

"What's wrong?" Was water pouring in?

"My field glasses!"

Theodosia searched around and finally spotted a brown leather case wedged against the gas pedal. It must have flown around like a miniature missile during the crash. She reached down and grabbed the case that held Aunt Libby's Zeiss field glasses. Gingerly, she opened the velvet-lined case, peered in, then handed the whole thing to Aunt Libby.

Aunt Libby turned the field glasses over in her hand, studied them carefully, then let loose a deep sigh of relief. "They're okay."

"Good."

Aunt Libby put a hand to her chest. "What was that all about?"

"I sincerely don't know," said Theodosia.

"Just a crazy driver?"

Theodosia wanted to ponder that question some more, since the whole incident had seemed so deliberate. But she said, to hopefully calm Aunt Libby's nerves, "I think so."

Aunt Libby frowned as she gazed out the passenger-side

window. "Are we going to be able to get out of this swamp? Or are we going to need a tow truck?"

"Let's find out," said Theodosia. She turned the key in the ignition and her engine caught immediately. Of course, she had no idea if she'd shut the engine off earlier, or if it had just quit on its own—just took a giant hiccup and shut itself off.

"At least it starts," said Aunt Libby. "But I fear we might be stuck tight."

Theodosia slid her gearshift into four-wheel drive. "Hope not." She goosed the engine, pretty much expecting they *would* be stuck tight. Instead, she felt her vehicle inch forward.

"Hallelujah!" cried Aunt Libby.

"God bless Chrysler Corporation," said Theodosia. She spun and torqued and judiciously goosed her car some more, taking it easy, but not letting up on the pressure, either. Gradually, they crept out of the muck, up the bank, and onto the road.

"We did it!" Aunt Libby gave an excited clap. "*You* did it!"

Theodosia blew out a glut of air and thought for a few moments. "Would you like me to take you home?"

Aunt Libby looked startled. "Home? I thought we were going to visit the bee people."

"You still want to do that?"

"I'm game if you are," said Aunt Libby.

"But are you really okay?" asked Theodosia. She was worried that Aunt Libby might have gotten bruised or shaken up when they spun down the embankment. And even though they'd landed in a bog full of muck, they'd hit fairly hard.

"I'm fine," Aunt Libby assured her. Then worry lines appeared. "But who would . . . why?" She gazed at the empty road ahead of them, anger clouding her normally placid expression. "Really. What kind of rude driver sideswipes someone like that? I mean, he didn't even stop to see if we were all right!"

"No, he didn't," said Theodosia. She knew darn well they hadn't been sideswiped. They'd been rammed hard from behind. And deep inside her was the unspoken thought, *I have a terrible feeling he didn't want us to be all right.*

22

❧

Dubose Bees was a third-generation farm that had been rais-
ing bees and producing honey for some sixteen years. It had
originally been a little bit of everything—apple orchard,
alfalfa fields, dairy farm. Now the fields were overgrown with
clover and tall grasses, and sturdy apple and cherry trees
dominated the landscape.

Harry Dubose and his family lived in a compact white
clapboard house set up on stilts and surrounded by a lovely
veranda. Two other buildings sat close by, a large hip-roofed
barn and a smaller, newer gift shop.

When Theodosia and Aunt Libby pulled into the yard,
they parked and headed immediately for the gift shop.

As the bell above the door tinkled, Harry Dubose looked
up from behind the counter. He wore khaki slacks, matching
shirt, and a long, yellow apron with a smiling honeybee logo.
He had a big grin on his face and a jar of tupelo honey in his
hand. "Welcome!" he cried. He set the honey down and came
around the counter to greet them.

Once Theodosia did the introductions, they snooped around the gift shop. She was amazed at the products Dubose Bees was selling. Cherry blossom honey, apple blossom honey, clover honey, cream honey, comb honey, honey mustard, and even beeswax candles. And a couple of jars of coveted melon honey, too.

"I hope you saved two cases of that for me," said Theodosia.

Dubose dipped his head. "I surely did."

"Excellent," Theodosia replied. "And I have a basket of honey scones for you as well as some of Drayton's vanilla honey tea."

"You don't say," said Dubose, clearly pleased by her generosity. "Honey tea?"

"It's a blend of white tea with hints of vanilla bean and honey," said Theodosia.

"Is that something I could retail here in our gift shop?" Dubose asked. "I mean, I think our customers might enjoy that. Honey tea."

"I'm sure that can be arranged," said Theodosia.

They pushed open the screen door and walked outside. Theodosia grabbed the basket filled with scones and tea and presented it to Dubose while Aunt Libby grabbed her field glasses.

"Say," said Dubose, looking at her car, "looks like you ran off the road somewhere along the way." Mud spattered the bottom half of her Jeep and a few matted weeds stuck to the wheel well.

"Something like that," said Theodosia.

"Guess that's what four-wheel-drive vehicles are for," said Dubose. "Off road." He grinned. "You want to see our operation, don't you?"

"You mean the hives?" asked Theodosia.

"Sure," said Dubose. "That's where all the magic happens."

"Are we going to need protective gear?" Theodosia asked.

"Naw," said Dubose, waving a hand. "Our honeybees are very well behaved."

They walked together down a well-trod path, through tall grasses and along a row of short, leafy trees.

"Those are Asian pear trees we planted a couple of years ago," Dubose pointed out. "We're hoping they'll bear substantial fruit this summer."

"So you're planning to have pear-flavored honey?" said Theodosia.

"That's the general idea," said Dubose.

They continued their walk. Sunlight streamed down as a warm breeze stirred across the meadow and gently lifted the hair off the back of Theodosia's neck. *Summer*, she thought. Always welcome and almost in full swing.

Ahead they could see white stacks of hives, lined up like mini condos.

"How many hives do you have?" Theodosia asked.

"Two hundred and forty," said Dubose.

"Good heavens!" Aunt Libby suddenly exclaimed. She lifted her trusty field binoculars to her face and tried to focus on a multicolored bird that had just flitted from one tree to the next. "Could that have been a painted bunting?"

"Could be," said Dubose. "They're rare, but we see them around here every once in a while."

"Sweet little gaudies," said Aunt Libby, smiling.

"That's cute," said Theodosia. After their earlier mishap, she was delighted Aunt Libby seemed to be having such a good time.

"I call them that because they *are* gaudy," Aunt Libby explained. "Particularly the males with their blue heads, bright green wings, and red underparts." She lifted her field glasses to her eyes again, studied the trees for an instant, then strode on ahead. She was anxious to catch a better look.

Next to Theodosia, Dubose's cell phone suddenly tinkled a sixties tune.

"Hang on," he told her.

Theodosia wandered a few feet away to give him privacy. She reached up into one of the pear trees and touched an index finger to a little green node. A potential pear. Hopefully, it would grow and ripen into a juicy, luscious fruit. Perhaps Drayton could even incorporate some of these locally grown pears into one of his proprietary tea blends. Maybe . . . Chinese black tea flavored with pear, honey, and a hint of ginger?

A rustle in the nearby brush suddenly caught Theodosia's attention. She turned and slowly walked toward what was a deeper, thicker woods adjacent to the apiary. Was someone out there? Was that what she'd heard? No, it was probably a whitetail deer stepping carefully through the woods. Or possibly even a wild boar. Amazingly, wild boar had been spotted rummaging and foraging not ten miles from Charleston!

Theodosia didn't know if wild boar were truly dangerous, but her curiosity was ramped up. She picked her way closer to the woods, resolving to scramble up into a tree if one of the wild piggies made its presence known and came scooting out to threaten her.

More rustling of leaves off to her right. She grinned. Something was definitely out there. But from the motion of the leaves and the sound of things, whatever it was had to be higher off the ground than a boar.

So . . . maybe a deer with her fawn? That would be a lovely sight.

As she stood listening, she heard a sudden clunk from about thirty feet away. A dull thud that sounded as if someone had pitched a baseball against a wooden fence. Or maybe a rock.

What?

Right on the heels of that came a frightened yelp!

Oh no . . . Aunt Libby?

Theodosia spun around and sprinted back to the path. She

hastily jogged left, heading for the stacks of hives she'd spotted earlier. To where she thought the strange sounds had originated.

Aunt Libby was there, all right. Field glasses still pressed to her face as she scanned the trees. What she didn't see was a stream of bees suddenly arcing upward into the air. Like a miniature cyclone, the gang of bees seemed to swell, and then they closed ranks and flew in a massive circle.

"Dear Lord!" Theodosia cried. "I hope they don't . . ."

She choked on her words as a group of bees suddenly veered from the main swarm and headed directly for Aunt Libby!

"Aunt Libby!" Theodosia's shrill cry rent the air. Startled, Aunt Libby dropped her field glasses, turned quickly, and, in an instant, took in the small storm of bees that was headed directly for her!

Aunt Libby started to run, then suddenly flung up both arms and began frantically swatting the air.

Without hesitation, Theodosia pounded her way toward Aunt Libby.

"Theo!" Aunt Libby cried out, as she flailed like crazy, trying to shield her face! "Help!" Her cries sounded shrill and pitiful.

Within seconds, Theodosia was in the thick of things, swatting at a small cloud of bees, pulling off the scarf from around her neck and trying to swaddle it around Aunt Libby's head so the bees couldn't get to her.

Twenty seconds later, Harry Dubose was beside them, squirting great drafts of water from a green hose that just seemed to materialize. And just as fast as they'd converged on Aunt Libby, the bees retreated and the incident was over.

"Aunt Libby!" Theodosia cried. "Oh, dear heavens, are you okay?"

Aunt Libby's eyes were open wide in panic and her lips seemed to move soundlessly.

No, it was obvious she wasn't okay. Not in the least.

"She get stung?" asked Dubose, panting from the exertion.

"On her face," said Theodosia. She placed her hands on each side of Aunt Libby's head and studied her carefully. "Maybe five, no I see eight distinct welts."

"What happened?" asked Dubose. "The bees don't usually . . ." He was worried and breathless, afraid for Aunt Libby, rattled that such an accident could take place when he'd assured them they'd be perfectly safe.

"I think somebody threw something at one of the hives," Theodosia said quickly, still clutching Aunt Libby to assess the damage. "A rock. Or maybe hit it with a stick." She tried to catch her breath, too. "To . . . to antagonize the bees."

"Caused them to defend their home," said Dubose. He turned his full attention to Aunt Libby again. "Is she allergic? Should we inject her with an EpiPen?"

Aunt Libby's eyelids fluttered. "I . . . I'm okay."

"No, she's not," said Dubose. "That many stings, she's gonna experience a drop in blood pressure and possible swelling of the airways."

Like the chemical reaction in a popover when its ingredients suddenly reacted to intense heat, Aunt Libby's face and hands were beginning to swell. It started with a small degree of redness and tightness of her skin, and then her face and hands began to puff with greater intensity. Even worse, Aunt Libby seemed to be hiccupping as she struggled with her breathing!

"Let's give her the injection, then run her to the hospital!" Theodosia cried.

Dubose leaned forward, swept Aunt Libby up in his arms, and carried her back to the parking lot. He ran all the way, puffing and sweating bullets.

"Hospital!" Theodosia cried again, but one of Dubose's assistants had seen them coming and he was already there with an EpiPen. Dubose grabbed it, shucked off the protective paper, and, with practiced hands, immediately jabbed the needle into Aunt Libby's upper arm. Hopefully, it would kick in fast and counteract the effects of the bee venom.

They loaded a slightly groggy Aunt Libby into Theodosia's Jeep, then Dubose jumped into his white 4Runner truck. "Follow me!" he yelled, grinding gears and taking off in a cloud of dust.

It was only six miles to the nearby St. Francis Hospital, but it felt like sixty miles to Theodosia. Aunt Libby slumped in the front seat, her skin pale, her breathing thready. Still, she managed a weak smile. The old gal was hanging in there.

They swept up the drive to the emergency room entrance and Theodosia jumped from her Jeep almost before it had ground to a complete stop. She rushed through a set of sliding glass doors, glanced at a bevy of nurses and med techs who were congregated behind a counter, and cried, "Emergency! Please help. I've got an eighty-two-year-old woman who's been stung by bees!"

23

❧

Theodosia's urgent pleas suddenly kicked everything into a blur of activity. A nurse sprinted out to check on Aunt Libby while an orderly followed close on her heels, dragging a metal gurney. Carefully, they transferred Aunt Libby from Theodosia's Jeep to the gurney. Then, moments later, amid a clatter of wheels on pavement and a flutter of blankets, she was rushed into the emergency room.

Theodosia sat on a purple plastic chair, feeling awful and a little alone. Aunt Libby was, after all, her only living relative.

"I feel responsible for this." Dubose had knotted his baseball cap in his big hands and was picking frantically at the brim. His eyes were red-rimmed and scared.

"It wasn't your fault," said Theodosia. She knew that if anyone was to blame, it was her. She was the one who'd let Aunt Libby go wandering off into the woods, doing her bird-watching thing right alongside all those hives. She was the one who'd heard something moving in the woods and never made a connection. Never figured that something—or someone—might foolishly stir up the bees.

"You said you thought somebody threw a rock at the hive?" Dubose asked.

"It sounded like it. Or maybe whacked it with a stick."

Dubose shook his head. "Why?" he muttered to himself, half in anger, half in amazement. "Why would someone do that?"

"I don't know," said Theodosia. "Maybe . . . kids? Just trying to act smart but up to no good?"

"Maybe," said Dubose.

"Has anything like this ever happened before?"

"No," said Dubose.

They sat together in silence for another five minutes until a nurse finally came out. She was dressed in green scrubs and looked tired, as if she'd just worked a twelve-hour shift. But her smile was genuine and her manner was solicitous and warm.

"The doctor's looking at your aunt right now," said the nurse, whose name tag read ANNE RILEY. "We have her on oxygen and she's receiving some additional medication."

Theodosia sprang up from her chair. "But is she . . . ?"

Nurse Riley interrupted. "You did the right thing, injecting her with that EpiPen. It was smart thinking."

Theodosia turned to Dubose and put a hand on his arm. "Thank you. For such fast thinking."

Harry Dubose looked like he was ready to cry. "I'm so sorry for all this trouble."

"Not your fault," Theodosia said again.

"She's holding her own," said the nurse. "And once the doctor finishes with her, he'll be out to talk."

"I'm not going anywhere," said Theodosia. But after thirty minutes of waiting, she sent Dubose home. He protested mightily at first but was finally convinced by Theodosia's words. Still, she had to promise to call him later on and give him a complete rundown on Aunt Libby's medical condition.

When the doctor finally emerged, Theodosia was composed but still concerned.

"Is she . . . ?" Theodosia began, then stopped. She suddenly couldn't ask the hard questions, couldn't fathom a world without her dear Aunt Libby.

But the doctor, a young, earnest-looking fellow by the name of Victor Prince, held up a hand. "Whoa, whoa, take it easy," he said. "Your aunt's in stable condition. We administered another dose of epinephrine along with some corticosteroids."

"So you're telling me she's okay?"

"Yes," said Dr. Prince. "She's resting comfortably and I don't foresee any complications as a result of this incident."

"Can I see her?" asked Theodosia. She was desperate to get to Aunt Libby.

"Of course." The doctor waved a hand. "Go right through those doors, then turn left."

"Thank you," said Theodosia. She walked a few steps, put a hand on the door to push it open, then stopped and turned back to the doctor. "Would it be better if my aunt stayed here overnight?"

The doctor pondered this for a moment. "What's her age again?"

"Eighty-two."

He considered this. "So she's up there. Maybe not a bad idea to keep her under observation." He nodded. "Sure, let's do it. I'll write the orders."

"Thank you," Theodosia said again. "Thank you very much."

Aunt Libby was propped up on one of the emergency room tables, a hospital-green blanket swaddled around her thin frame and an oxygen cannula stuck in her nose. She looked both alert and relaxed as a med tech in green scrubs hovered nearby, dabbing tiny circles of white, gooey cortisone cream on the bites that covered her hands and face.

"You scared me to death!" Theodosia cried as she rushed to Aunt Libby's side. She wanted to throw her arms around her and hug her tight but was afraid she'd irritate the bee stings.

Aunt Libby grabbed for Theodosia's hand and squeezed it. "I didn't mean to," she said, her voice sounding dry and a little scared. Then she shook her head, as if to clear it. "I guess I scared myself, too. I sort of . . . conked out there for a while."

"You sure did," said Theodosia, her voice sounding shaky, too. Then she decided it might be better *not* to replay the bad parts of today's bee event. Better, instead, to bolster Aunt Libby's spirits with positive news. "But the doctor says you'll be fine. That you *are* just fine."

"I *feel* fine," said Aunt Libby. "Just peachy now." But her pallor belied her hearty declaration.

"I suspect you'll be good as new in a couple of days," said Theodosia. "But the doctor wants to keep you here overnight. Purely for observation, of course."

The med tech, whose name tag read BEVERLY, finished administering the cortisone cream and nodded. "You can never be too careful about these things."

"And I'm going to stay with you," Theodosia told Aunt Libby.

Aunt Libby shook her head in protest. "Nonsense. You've got your Japanese tea ceremony tonight. Your *chado* at the Heritage Society."

"Drayton and Haley can handle it just fine without me."

"No, no," said Aunt Libby, firmness seeping into her voice. "You have to be there tonight. Show the flag. I'll be okay. Better than okay, especially if I'm staying here tonight. Lots of nice people to look after me."

"We'll take good care of her," Beverly promised.

"Well . . ." Theodosia was hesitant to leave her.

"Really," said Aunt Libby, and this time she did sound more like her old self. "You can come pick me up first thing tomorrow morning. I'll stay here, order room service, and enjoy the five-star treatment."

Theodosia still wasn't convinced. "Did you know you'd have such a violent reaction? I mean, did you know you were seriously allergic to bee venom?"

"Never suspected it in a million years," said Aunt Libby. "I've been stung before, but only once or twice at the same time." She sighed deeply, then held a hand to her heart. "But this . . . I don't like to admit to my own mortality . . . this was very frightening. It felt like I was under siege!"

"That's because you were," said Theodosia. There was no need to cause Aunt Libby any more worry or excitement, but the question that burned like fury in the back of Theodosia's mind was, *Why did the bees suddenly launch an all-out blitz against Aunt Libby?* Did normally docile honeybees get suddenly cranky and decide to harass an old lady?

No. Hardly.

Driving back to Charleston, Theodosia called Dubose on her cell phone to tell him that Libby was okay.

"I feel awful," said Dubose, repeating his mantra. "Completely responsible."

"It wasn't your fault," said Theodosia. "Something frightened the bees."

"Never seen anything like it," said Dubose.

But fresh in Theodosia's mind was the loud crack she'd heard just before the bees had taken wing. The crack of something heavy, a rock or a baseball bat or a piece of wood, smacking against the hive. The sound of someone *deliberately* upsetting those bees.

Theodosia sailed into her house, still thinking about how someone must have provoked those bees, wondering how it all tied in.

Had the bee attack been meant for her?

She hated that idea, but had to admit it was a possibility. If she'd upset the proverbial apple cart by investigating Parker's death, then maybe someone wanted to slow her down for good?

Had the bee attack been launched as a second phase? The first being her car forced off the road?

Thinking about it made her shudder. Still, Theodosia wasn't about to call off her hunt and back down. Retreat was not an option. It just wasn't part of her nature.

Toenails clicked against parquet floors as Earl Grey padded into the kitchen to greet her.

"Boy, did you miss a piece of excitement today," Theodosia told him. "First we got run off the road into a swamp, then a bunch of bees came swarming after Aunt Libby."

Earl Grey flipped an ear up and gazed at her with serious brown eyes.

"That's right, although I guess she's your Great-Aunt Libby. In dog terms."

Earl Grey watched carefully as Theodosia bustled about her kitchen, filling his bowl with fresh, clean water and pouring out a cup and a half of kibble.

"What time did Haley bring you home today?" Theodosia asked.

"Rwrrr."

"Four?" said Theodosia. "Did she let you wander through the tea shop, too, once everyone had left? Did you get to play tea shop dog?"

At the words *tea shop* Earl Grey wagged his tail.

"So she did. Yeah, Haley loves to push the envelope, doesn't she? Good thing the health inspectors didn't drop in for a surprise visit." She set the bowl of kibble down on a place mat that said BLESS THIS FOOD. "Oh well. No harm done."

Five minutes later, Theodosia was upstairs, tearing through her walk-in closet. She needed something sort of Asian-inspired to wear tonight and she thought she had the perfect top. Except right now . . . she wasn't finding it. She pounded into her bedroom, rummaged through the dresser drawers, and finally found it. A sort of kimono top, done in pale blues and greens with a lovely crane motif.

Back in the closet she pulled out a pair of tapered white silk slacks. Perfect. She put on the top and slacks, then shucked her feet into a nice pair of leather thongs. A string of pale jade beads went around her neck.

In the bathroom, Theodosia brushed out her hair, gathered it into a loose ponytail, and twisted it around. She pinned it carefully and gazed into the mirror. Hustling back into the bedroom, she rummaged through a basket piled with strands of pearls, antique brooches, and bangle bracelets. Selecting a pair of blue-and-gold lacquer chopsticks, she stuck them in her bun. Then she gazed into the mirror at her reflection and wrinkled her nose. Too much? Maybe. Maybe not. She'd have to ask Haley.

24

Jumbo shrimp wrapped in blankets of tempura batter sizzled and bobbed in Haley's electric deep fryer. Perfectly wrapped tuna and avocado rolls were artfully arranged on a black lacquer tray. Theodosia, Drayton, and Haley had crowded into the small utility kitchen at the Heritage Society, preparing the appetizers and tea for the evening. Outside, on the patio, Drayton's bonsai had been positioned on stone pillars that surrounded a pattering fountain, and a backdrop of tall, emerald-green stalks of bamboo swayed in the night breeze. Japanese lanterns cast an intimate orange glow as guests began to trickle in.

As Theodosia assembled miniature skewers of chicken teriyaki, she shared the afternoon's dramatic (and traumatic) events with Drayton and Haley.

"How utterly terrifying!" Drayton exclaimed. He'd hung breathlessly on every single word of her story. "Did you call the police?"

"What would they have done?" said Haley. "Arrest a bunch of bees?"

"I'm talking about reporting the truck that ran her off the road," said Drayton.

"Oh," said Haley.

"I thought about calling local law enforcement," said Theodosia. "Until I realized I wouldn't be able to give them a decent description. I never even caught a couple digits from the license plate, and I figured 'dark-colored truck' might be a bit obscure."

"Are you sure you were *deliberately* run off the road?" asked Haley.

"It sure felt like it at the time," said Theodosia.

"And then someone startled the bees," said Drayton. "That all sounds extremely deliberate to me. As if . . ." He paused to measure out several scoops of green tea. "As if someone was seriously harassing you. Or wanted to inflict bodily harm."

"It could just be a bad coincidence," said Haley.

"It could be," said Theodosia.

"Or someone wants you out of the way," said Drayton, in a low tone.

Haley looked suddenly worried. "Why would that be? Because Theodosia's been investigating Parker's death?"

"That's exactly what comes to mind," said Drayton.

"But who would be after her?" asked Haley. She turned to Theodosia. "Who do *you* think it was?"

"No clue," said Theodosia.

"That's really the crux of the matter, isn't it?" said Drayton. "No definitive clues. Concerning Parker's murder, I mean."

"Certainly nothing concrete," said Theodosia. "Nothing that could lead to an arrest."

"Frustrating," Drayton murmured. "And now it's turning dangerous for *you*." He gave Theodosia a long, knowing look.

"Now that you mention it," said Haley as she mulled over their words, "stirring up those bees does sound downright intentional." She used a pair of long wooden chopsticks to flip her shrimp over in the bubbling oil. "Poor Aunt Libby! Getting stung must have been awful!"

"If it makes you feel any better," said Theodosia, "poor Aunt Libby was eating chicken piccata and watching a Julia Roberts movie when I left."

"Oh," said Haley. "That does sound kind of relaxing. So she really is okay?"

"They're keeping her overnight for observation," said Theodosia. "But, yes, all things considered, I think she'll be just fine."

"Aunt Libby is tough," said Drayton. "She's a little woman with a backbone of forged steel."

"That's true," said Theodosia, "but she is eighty-two."

"She lived through World War Two," said Haley. World War II was Haley's benchmark for rock-bottom courage. Anybody who'd been alive during that era, whether they were a soldier, a factory worker, a farmer, a homemaker, or just a kid, was, in her eyes, a genuine hero.

"She didn't exactly fight *in* the war," Drayton pointed out.

"Well, I know that!" said Haley. She dipped a flat bamboo-and-mesh scoop into the oil and snagged a dozen golden shrimp. Then she deposited them on thick paper towels. "Okay, these are ready. Just stick toothpicks in them and pile them on the end of that platter, next to the California rolls."

"Then I can take the platter out?" asked Theodosia.

Haley bobbed her head. "Set it on the tea table and people can just help themselves. No need to circulate among the guests or anything since this isn't black tie."

"Just black kimono," said Drayton. He was wearing a short, black silk kimono jacket over his white shirt and black slacks.

"You, my friend," Haley chuckled at Drayton, "look like some sort of disreputable waiter in that getup."

Drayton pulled himself to his full height and peered

down his aquiline nose. "I'll have you know this is an authentic *haori* coat from the Meiji period."

"Is that so?" said Haley, squinting at him.

"And I brought along kimonos for both of you to wear," continued Drayton. "Borrowed from a friend who has a rather extensive collection."

"Really?" said Haley. "You think kimonos are better than what Theodosia has on?"

"Just more authentic," said Drayton. He reached around behind him and pulled a rustle of silk from a shopping bag. When he unfurled it, they were looking at a full-length peach-colored kimono decorated with purple flowers.

"That's absolutely gorgeous," said Theodosia.

"Then this shall be yours," said Drayton. He adjusted his tortoiseshell half-glasses. "That floral motif happens to be wisteria, by the way. A harbinger of spring in Japan."

"What about my kimono?" asked Haley, suddenly interested.

Drayton pulled out a second kimono, a red one. "Red to match your temperament, but adorned with lovely white cranes, which are always an auspicious symbol."

"Kinda neat," said Haley.

"Neat," said Drayton, the word dripping off his tongue.

Haley watched as Theodosia stepped into her kimono, then let Drayton tie a long, cream-colored obi around her waist. "You look like some sort of vision in that," Haley observed. "Like you should be swooping down from Mt. Fuji on the back of a fire-breathing dragon."

"No fire breathing tonight," said Drayton, "except for the hot coals in my hibachi."

Theodosia adjusted the obi, pulling it a little tighter, then scooped up the tray of Japanese goodies. "Okay?" she asked. She was just happy Drayton didn't expect her to totter around an uneven patio wearing wooden geta.

Drayton and Haley both nodded their approval.

"Hey!" Haley exclaimed, just noticing Theodosia's updo. "I like what you did with those chopsticks. In your hair, I mean. A little bit of Harajuku hip mingled with the elegance of a geisha!"

"Good heavens!" exclaimed Timothy Neville, the moment Theodosia stepped out onto the patio. "Don't you look lovely!"

"Thank you," said Theodosia. Timothy was the octogenarian executive director of the Heritage Society, a small, simian-looking man with a cap of thin, white hair above his tightly stretched countenance. Well-connected, with a lineage that ran all the way back to the early Huguenots, Timothy was rich as Croesus and ran the Heritage Society with an iron fist. He was also, Theodosia knew for a fact, a permanent fixture. In fact, Timothy had let it be known that when he finally departed the Heritage Society, it would be feet first in a horizontal position. Though several members had chuckled at this, Theodosia didn't doubt Timothy for a moment.

"Tell me," said Timothy, looking rather elegant in his trim white dinner jacket, "since Drayton was the one who set up this event, what exactly is on the program for tonight?" His spidery fingers hovered above a piece of sushi, then switched direction and grabbed a plump shrimp.

"As soon as all our guests arrive," said Theodosia, "Drayton's going to perform a tea ceremony."

Timothy grimaced. "This is going to be an elaborate ritual?"

"Actually, it's rather simple," said Theodosia. "More of a demonstration than anything."

"Excellent," said Timothy, his eyes drifting away, taking in the crowd of people who continued to gather and exchange air kisses. He was thinking, no doubt, that there had to be *some* donor still untapped whose arm could be twisted into ponying up substantial money for his beloved institution.

"Thank you for letting us use your patio," said Theodosia. This wasn't exactly a Heritage Society–sanctioned event. It was really more of a favor to her and Drayton and the sponsors of the Coffee & Tea Expo.

Timothy waved a hand. "Think nothing of it." He lowered his voice. "Oh, good gracious, here comes that crazy woman Delaine. A prodigious fund-raiser, to be sure, but such a dreadful gossip." And off Timothy darted, disappearing into the crowd.

Delaine had already spotted Theodosia and was waving madly, her wrist clanking with glittering bracelets. "Theodosia!" she cried, taking little baby steps, all her tight gold sheath dress and matching four-inch stilettos would allow. Then, drawing closer, she whooped, "Oh, Theo! Don't you look all colorful and delicious and exotic! Dare I say it? Like a courtier who just stepped out of some marvelous *Ukiyo-e* print!"

"Uki-what?" said Dougan Granville, who had been dragged along in Delaine's frothy wake.

"*Ukiyo-e* literally translates as 'pictures of a floating world,'" Theodosia explained. "It's a term that refers to the Japanese woodblock prints of the seventeenth through nineteenth centuries."

"Oh," Granville grunted. He'd turned to eye the crowd. Looking for a means of escape, perhaps? But Theodosia had a few questions for Dougan Granville.

"Dougan," Theodosia began, "since you're on the board of the Neptune Aquarium, I was wondering if you knew exactly how the restaurant franchise was awarded?"

"Huh?" Granville was distracted and still looking around.

"Dougan?" said Delaine, gazing lovingly up at him. She gave his arm a little tug. "The restaurant franchise?"

"The one that was awarded to Lyle Manship?" said Theodosia, giving him a prompt. "Can you explain why he was the recipient?"

Granville pulled a Cohiba cigar from the breast pocket of

his finely tailored navy jacket and twiddled it between his fingers. "No idea," he said.

"But you're on the board," said Theodosia.

Delaine sidled even closer to Granville, suddenly in a defensive posture. "Dougan serves on *several* boards."

"There are boards and then there are working boards," said Granville, as if that were explanation enough.

"Are you telling me you're a board member in name only?" said Theodosia.

"Something like that," said Granville. "In the case of the Neptune Aquarium, where funding came from individuals as well as the city and the federal government, they have a top-notch executive committee already in place. You know, an executive director, assistant director, financial officer, marketing guy, that sort of thing."

"The thing is," said Theodosia, "Lyle Manship, who received the restaurant franchise, is a bit of a sleazeball. I understand there's even been some impropriety in his past."

"You don't say," said Granville. He looked surprised, as if this were the first he'd heard.

"So I was wondering," said Theodosia, "why his past business dealings wouldn't have been investigated a little more thoroughly."

"You'd have to talk to the executive director about that," said Granville.

"You mean David Sedakis," said Theodosia.

"That's right," said Granville.

"It's a known fact that Manship does have a checkered past," said Theodosia, "so do you think David Sedakis might have overlooked that?" She took a deep breath, then asked, "Do you think money might have changed hands?"

"I don't know," said Granville. But his body language and squared shoulders clearly stated, *And I don't want to know.*

Still, Theodosia pushed him. "Do you think you could try to find out? Do a little digging?"

Granville looked pained. "Perhaps."

"My pumpkin-poo is frightfully busy right now," said Delaine.

"I know you want to be a responsible board member," Theodosia continued, "even if you're there in name only."

Granville looked even more pained.

"Because if there had been some sort of under-the-table deal," said Theodosia, "you certainly wouldn't want your name attached to it. You wouldn't want to have your stellar reputation impugned. After all, you've worked long and hard to establish your law firm as one of Charleston's preeminent firms." Theodosia pretty much choked on these last words, even though they seemed to be effective in hitting their target.

Granville looked like he was turning green, while Delaine clenched her jaw so hard she looked like she'd pop a filling. Theodosia had touched upon the one thing that everyone in the upper reaches of Charleston society feared most. Scandal.

"I'll look into it," Granville muttered.

"Thank you," said Theodosia. "I appreciate it."

25

❧

The tea ceremony was beautiful. With everyone seated on folding chairs, and a musician plucking out a simple, haunting tune on a Japanese koto, Drayton stepped to a small raised platform and began.

"My *tetsubin . . .*" he said, indicating a black iron teapot that was heating on a small hibachi, "is filled with water and about to come to a boil. But, as in the preparation of any fine tea, one never allows the water to reach full boil."

There were murmurs and nods from the crowd as they gave him their rapt attention.

"In fact," Drayton continued, "there's a famous Japanese adage that serves as a perfect reference." He gave a quick smile, then said, "'Carp eyes coming, fish eyes going, soon will be the wind in the pines.' You see," he explained, "the fish eyes are the tiny bubbles, and the carp eyes are the large bubbles that generally herald a good roiling boil. And the wind in the pines is, of course, the beginning rush of the teapot's whistle."

This charming metaphor drew a round of applause from the tea-loving crowd.

Lifting his teapot off the glowing coals of the hibachi, Drayton poured water into a small, sea-green ceramic bowl. Then, opening a matching ceramic jar, he used a long wooden spoon to extract several spoonfuls of green tea powder. This was then added to the water in the bowl. With a bamboo whisk, Drayton whipped the tea and water together until it turned into a lovely green froth.

"We turn the bowl three times," he said, rotating the bowl, "and then our cup of tea is ready to drink." He handed the bowl to Theodosia, who was standing nearby. She accepted the bowl with both hands and took a tiny sip. "*Chado* means 'tea house,'" said Drayton, with a smile. "And every cup of tea is singly and individually prepared for each person."

Theodosia handed the cup back to Drayton as he continued. "Because tea, music, and poetry blend together so well," he told everyone, "I shall share with you a simple haiku written by Kyoshi Takahama."

> *Ikiteiru*
> *Shirushi ni sin-cha*
> *Okuru toka*

"Which translates to," said Drayton, "He will send green tea, as a token of living, my friend's letter reads." He spread his arms wide and nodded toward his audience. "And now, we shall serve freshly made Gyokuro tea, also known as 'Precious Dew,' as well as Japanese rice cookies and appetizers. And bid everyone to partake of this beautiful evening of peace and friendship."

"Don't you think you were a little hard on Dougan?" Delaine asked Theodosia. Her mouth was tightly pursed, her eyes flashing a warning.

Theodosia had finished pouring tea for all the guests at the party and was now enjoying a well-deserved cup of tea herself.

"I didn't mean to be," said Theodosia. "I'm just trying to get to the bottom of things."

"This *investigating* thing you do," said Delaine. "It can be a bit tedious." Delaine took a quick sip of tea, then scanned the throng of guests, obviously keeping an eye out for Dougan.

"I'm sorry you feel that way," said Theodosia. "But when you lose someone who's near and dear to you, it's only natural to want to see his killer brought to justice."

Delaine pretended to look shocked. "Killer? I thought Parker's death had been deemed an accident. At least that's what the newspapers reported."

"Well, they were wrong."

"But you do have confidence that the police will solve this crime, don't you?"

Theodosia kept a placid look on her face, mostly to keep peace. "I'm sure they're doing their best."

"Of course they are, dear," said Delaine. "Now please try to relax, will you?"

"Delaine," said Theodosia, "I am relaxed. You're the one whose eyes keep darting every which way."

Delaine's brittle façade suddenly collapsed and she gasped, "Frankly, Theo, I'm an absolute wreck. When I got involved with Dougan I had no idea how many ex-girlfriends the man had! It's like a veritable minefield out there. Every time we go to a restaurant or theater, some woman pops out of the woodwork and starts prowling after him like some kind of hungry alley cat. I don't know what to do!"

"Only one thing to do," said Theodosia.

Delaine gazed at Theodosia in desperation. "What's that?"

"I'm paraphrasing Beyonce's song 'Single Ladies,' but if he likes it he oughta put a ring on it."

"Yes!" Delaine shrilled. "You're probably right!"

"You two get along beautifully," said Theodosia. "In fact, you're pretty much two of a kind." Were they ever!

"We are!" Delaine agreed. "Pooh Bear and I are soul mates of the first magnitude!"

"If that's the case," said Theodosia, "maybe you and Pooh Bear should think about taking the next step."

"That's an awfully big step," said Delaine. She looked suddenly thoughtful.

"Entirely up to you," said Theodosia.

"Yes, it is," said Delaine.

"But like you said. There are ex-girlfriends everywhere . . ."

"To say nothing of all the *potential* girlfriends lurking in the wings!" Delaine groused. "Just waiting to jump out and dig their sharp little talons into him!"

"Think about it," said Theodosia. "You might have to strike while the iron is hot."

Making a quick trip back to the tea table, Theodosia encountered a tight cluster of men that she wouldn't have imagined in her wildest dreams.

Lyle Manship and David Sedakis were standing there, chatting very matter-of-factly with Timothy Neville.

Why are they here? was Theodosia's first thought. And then, a half heartbeat later, she knew exactly why. Manship had attended the Coffee & Tea Expo and, thus, had wandered over with the group. And Sedakis was a board member with the Heritage Society.

Timothy spotted her immediately and extended a warm invitation to join them. "Theodosia," he said, sounding hale and hearty for such a small, elderly man, "come chat with us. I trust you know everyone?"

"Yes, I do," she said, sidling up to the group.

"A charming demonstration," said Manship, giving his barracuda's smile. He was dressed in a black jacket with a mandarin collar, which made him look like he'd just stepped out of a bad Steven Seagal movie.

"And you're wearing such a lovely kimono," said Sedakis. His eyes burned into her and, for an instant, Theodosia wondered if Dougan Granville had already confronted him. Maybe. Hopefully.

"Drayton did a fine presentation," said Timothy. He seemed oblivious to the tension that ran like an electric current between Theodosia, Manship, and Sedakis.

"Drayton was very much in his element," said Theodosia.

"He obviously likes to proselytize on tea," Sedakis said in a dry tone.

"Nothing wrong with having keen interests," said Theodosia. "But you're aware that Drayton is extremely well-rounded in all his interests. After all, Mr. Sedakis, you serve as a board member with him here at the Heritage Society."

"Indeed I do," said Sedakis.

Theodosia pretended to look puzzled. "But now that you're executive director at the Neptune Aquarium and are frightfully busy with administration as well as the new restaurant, I imagine you'll pretty much have to throw your heart and head into all of that. Which will leave you stretched awfully thin."

"That's true," said Timothy, suddenly paying closer attention.

"In fact," said Theodosia, "I can't imagine you'll want to continue serving on this board." She let a couple of beats go by, then said, "A halfhearted board member might not be so . . . welcome?"

"We should discuss this further," said Timothy, holding up an index finger.

Theodosia didn't often harbor unkind thoughts. But these two men, Manship and Sedakis, brought out the worst in her. Scum and scummer, that's what they were. However their little arrangement had come about, it stank. Stank to high heaven.

Theodosia turned away from them and sped across the patio. And ended up walking right into the open arms of . . .

"Max!" Theodosia cried. "You're back!"

Tall and broad shouldered, with a tousle of dark hair, Max wore a slightly sardonic grin as he wrapped his arms around Theodosia in an enormous bear hug and gave her a kiss.

"And just in the nick of time, it looks like. I was just in the kitchen looking for you and Haley told me some crazy story about bees attacking your Aunt Libby?"

"It was awful," Theodosia said. She grabbed Max by the hand and led him over to a low stone bench. They sat down together, still holding hands, shoulders and knees touching and bumping.

"Tell me everything," said Max. "Wait, you have to give me another kiss first."

In the shadow of a grove of rustling bamboo, they shared a longer, lingering kiss.

"Worth the wait," said Max, pulling away reluctantly. "Okay, now tell me everything."

And so Theodosia gave him the 411 on getting run off the road that afternoon. And then the story about somebody, at least she *thought* it was somebody, stirring up the bees, and Aunt Libby getting stung, and their heart-stopping ride to the hospital.

"This all didn't just happen out of the blue," said Max. "This isn't cause, it's effect."

"Yes," said Theodosia. "I suppose it is."

"So I'm going to have to hear your whole week's saga from the very beginning."

"Okay."

"But first I need to kiss you again," said Max.

"Okay," said Theodosia. No objections there!

They kissed, nuzzled, and then grinned at each other like a couple of long-lost lovers who'd finally been reunited.

"I love your kimono," said Max.

"Drayton's idea."

"Of course. And your hair is cute, too."

"My idea," said Theodosia.

"So . . ." said Max. But he seemed to be suddenly swaying, even as he sat there talking, and was fighting valiantly to keep his eyes open.

"You know what?" said Theodosia.

"What?" said Max, sounding more than a little groggy.

"You need to go home."

"Aww . . . I just got here. Besides, I want to hear . . ."

"And get some sleep," said Theodosia. "You're dead on your feet and about to pass out."

"Sweetheart," he pleaded, but he still couldn't stifle his yawn.

"See what I mean?" said Theodosia. "Too many planes, trains, and automobiles. Besides, I can rehash the whole thing with you tomorrow." She gave a quirky grin. "It'll give us something to talk about when you go along with me on round two of the scavenger hunt."

"*I see your* boyfriend is finally back in town," Delaine called in a singsong voice.

Theodosia turned and grinned at Delaine, who was standing there, her arm linked with Majel Carter's. Both of them were grinning like devilish little co-conspirators.

"What are you two up to?" Theodosia asked. *Probably watching Max and me kiss. Or else Delaine has been plotting wildly as to how she's going to capture Dougan.*

Delaine said, with mock seriousness, "I've been telling secrets of the heart." She held a finger to her lips but couldn't stifle her own merry laughter.

"Has she ever!" agreed Majel.

Theodosia decided they both looked like proverbial Cheshire cats. Lots of that going around tonight.

"And I'm making big plans," Delaine tittered, "that just might include my two favorite BFFs!"

I think Delaine's going to try to get Dougan Granville to marry her," said Theodosia. They were driving through the purple-black twilight down Archdale Street, Drayton riding in the passenger seat and three of his prized bonsai loaded in the way back of Theodosia's Jeep.

"Are you aware your car smells like rotten eggs?" he said.

"Sorry about that," said Theodosia. "It's from when I got run off the road. We ker-plopped into some swamp water and I haven't had a chance to run it through the car wash yet." She paused. "Drayton, did you hear what I said?"

"About Delaine?"

"Yes, about Delaine."

"That she might be getting married," said Drayton. He picked an imaginary piece of lint off his black trousers. "Excuse me, but Delaine falls in love every six and a half minutes. She's got the mating instincts of a tsetse fly."

"That's not very nice." They rolled past Timothy Neville's palatial mansion, where lights twinkled from a bay window, then drove under a spreading canopy of oaks that closed in on them like a verdant tunnel.

"Apologies then," said Drayton. "It's just that I'm . . . skeptical."

"Skeptical that Delaine's truly in love or skeptical that she'll really get married?"

"Yes," said Drayton. He shifted in the passenger seat. "But let's get back to this afternoon. The story you tell is . . . upsetting to say the least."

"It really happened," said Theodosia.

"I never doubted you," said Drayton, "though I thought it might be possible that you overreacted a touch. Especially since you had Aunt Libby aboard as passenger."

Theodosia pulled to the curb in front of Drayton's small house. It was a small cottage, even smaller than hers, that had once been occupied by a rather famous Civil War doctor. "Someone clearly ran us off the road. And then, at the apiary, someone disturbed the bees."

They sat in the dark of Theodosia's car, the engine ticking down.

Finally, Drayton said, "That's it, then. You have to stop investigating."

"I can't do that."

"Of course you can. It's like deciding to stop eating bacon or some equally unhealthy food. Or forgoing candy for Lent. You simply . . . quit."

"No," said Theodosia. "I'm not a quitter."

"Someone, I have no idea *who*, is feeling decidedly threatened by you."

"And so they're threatening me back," said Theodosia.

"That's right," said Drayton. "Only they have the advantage of anonymity and stealth."

Theodosia thought about this. Drayton was right, of course. She had no idea who she was dealing with. While someone, possibly even someone rather close to her, held all the cards. Or did they?

"You know what?" Theodosia said to Drayton.

"What?"

"Whoever is making trouble for me does have one huge disadvantage."

"What's that?" asked Drayton.

"They're crazy."

Theodosia did three things when she arrived home. First she kissed Earl Grey on the top of his furry head and put him out in the backyard for a final romp. Then she called Aunt Libby at the hospital and determined that she was just fine, had to get back to her movie, in fact. And then Theodosia brewed a cup of chamomile tea and sat down at her kitchen table to think.

Because that's where the real dilemmas are hashed out in everyone's life. There's never a plush boardroom where critical data can be analyzed, there's never a White House situation room where hundreds of well-trained operatives feed you up-to-the-moment information.

When your life is in crisis, or you've hit some horrible, personal roadblock, you plunk yourself down at the kitchen table and try to work it out. You lay out your cards, the hand you've been dealt, and try to puzzle out the answer.

Or, as Drayton had said, you figure your next move. Of course, even better would be to strike a final declaratory blow and win. Just like that. Checkmate.

So, Theodosia wondered, *how do I win? How do I beat this guy—or this person (because it could be Peaches or even Shelby) at their own game?*

The answer drifted back to her. *I don't know.*

Theodosia shook her head. Not good enough. She knew she had to figure this out. Or at least inch ahead and gain some insight.

She bent over her tea, inhaled the sweet, almost green-apple scent, and willed her brain to edge forward and explore the various possibilities. To be logical, non-emotional, and, hopefully, very, very clever.

Okay, she thought, *what was the first inkling I had that somebody might be dogging my footsteps?*

Closing her eyes, Theodosia tried to picture the one point in time over the last couple of days when she'd first been aware of being shadowed. She thought hard, trying to flip through her relatively mundane activities as if they were a stack of picture postcards. There wasn't anything.

Or was there?

Theodosia's eyes peeped open.

What about the truck parked at the oyster shack last night? The one with the smoked windows and muffled music?

Had the driver of that truck been following her?

Could it have been the same truck that ran her off the road today?

She took a gulp of tea, set her cup down, jiggled her foot, and considered this.

Maybe.

But she knew it was a big maybe.

A scary maybe.

Theodosia gritted her teeth, mustering up a little inner fire. If somebody had been following her, who was it? And what did they want? Had they intended to harm her? Or just throw her off the track?

Or was something else going on? Something peripheral that she'd somehow gotten herself involved in? Somehow stumbled into?

This last notion gave her pause.

Had her picture taking triggered someone's paranoia about something?

If so, what?

She pondered this for a few more minutes as she finished her tea. Then, when she heard the click-click of toenails coming across the patio, she walked to the back door and let Earl Grey inside. As she was turning the lock, Theodosia decided to take a quick look through her photos.

She pulled her cell phone from her bag and scanned through the mini gallery.

There was the Hobie Cat, the art gallery, the Angel Oak tree, a moody photo of a trawler off the coast, and the Hot Fish Clam Shack. All pretty garden-variety stuff.

No, she didn't think there was a thing here that would get anyone riled up. Not a doggone thing.

26

❧

Aunt Libby was just fine this excellent Saturday morning. In fact, it practically took an act of Congress to get her to leave the hospital. She chatted with the orderlies, hugged the nurses, kissed a second-year intern, and blew air kisses to the lady who'd delivered her breakfast.

"You're sure Margaret Rose is going to be at Cane Ridge?" Theodosia asked.

"I just spoke with her ten minutes ago," said Aunt Libby. "She's there now, waiting for me. She's got DVDs of *Steel Magnolias* and *Sex and the City*, so we're going to have ourselves a movie marathon. Popcorn included."

"You're going to watch *Sex and the City*?"

Aunt Libby gave a sly grin. "That language doesn't shock me."

"Glad to hear it," said Theodosia, "because it shocks the heck out of most people."

"I'm not most people."

"No," said Theodosia, "you're certainly not."

They walked out the front door of the hospital to where Theodosia was double-parked.

"Listen," said Theodosia, who was having second thoughts about Aunt Libby's health. "I can stay with you today if you want me to."

"No," said Aunt Libby, as Theodosia helped her into the passenger seat, "you've got your scavenger hunt."

"I know," said Theodosia, "but I can blow that off." She leaned in and gave her aunt a gentle squeeze. "You're much more important to me than some little contest."

"But you said you were doing it for charity?"

"That's right," said Theodosia. "At-risk youth."

"Then you have to do it," said Aunt Libby. "Besides, you always finish what you start. That's one of your endearing qualities."

"You think?" said Theodosia. She felt like she had loose ends strewn all over the place.

"I know," said Aunt Libby.

Exactly one hour later, Theodosia pulled into the circular drive behind the Gibbes Museum. She hit Max's number on her speed dial and, thirty seconds later, he came bouncing out the back door. He looked well-rested, adorable, and strangely intense.

"Hello, sweetheart," he said, settling into the passenger seat, "I take it you're still investigating?"

Theodosia had pretty much figured that, after sleeping on the information she'd given him, Max would want to know every niggling little detail. And to sort of manage things and keep him from going completely postal, she'd run through a couple of diversionary answers in her mind. But in the end she felt compelled to simply tell the truth. "Yes. Yes, I am."

Max digested this for a moment, then said, "Because you still care about him?"

"Parker was a friend, but it's not what you think. There

was no romantic entanglement, I can promise you that." She reached over and took his hand. "That was all . . . in the past. Ancient history."

"Good." Max did a little more digesting, then said, "I kind of hate to ask this, but are you getting anywhere?"

Theodosia sighed deeply. "Not as far as I'd like. There have been a few problems."

Max squeezed her hand, then seemed to relax. He leaned back and pulled his seat belt across. "We've got a couple hours of driving and picture taking ahead of us, so maybe you'd better tell me all about it."

"Really? You really want to know the whole sorry mess?" Theodosia felt such enormous relief she wanted to burst into tears.

"If it involves you, I want to know," said Max.

The day turned into a magnificent spring afternoon. The sun shone down like an enormous yellow orb, wispy white tuffets of clouds twirled lazily across azure-blue skies, and Theodosia talked her heart out. She started at the beginning, that dreadful opening party at the Neptune Aquarium, and continued with every little nit and nat that had followed in its wake. She laid out her suspects—there was a virtual smorgasbord of them—and carefully explained why each had earned a place of honor on her list. As she talked, she glanced at her scavenger hunt checklist, negotiating the twists and turns of the Maybank Highway until it led them right to the door of the Charleston Tea Plantation.

"Tea," said Max, glancing out the window. "I should've known there'd be tea," he chuckled.

"But no tea drinking," said Theodosia. "Unless you want to open that thermos bottle I stashed in the backseat. I'd love to take you on the grand tour, but today we just need to snap a quick photo and be on our way."

Max turned and stared at her with genuine curiosity. "Tell me," he said, "did you figure all this out on your own?"

"All this . . . ?"

"Everything you've been telling me for the past half hour. About the suspects and, I guess, what would technically be called motives."

"Drayton put in his two cents' worth along the way," Theodosia said, slowly. "And Detective Tidwell told me about Shelby being named beneficiary. That got my brain pinging, too."

"Hmm."

Theodosia wasn't sure how to interpret this. "*Hmm* meaning not good?" she asked.

But a smile creased Max's face. "It means I can't quite believe I'm having a romantic relationship with my very own Nancy Drew."

Theodosia blushed. "I don't think poor Nancy ever had much romance in her life. Probably too young, I guess."

Max made a Groucho Marx gesture with his eyebrows. "But we're not." He unsnapped his seat belt and reached for her. Pulled her into a kiss and then continued with a caring, gentle hug. "Poor dear, you've been through the wringer this last week. Now I feel awful about being gone. Missing in action."

"But now you're back," said Theodosia.

"Willing and able to help," said Max. "If you want me to, that is."

"I think," said Theodosia, reaching for her cell phone, "I can use all the help I can get."

Fenwick Hall was their second stop, a brick manor house at the end of a broad avenue of oak trees. Though no longer a private home, it was reputed to have a tunnel leading from the basement to a nearby creek. John Fenwick, the owner and builder, had been known to have sneaky dealings with pirates as well as local riffraff.

"Okay, got it," said Max, as Theodosia stopped just outside the impressive wrought-iron gates. He double-checked his photo, then said, "Where to next?"

"Down Bohicket Road to Kiawah Island," said Theodosia. She glanced at her scavenger hunt list. "We need to get a shot of Beachwalk Park. And then swing back to Johns Island and find the Johns Island Presbyterian Church."

"It's historic, I take it?"

"Founded in the early seventeen hundreds," said Theodosia.

"I've been noodling all your information around," said Max, "and as far as the suspects on your list—Manship; the lawyer, Beaudry; the ex-girlfriend, Shelby; and the aquarium guy, Sedakis—well, I can see why you'd want to keep an eye on them. But the one that seems sort of far-fetched is Peaches Pafford."

"You think?"

"She's just a businessperson who knows how to jump on a good deal when she sees it." He paused. "Unless she's really the whacked-out character you say she is," said Max.

"She's one tough nut," said Theodosia. "In fact, if Peaches had a nickname it would probably be Old Ironsides."

A sly grin stole across Max's face. "Sounds like I'm going to have to meet this Peaches Pafford for myself. And the sooner the better . . . tonight even."

"I can pretty much guarantee it's not going to be tonight," said Theodosia. "Tonight Peaches is having a private oyster fest at her restaurant."

"So I heard. Which makes it perfect."

Theodosia shook her head. "No, it doesn't. Because I hear the event's completely sold out. You can't possibly get in without a ticket."

Max reached into his jacket pocket and pulled out four orange tickets. "Wanna bet?"

Theodosia did a double take, then focused her eyes back on the road. "Seriously? You have tickets? For the Oyster Fest at Aubergine?"

"Never underestimate the power of a PR guy," said Max.

Theodosia grinned. "The big schmooze, huh?"

Max's eyelids fluttered in a gesture of mock tribulation. "You have no idea how hard I have to work."

"Well . . . great," said Theodosia. "Then I guess we *are* going." She'd never been to Aubergine before and figured it might afford her a chance to toss a few more probing questions at Peaches. Maybe catch her off guard.

"There's only one small problem," said Max.

"Oops," said Theodosia. "I knew there'd be a catch. What is it? The tickets are promised to somebody else?"

"Nope. We can go, but only for a short while. The thing is, I also have a donor's dinner tonight. Eight o'clock sharp. It's practically a command performance."

"So if you don't show up by eight you turn into a pumpkin?" Theodosia turned into the parking lot of the Presbyterian church and eased to a stop.

"Or, worse yet, I get fired," said Max. "So, my dear, like the proverbial bad date I'm going to have to duck out on you."

"Man," said Theodosia, "you've been home for, like, one day and you're already dreaming up excuses to dump me."

"Dump you?" said Max, leaning across the front seat and putting his arms around her. "Never. Not on your life." He kissed her slowly then, in a dreamy, easy way. And Theodosia responded—although the fact that they were sitting outside a church gave her pause.

"Okay, so here's what we're going to do," said Max. "I'm going to give you three tickets. Maybe you can get Drayton and Haley to come along, too. Seeing as how I have to run off like the scoundrel you think I am."

"Mmm . . . okay."

Max gave her an earnest stare. "Are you sure? Are you sure

that works for you? You're not going to feel cheated or something?"

"Not in the least. Besides, it'll give me another chance to harass Peaches."

Max shook his head. "You really are incorrigible."

By five o'clock that afternoon, Theodosia had dropped Max at his apartment and headed for home. She was planning to meet him at Aubergine at seven, so she had a little time to hang with Earl Grey, then laze in a bubble bath.

But just as she stuck her toe into a frothy soup of T-Bath Bubbles, she remembered she had to call Drayton and Haley.

Okay, gotta do that first.

Turns out Haley already had plans to attend a rock concert with her boyfriend du jour. Some hot new group called the Smoke Jammers. But when Theodosia got Drayton on the line, he jumped at the chance to attend the Oyster Fest.

"Have you ever known me to say no to eating oysters?" asked Drayton.

"I had a hunch you might be up for it," said Theodosia.

"But . . . won't I be a third wheel? I mean, your friend Max just returned from New York. You two haven't seen each other for an entire week."

"We spent the afternoon together doing the second leg of the scavenger hunt," said Theodosia.

"Better him than me," said Drayton.

"Hey, don't sell yourself short," said Theodosia. "Your photos were great. But here's the thing . . . Max has to run off to a donor's dinner at eight. So you'd be my date, too."

"A backup date," said Drayton.

"Something like that."

"And we'd get an opportunity to see Peaches again," said Drayton.

"Exactly my thought. I figured it might be a sort of lucky-strike extra."

"Then it sounds like a plan," said Drayton.

"Excellent."

"So I should meet you there?" Drayton asked. "Where exactly is this chichi restaurant of hers?"

"Tell you what," said Theodosia. "Max and I have to drive separately anyway, so I'll drop by your house and pick you up."

Theodosia allowed herself ten minutes of bubble bath reverie while she listened to an Alicia Keys CD. Then, refreshed and relaxed, she jumped out of the bathtub, ready to get duded up.

Or should she? How formal was this event tonight? Should she slip into her de rigueur black cocktail dress or switch things up and go boho-chic? Fun and funky was always better, she decided, so she stepped into her closet to see what garment tickled her fancy.

Ah. She had a terrific, floaty raspberry-pink top that would look great with gobs of pearls and a pair of white, tapered silk slacks. Really perfect.

Or was it? Could she wear white? Should she wear white? Only one way to find out. Phone up the arbiter of taste for the Greater Charleston metropolitan area.

Delaine sounded perturbed when she took Theodosia's call. "You're asking me if you can wear white?"

"Yes, I am," said Theodosia. And then added, "You know, because it's before Memorial Day and all that."

"Theodosia!" Delaine sounded supremely exasperated. "Those tired old dictums went out the window years ago! In fact, practically every fashion rule that ever existed has been tossed out."

"Then how come you're always telling me never to wear brown with black or wear tights with peep-toe shoes?"

"*Excuse* me!" Delaine bellowed. "Did you call to harass me or ask for advice? Because, if you must know, Dougan and I are also attending the Oyster Fest tonight. And I'm hurrying to get ready, too."

"Sorry," said Theodosia.

Delaine's mood shifted, as it always did, just like the swirling tides of the nearby Atlantic. "Oh, don't worry about it, sweetie. I'll just take it out on you later."

At six thirty that Saturday night, with Drayton sitting next to her wearing a cream-colored linen jacket and dove-gray slacks, Theodosia pulled into the parking lot behind Aubergine. She cruised the first three rows, past BMWs, Mercedes-Benzes, and Audis. Deciding this was a fairly tony crowd and that this part of the lot was parked up solid, she figured she'd have better luck at the back of the lot.

Circling back, she bumped off the smooth asphalt and onto crunchy gravel, still searching for a parking spot.

"I think there's a spot over by the Dumpster," said Drayton.

"Just our speed," said Theodosia. She cranked the steering wheel hard, pulled into a narrow slot between the hulking brown Dumpster and a pickup truck, then did a double take and cried out, "Holy crap!"

Drayton's brows lifted slightly. "Excuse me?"

"You see that truck?" Theodosia was pointing and gesturing like crazy.

Drayton glanced out the window. "Yes?"

"If I'm not mistaken," Theodosia cried, "it looks exactly like the truck that ran me off the road yesterday!"

27

❧

They stared at the black truck as if it were a Magic 8 Ball, able to magically produce an answer. *Very probable.* Or perhaps *Explore all possibilities.*

Finally, Drayton said, "Do you think it's also the same truck that pulled in when we were at the clam shack?"

I don't know," said Theodosia, squinting at it. "All trucks look pretty much alike to me. I'm not exactly a motorhead."

"This one's a what?" asked Drayton.

"Um . . . maybe a Chevy?"

"Okay," said Drayton.

"That still doesn't help much, does it?"

"Do you think maybe you'd recognize the driver?" Drayton asked.

Theodosia shook her head. "Unfortunately, I never really got a good look at him."

"Or her," Drayton muttered. When Theodosia registered surprise, Drayton added, "Well, the truck *is* parked behind Peaches's restaurant."

Theodosia considered this. "Good point."

"Though it could be the wrong truck. Or just a weird coincidence," Drayton hastened to add.

"I've got an idea," said Theodosia. "Let's go in and find out."

Aubergine was a luxe, upscale eatery that had received four stars from Michelin and a twenty-four-point rating from Zagat. In other words, it was your basic white-linen-tablecloth fine-dining restaurant with prices that soared to astronomical heights.

The expansive lobby was paneled in dark cypress and featured a giant stone fireplace, two curved sofas upholstered in—what else?—aubergine-colored velvet, and a series of gold-framed etchings on the walls that depicted turn-of-the-century Parisian street scenes.

"Very nice," said Drayton as they stood in a short queue at the maître d' stand.

Aubergine was pretty much what Theodosia had expected. Peaches Pafford always went for over-the-top glam, so it would stand to reason her restaurant would be showy as well.

"Look," said Theodosia, nodding toward a gilt plaque that was engraved with several lines of flowing calligraphy. "Peaches even has a corporate philosophy."

Curious, Drayton put on his glasses to read it.

"Well?" said Theodosia.

"Platitudes," said Drayton. "And wishful thinking."

"Not up there with Kierkegaard?" grinned Theodosia.

Drayton's mouth twitched upward. "Hardly. Then again, who is?"

Moments later, a tuxedo-clad maître d' flashed his broad smile at them. "Good evening," he said in a brisk tone. "Might I see your tickets?"

Theodosia produced two of the orange tickets and the maître d' nodded his approval. "Ah yes, table twenty-two. Please go right in. If you prefer to begin your evening with a libation, our cocktail lounge is directly to your right." He made a quick hand gesture. "Off to your left is our dining room. Tonight, in honor of our special event, we're offering a seafood raw bar as well as a station where Chef Oliver is roasting oysters. Please. Enjoy."

Opting for the dining room, Theodosia and Drayton pushed their way through an aubergine-colored velvet curtain and suddenly found Peaches's restaurant spread out before them.

Everything had been designed on a grand scale. Large, circular tables; enormous, upholstered chairs that looked like they'd been liberated from a French castle; another large fireplace made up of almost perfectly rounded stones; and not one but three huge crystal chandeliers. And everything, everywhere, dripped with gold. The chairs were edged with gold, the chandelier sparkled with gold, gold edged the rims of the plates and glasses, even the flatware was gold.

"Goodness," said Drayton, slightly taken aback. "What would one call this style of decorating?"

"Gilt trip?" said Theodosia, with a wry smile.

Her words tickled Drayton's fancy. "Ha! Clever."

"Let's go find table twenty-two," said Theodosia, "and see if Max is here yet."

They eased their way between the various tables, mumbling excuse-me's and occasionally stopping to greet a familiar face.

"Everyone who's anybody is here tonight," noted Drayton. "That table over there? The executive director of the Charleston Symphony and the chairman of the Art Association."

"Why is Peaches such a hot ticket?" Theodosia wondered.

"She's a schmoozer," said Drayton. "She ingratiates herself

all over town and donates just enough money to all the popular arts organizations and social causes. And, probably, her restaurants do turn out some very fine food."

"At least her chefs do," said Theodosia. They'd arrived at table twenty-two and found it empty. Two chairs had white dinner napkins dropped onto the seats, an obvious sign that someone had been here and staked their claim. "So now what?"

"Now we eat," said Drayton. "Any sort of investigation, no matter how trifling, must always be conducted on a full stomach."

The raw bar at Aubergine was a thing of pure beauty—a twenty-foot-long table mounded with crushed ice and topped by a glittering ice sculpture of a half-naked woman rising from an oyster shell. But the shellfish were the real attraction. Gigantic pink shrimp curled on silver platters. Fresh oysters, practically quivering in their brine, were scattered atop the crushed ice. Lobster tails, crab legs, and even tiny imported periwinkles were enticingly displayed.

"This is amazing," said Drayton.

"A feast," agreed Theodosia.

Drayton brightened. "And look over there, they're roasting fresh oysters over charcoal."

"Yum," said Theodosia. She smelled the mingled aromas of oak wood, sea salt, and hot sauce and could almost hear the oysters popping inside their shells. But first she was going to help herself to the chilled portion of the dinner. Specifically, the raw oysters.

"We're two of a kind," said Drayton, as they both placed oysters on their plates. "Love the briny little mollusks."

"In the right season," said Theodosia, "I think our local oysters are even tastier than blue crab." Blue crab was also a local delicacy.

"It's so interesting," remarked Drayton, "that oysters actually derive their flavor from the region where they're harvested." He dribbled a dollop of creamy horseradish sauce onto his plate, then added, "Just as grapes take on the terroir, or taste of the land."

"What would be the water equivalent for oysters?"

"Not sure," said Drayton. *"Aquoir?"*

Theodosia giggled. "Nice try, but I don't think that's an actual word."

Unfazed, Drayton said, "It should be."

Max was lounging at their table when Theodosia and Drayton returned with their plates of seafood. He wore a snappy checked jacket and gray slacks and looked adorable (in Theodosia's eyes, anyway) with his half-amused grin and carefully tousled hair. He was sipping from a flute of champagne and chatting casually with an older couple who were picking genteelly at small mounds of tiny pink shrimp.

Max made introductions all around, then turned his full attention on Theodosia. "Have you talked to Peaches yet?" he asked.

She shook her head. "Haven't seen her."

"You put up a fairly convincing argument," Max told Theodosia, in a low tone, "that Peaches might be involved in your friend's murder."

"Did I?" said Theodosia. She wasn't sure she'd convinced Max of anything. Or, at the very least, she'd managed to reveal what was probably her overly suspicious nature. Which might or might not be a turn-on or turnoff.

Max picked up a tiny gold seafood fork and speared an oyster from Theodosia's plate. As he popped it in his mouth, his eyes widened then focused on some point across the room. "There she is now," he said.

Theodosia followed Max's gaze across the vast dining

room. Peaches Pafford had made her grand entrance, strolling through her dining room like the lady of the manor. Wearing a floor-length shimmering gold dress, Peaches projected the overall impression that she was garbed to look like some kind of award statue. The drapey dress fell to her ankles, where gold shoes peeped out from beneath the hem. Her ears were dripping with long gold earrings; chunky gold bangles clanked on both wrists. Even her hair, which always seemed to carry a pinkish luster, seemed to be threaded with streaks of gold.

"She looks like she's been dipped in gold dust," whispered Max.

Theodosia watched as the effusive Peaches greeted guests, blew air kisses, and administered hugs to a chosen few. Then Joe Beaudry emerged from the crowd and became the recipient of one of those hugs.

"Or maybe she's the golden calf," Theodosia remarked.

"Huh?" said Max.

"That's Joe Beaudry," Theodosia said, sounding both terse and tense. "The lawyer I was telling you about."

Drayton leaned in to add his two cents. "The lawyer who brokered the deal between Shelby and Peaches. To buy Solstice."

"Shelby," said Max.

"The more *recent* girlfriend," said Theodosia.

"Ah," said Max. He sat back in his chair and a frown flickered across his face. For the first time, Max seemed to comprehend the fact that perhaps one of these players really was a real-life killer.

"I think," said Theodosia, getting to her feet, "I'm going to wander over and get myself a couple of roasted oysters."

"And do a little chitchatting as well?" asked Drayton.

"You never know," said Theodosia.

"For gosh sakes, be careful," warned Max.

But by the time Theodosia arrived at the oyster roast station, Peaches was nowhere in sight. And neither was Joe Beaudry.

She turned her attention to the chef. "You're roasting them over oak?" she asked.

"Yup," he told her. "Just for a couple of minutes. Then I cover 'em with damp burlap and move them off to the side so they can sort of stew in their own juices." He paused. "How many would you like?"

"Four to start with," said Theodosia.

The chef looked past her. "And you, sir?"

"A half dozen," said Lyle Manship.

Theodosia took a step back in surprise. Manship was the last person she expected to see here!

Manship gazed at her and said, in a neutral tone, "Hello, Theodosia."

"Are you still in town?" Theodosia asked. "When are you going back to Savannah?"

"That's awfully rude," Manship told her. "Where's that fine Charleston hospitality?"

"Not here," said Theodosia. She wondered briefly if the black truck parked outside belonged to him. She had a sudden and murderous urge to stab him in the middle of his chest with her index finger and scream, *Are you the jackhole who ran me off the road yesterday? Who basically tried to kill me and my Aunt Libby? Then did you stalk us and purposely frighten the bees so they'd swarm and sting her?*

But she didn't say that. She kept her composure and cool. Because losing your head rarely advanced you from point A to point B. Hardly ever, anyway.

But there were more surprises in store for Theodosia that night. Returning from the roast oyster station, slipping between tables, Theodosia bumped into Detective Burt Tidwell.

Taken aback, all she could stammer out was a somewhat blunt, "What are you doing here?"

Tidwell looked both bemused and a little startled. "Excuse me," he fired back, "why are *you* here?"

"I have an invitation," said Theodosia. It was the only benign answer she could come up with at the moment.

"Certainly not from the illustrious Mrs. Pafford," said Tidwell.

"No, we're not that close."

Tidwell clenched his jaw and adjusted his mouth into a stolid frown. "You realize, your being here puts you in a somewhat sticky situation."

"Excuse me?"

"You heard me," said Tidwell. "And I seriously hope you don't think you're here to conduct any sort of investigation."

"No," said Theodosia, "I wouldn't do that."

"Of course not," said Tidwell. He knew she wasn't being truthful, and Theodosia knew that he knew.

Theodosia gazed at Tidwell, trying to figure out his real mission. He was dressed in one of his extra-large sport jackets, this one looking a little frayed at the elbows with a button hanging loose, and his tie was askew. Was Tidwell here to partake of the Oyster Fest? Was he someone's grudging guest? Yes, of course Tidwell was here to eat. No matter where he went, Tidwell managed to eat. But Theodosia suspected there might be something else going on. Some other reason for his larger-than-life presence. Not only were Tidwell's eyes shining brightly, but he looked like he was fairly quivering on the balls of his feet. As much as someone his size could quiver. Jiggle, maybe?

"What's going on?" she asked him. Her inner radar was pinging like crazy, telling her something big was about to happen. Had there been a break in the case? Was Tidwell close to making an arrest? Better yet, was he going to stage a very public takedown of Peaches Pafford? Arrest her for Parker's murder?

"You're way too suspicious for words," Tidwell barked, then quickly slid past her.

"You bet I am," said Theodosia.

28

❧

"*Were you able* to talk to Peaches?" asked Max, when Theodosia returned to their table.

"No, I couldn't find her," said Theodosia.

"But you brought back roast oysters," said Drayton, looking pleased. "Nice plump ones, from the looks of it." Drayton really was an oyster fanatic.

"Help yourself," said Theodosia.

"No, that's okay," said Drayton, waving a hand. "I'll . . . well, perhaps just one."

Max suddenly reached for Theodosia's hand and gave a quick squeeze.

"Hmm?" she said.

"With a puff of smoke and a whiff of sulfur she materializes," said Max.

"Who does?" said Theodosia.

"Delaine," said Max, under his breath. "The she-devil. Ten paces and closing in." Max had dated Delaine a couple of

times, before he'd fallen hard for Theodosia and Delaine had
gone gaga for Dougan Granville.

Theodosia glanced up, hoping there wouldn't be any kind
of rehashing of old alliances. Because you never knew with
Delaine; the teeniest bit of stored hurt or resentment could
fester and percolate, and then, just like that, be spit up. But
tonight, in her sleek black cocktail dress, with her long hair
wound up on top of her head in a Psyche knot, hanging on
the arm of Dougan Granville, Delaine looked happier and
more radiant than Theodosia had seen her in a long time. In
fact, Delaine had a broad, practically simpering grin on her
face. A grin that seemed to convey, *I have a major announce-
ment to make.*

"Delaine," said Theodosia, who was getting curiouser and
curiouser by the moment, "what . . . ?"

Delaine thrust out her left hand, and Theodosia was suddenly dazzled by the brilliance of the four-carat yellow diamond that blinged and blanged on her ring finger!

Theodosia leaped to her feet. "Oh, my gosh! You got . . ."

"Engaged!" whooped Delaine. "We did it! Isn't it amazing! Isn't it grand?"

There was a minor furor then, as everyone began talking
and babbling at once, complimenting Delaine, and extending hearty congratulations to Dougan Granville.

Though Granville did his part to keep his game face on,
Theodosia thought he looked like some poor animal who'd
just been caught in a leg trap.

Max quickly summoned a waiter and had a bottle of
Perrier-Jouet Champagne brought to their table.

"When's the big day?" asked Drayton, as the waiter poured
and everyone hoisted flutes of champagne.

"Soon, very soon!" promised Delaine, which prompted
another round of glass clinking, well-wishes, and hearty congratulations. This time, people from the surrounding tables

chimed in. After all, who doesn't love an engagement? Or a wedding? Especially between two such flamboyant people.

When things began to quiet down, Delaine slipped around the table and knelt next to Theodosia. "This is all because of you!" she said in a loud whisper.

"This should be about *you*," said Theodosia. "And Dougan, of course."

Delaine held out her left hand and waggled her fingers, the better for the light to catch and bounce off her spectacular diamond. "Oh, he'll go along with whatever."

"Delaine," said Theodosia, suddenly serious, "this has to be better than whatever. This is *for*ever."

"I know that," said Delaine, but she still seemed enraptured by the diamond ring and the fact that Dougan had popped the question, if that was how it had really gone down. "What I truly want to know is, what does your calendar look like this coming July? Preferably on a nice Saturday morning?"

"You're going to get married that soon?" said Theodosia. "That's only a two-month engagement." Didn't they need a little more think time? A little planning time? Maybe even some cooling-off time?

"Life is so short," Delaine chortled. "So I want to grab all the gusto I can."

"Delaine," said Theodosia, gripping her friend's hand, "this is reality, not a beer commercial."

But Delaine was not to be dissuaded. "Theo," she said, "I'm a big girl. A successful entrepreneur and a woman of the world. And I know *precisely* what I'm doing."

"Then I'm incredibly happy for you," said Theodosia.

"So what I wanted to ask you," said Delaine, "was would you please be my maid of—"

"Hands up!" came a thunderous shout. A shout so loud and determined that it rattled the chandeliers, startled the waiters, and brought more than a few people leaping to their feet. Seconds later, three uniformed police officers charged through the crowd, guns drawn!

Women shrieked, men cried out in protest, but the officers swept between the tables with precise and careful choreography. Then, just as quickly as the din had risen, the noise level dropped to zero.

"What are you *doing*?" screamed a strangled male voice.

Theodosia popped out of her seat like a manic gopher, straining to see just what on earth was going on. And what she saw stunned her. Buddy Krebs, the seafood purveyor she'd met at Dougan Granville's house, was being roughly spun around and patted down, just like a prime suspect on *Law & Order*.

Buddy Krebs? The seafood guy? What's this about?

Following on the heels of that bizarre shocker, like a scene straight out of *Eliot Ness and the Untouchables*, Detective Burt Tidwell burst across the room with four more officers in tow. Only these officers were garbed in brown uniforms with badges and shoulder patches that identified them as officers of the SCDNR, the South Carolina Department of Natural Resources.

The four DNR guys, all with guns on their belts, hurriedly took over from the Charleston police. They grabbed Buddy Krebs, flung him hard against a wall, and pulled out a pair of handcuffs.

This drew more screams and a few cries of protest.

Then, like a foghorn cutting through the din, a shrill voice cried out, "Just what do you think you're doing?" Then the crowd parted and Peaches Pafford came striding to the forefront, like an eighteenth-century warship under full sail.

"We're here to serve a warrant," said Tidwell, barely casting a glance her way.

But Peaches was not to be upstaged. "How *dare* you come storming into my restaurant right in the middle of an important event!" She glanced at Krebs, who was now spread-eagled and handcuffed, and let loose an audible gasp. "I demand you release my guest immediately!"

"He's not your guest anymore, ma'am," said one of the DNR officers. "He's our prisoner."

"This can't be happening!" Peaches wailed. She spun around like a children's top that had been wound too tight and sputtered at Tidwell, "Stop this! Stop all of it right now!"

This time, Tidwell didn't bother to acknowledge her. "Read Mr. Krebs his rights," he instructed the DNR officers.

One of the DNR men pulled a small, plasticized card from his back pocket and launched into a hurried mumble.

"But what . . . why?" Peaches squealed.

Tidwell sighed, then loudly announced to the room, "Illegal seafood operation."

"What!" screamed Peaches. She reeled back as if Tidwell had socked her hard in the jaw. "Illegal . . . seafood?"

"Krebs has been trawling in the protected Cape Romain area," said Tidwell. "He's been under surveillance by the DNR for the past two and a half months."

Peaches was still crazed. "That can't be! Buddy Krebs is a respected seafood supplier. In fact, he's my *premier* supplier!"

"Indeed," said Tidwell. His beady eyes shifted toward her seafood bar, piled high with crab claws, shrimp, and oysters. Theodosia saw the wheels turning in Tidwell's brain but wasn't sure if his intent was to confiscate the purloined seafood or happily chow down on it.

Peaches suddenly saw where this might be leading and jumped to lodge a protest. "I hope you don't think *my* oysters are illegal!" she blustered. "We only buy from reputable purveyors."

"Of course you do," Tidwell grunted.

The DNR officers started to lead Krebs out, but Peaches sprang in front of them, attempting to block their path.

This was the final straw for Tidwell.

"If you continue to obstruct the law," said Tidwell, "we'll

arrest you as well. And haul each and every mollusk back to our lab for testing. To ascertain if, perhaps, your seafood *did* come from an area where harvesting is prohibited."

"You don't have to do *that*!" Peaches cried. "I . . . I can personally vouch for my seafood!"

A ripple of laughter traveled through the crowd. Now Peaches's antics were almost amusing.

"She can personally vouch for her oysters," Theodosia whispered to Drayton.

"Sure," said Drayton, "but what about her clams? They could be contraband clams."

"Do you believe this?" said Max. He was fascinated by the scene being played out in front of them.

"Buddy Krebs," Theodosia murmured. "And he's on the board of the Neptune Aquarium." She turned to Drayton and whispered, "When I was at Dougan Granville's house, Krebs gave me a big song and dance about responsibility and how he wanted to be a watchdog for our oceans." She let loose a derisive snort. "What a crock."

"The aquarium's reputation is diminishing rapidly," said Drayton. "First Parker's death, then the questionable restaurant lease, and now one of their board members is under indictment."

"Krebs isn't under indictment yet," Theodosia pointed out.

"But he will be," said Drayton.

Theodosia suddenly grasped Drayton's arm. "Oh, my gosh!" Her eyes flew open wide and she looked positively thunderstruck.

"What?" said Drayton.

"I think I just put two and two together!" said Theodosia.

"And you came up with . . . ?"

"The night we were at the Hot Fish Clam Shack? When I took the photos?"

Drayton nodded, as Max listened intently.

"There was a fishing boat in the background. It must have

belonged to Krebs! He must have thought the photos I took would get posted . . ."

"Which they were," said Drayton.

"And that the DNR would be on to him!" said Theodosia. She put a hand to her mouth. "Oh, my gosh, Krebs knew I took the photos and that's why he was after me. And Aunt Libby!"

"I think you may be right," said Drayton, excitedly.

"Wow," said Max.

The wheels continued to crank in Theodosia's brain and she suddenly looked mournful. "And that had to be why Krebs killed Parker," she said in a slightly strangled tone.

Max looked suddenly confused. "Wait a minute, now you're saying your friend Parker was on to Krebs's illegal operation?"

"He had to be," said Theodosia. She sat stolidly for a few moments, then her hands flew up. "Oh, my gosh, I have to talk to Tidwell! Right now!" She stood up so fast, her chair almost flew over backward.

"Better hurry!" urged Drayton.

"Be careful!" Max called after her.

Theodosia caught Tidwell out in front of Aubergine. He was sprawled in the front seat of his burgundy Crown Victoria talking on his radio.

"What?" he rumbled, when she came stumbling up to him.

Theodosia stood on the street, letting her suspicions and conclusions tumble out in a glut of words and gestures.

Tidwell listened carefully and nodded a couple of times, seemingly, she thought, to encourage her brilliant conclusion that Buddy Krebs had murdered Parker Scully.

"And that's Krebs's black truck parked out back, right?" said Theodosia.

"Correct," said Tidwell.

"Well, I think he chased me yesterday. Tried to run me off the road!"

But, in the end, Tidwell didn't quite share her enthusiasm. And, much to Theodosia's consternation, he never once cried out, "Aha, Krebs is definitely the culprit!"

But Theodosia was dogged in her argument. "Krebs is the killer," she said, pressing her point. "I just know it. I can *feel* it."

Tidwell was polite, but neutral. "We'll interrogate him," Tidwell promised, "and see if we can connect the dots."

"Please try very hard!" Theodosia begged.

Ten minutes later, half the guests had departed Aubergine and Peaches was nowhere to be found. A scattering of guests, the half that didn't embarrass quite as easily, remained at their tables, eating and chatting about the strange events that had just taken place.

Unfortunately for Theodosia, Max was one of the guests who now had to take his leave. It was time for him to dash off to his donor's dinner.

She walked him to the front door and gave him a good-bye kiss.

"I'm sorry about your friend," said Max. "It really does sound like this Krebs guy was the killer."

"I think so, too," said Theodosia. "And thank you."

"You're very good at this amateur sleuthing thing," said Max.

"I'm not so sure about that. This thing with Krebs kind of came zinging out of left field."

"But now it's over," said Max.

Theodosia heaved a sigh of relief.

With his arms still wrapped possessively around her, Max said, "But please realize, Theo, we never have, like, a normal date."

Theodosia's eyelashes fluttered and she said, "Define *normal*."

But Max was dead serious. "I'm talking about a calm, relaxing evening wherein state troopers don't come crashing through the door to arrest someone."

Theodosia thought for a moment. "Oh, I see. You want calm and sedate. Okay, how about two weeks ago when we attended that concert of chamber music?"

Max held up a finger. "That was an exception to the rule. But, generally, our encounters tend to be marked by chaos and arrest warrants."

"Don't you think it keeps things interesting?" asked Theodosia. She was teasing him now, trying to defuse the situation a little bit.

"Interesting, yes," said Max. "Romantic, no."

"Oops," said Theodosia. She liked romantic. Romantic was good, especially where Max was concerned. "Then what can I do to get things back on a much more romantic keel?"

"Ah," said Max, "I thought you'd never ask." He grinned. "I have a simple request."

"Name it," said Theodosia.

"You, me, dinner at your house tomorrow night."

"Done," said Theodosia.

"But I'm not," said Max. "Because there are going to be some conditions imposed."

"Okay," said Theodosia, wondering where this was leading.

Max focused his gaze on her. "There will be no writs, warrants, or arrests. There will be no intrusion by police officers or SWAT teams. There will be no handcuffs. There will be soft music and . . ." He suddenly relented and gave a crooked grin. "Well, on second thought, maybe the handcuff part *is* okay."

"Max!" Theodosia squealed. "Really!"

* * *

By the time Theodosia fought her way back through the departing crowd, feeling pretty much like a salmon swimming upstream, Drayton was the only one left at their table.

"What happened to Delaine? And Dougan?"

"Gone," said Drayton. "She and Granville bolted like a couple of frightened jackrabbits."

Theodosia looked around the room. "*Some* people stayed."

"Probably because they paid good money for all this fine seafood." In her absence, Drayton had gone back to the raw bar and helped himself to a pile of crab claws and a ramekin of melted butter.

"I see this brouhaha didn't put a curb on your appetite."

"Not when I'm eating seafood," said Drayton. He glanced left, then right, as if making sure he wouldn't be heard. "Even if it is illegal."

Theodosia plopped down in the chair next to him. "I don't think I could eat a bite now," she told him. "When I think about that horrible man murdering Parker, I feel sick to my stomach."

"You really think Krebs killed him?"

She nodded. "I do. And I think it was over something as stupid as Parker giving him a warning or threatening to turn him in."

Drayton put an arm across Theodosia's shoulders and gave her a quick hug. "Poor dear. You've been so upset over this."

"I don't . . ." began Theodosia. Then she heard a faint tinkling in her purse. "Cell phone," she said. Maybe it was Tidwell calling to tell her they'd sweated a confession out of Krebs? Or Krebs had suddenly confessed in a mighty purging of his soul.

But, no, it was Majel Carter. Sounding a little rattled.

"Theo? Theo!" cried Majel.

"Yes?" said Theodosia, sensing apprehension in Majel's voice. "Sweetie, what's wrong?"

Majel was practically beside herself. "You're not going to believe this," she said, a rising note of panic coloring her voice, "but your team is missing a photo! The City Charity organizers just called me!"

Oh no.

"My gosh, what is it?" asked Theodosia. She opened her purse and pawed through the contents, searching for the scavenger hunt list. But it wasn't there.

"What was the item, Majel? What did I miss?"

"The front gate of Angel's Rest!"

"Your summer camp?"

"Yes," bawled Majel. "Out on Hopper Road."

Ouch.

"Oh, my gosh, I guess I seriously screwed up," said Theodosia. "I'm so sorry!"

"Is there any way you can still get to it?" Majel pleaded. "I mean, I know it's late, but there's ten thousand dollars at stake for Tuesday's Child!"

"Don't worry," Theodosia assured her, "I'll get the photo and send it in, okay?" She paused. "When's the deadline?"

"Ten o'clock tonight," said Majel.

Theodosia stole a quick glance at Drayton's old Patek Phillipe. "I'm going to try my best," said Theodosia. "So . . . don't worry."

"Theodosia," said Majel, "you are a total dear!"

29

❧

"You see?" said Drayton, "I said you had a kind soul and you do. This extra effort proves it."

"I also have a scattered brain," said Theodosia. "I can't believe I missed one of the shots on the scavenger hunt list. The money shot, at that!"

They'd been driving a good forty-five minutes and had just passed through the sleepy little town of Early Branch. It was pitch-dark now and quiet, no houses, no nothing in sight. Only blue-black flashes of woods and water, as they whipped by. Stands of alder and straggly pine and turgid little streams. Overhead, a thin sliver of moon shone down amid a faint scattering of stars.

"You've had a lot on your plate this past week." Drayton smiled. "Besides oysters."

"No, that's *your* plate," Theodosia told him, as she goosed her speed up to sixty, in a hurry to get to Angel's Rest.

"Touché," said Drayton.

"Thanks for coming with me," said Theodosia.

"It was the least I could do," said Drayton. "I figured you could use a little company tonight." He hesitated. "I know how upset you've been. How upset you are."

Theodosia gritted her teeth. "Krebs killed him, Drayton. Krebs pushed Parker into that fish tank and held him under water until he drowned." Her hands gripped the steering wheel so hard her knuckles turned white. "That slimy Krebs was fishing and dredging where he wasn't supposed to, probably taking out hundreds of thousands of dollars' worth of illegal seafood. And Parker, God bless his honest soul, was somehow on to him."

Drayton shook his head. "Another senseless murder for profit."

"It's not the first time, it won't be the last," said Theodosia. "Today people kill for nothing. Sometimes for a few dollars. A *pittance*," she spat out.

They drove along in silence for a good five minutes.

"But don't you feel slightly vindicated?" Drayton asked. "Maybe even hopeful about Krebs being brought to justice?"

"Tidwell played his cards close to the vest," said Theodosia, "but I'm fairly confident he'll sweat a confession out of Krebs. Or get one of Krebs's crew members to spill his guts. You know Krebs didn't work his boat alone."

"Good point," said Drayton. "It had to be a fairly large operation. Certainly more than just one trawler."

"And if the seafood was harvested in international waters or was transported interstate," said Theodosia, "then I think the feds get involved, too."

"One never wants to mess with federal agents," said Drayton. "They've got those super-security prisons with cameras and razor wire and concrete walls that are fifteen feet thick."

"Don't you love it?" said Theodosia. "Our tax dollars at work."

They swung through a series of S-turns, and suddenly low swampland spread out on either side of them.

"I haven't been out this way in a long time," observed Drayton.

"I'm not sure I've ever been out this way," said Theodosia.

"We're a far enough piece from Charleston now," said Drayton, "that's for sure."

Theodosia reached into the bin between the seats and grabbed her cell phone. "I entered our destination address, but it feels like we're somehow off course."

"You think?"

"No," said Theodosia, "I'm still hopeful. But my confidence would be seriously boosted if I could find Hopper Road."

"Could have been that last turn back there. We flew by it kind of fast."

"Maybe," said Theodosia. She eased off the accelerator and crept along a little slower, as they both stared ahead into the darkness.

"It does feel like we're in the middle of nowhere," said Drayton. "I haven't seen a house or yard light for miles."

"Just pristine wilderness out here," said Theodosia. "Probably the perfect setting for a children's camp."

"Get the kids out of the big bad city," said Drayton, "so they can marvel at God's creations."

"That's a lovely, poetic thought," said Theodosia. She suddenly perked up, said, "Whoa, wait a minute, there's a signpost up ahead."

"Easy, easy," said Drayton.

Theodosia slowed to a crawl. "Ah, here it is. Hopper Road. Whew. Looks like we're still on course."

"So now what?"

Theodosia squinted at the green screen of her cell phone. "Directions say turn left."

"Okay, then."

They bumped off the blacktop road and down a gravel road.

"Definitely out in the boonies," said Drayton.

"Pristine," said Theodosia, as she swung around a curve and a pair of yellow eyes glinted at them from out of the darkness.

"What was *that*?" said Drayton, as they rumbled past.

"Not sure. Maybe a fox or raccoon? Something nocturnal."

"What else is out here?"

"Deer, opossum, wild boar?" Theodosia smiled. "You were the one who said the kids could marvel at God's creations."

"I just didn't think the creations would look so spooky at night," said Drayton.

"It *is* spooky out here," said Theodosia. "And this road is getting worse. Even the ruts have ruts."

"Torturous," said Drayton, reaching forward to brace his arms against the dashboard. "But we must be almost there." He jumped slightly. "What did we just go by?"

"Relax," said Theodosia, "you're letting your imagination get the best of you."

"I thought I saw . . ." Drayton began.

"There! Up ahead!" said Theodosia. They rounded a turn, overhanging branches and tall grasses swishing against the sides of the car.

"Thank goodness," said Drayton.

Out of the gloom rose a pair of stone pillars and a rusted gate.

"Bingo," said Theodosia, "I'm pretty sure this is it."

Except it wasn't. Not by a long shot.

Theodosia and Drayton sat staring at the crumbling stone pillars for a few moments, completely taken aback. Then Drayton said, in a squeaky, almost quavering voice. "This looks more like a cemetery."

Theodosia frowned, trying to make sense of it, trying to figure out where they went wrong. "Yes, it does," she said, slowly. "But . . . that can't be right, can it?"

"It says *Angel's Rest*," said Drayton. He pointed toward the rusted iron gates that hung lopsidedly off their hinges. A twisted archway snaked across the top, with Gothic script that scrolled out ANGEL'S REST.

"I know what it *says*," said Theodosia. But this place doesn't jibe with what it's supposed to *be*." She drummed her fingers against the steering wheel, thinking. "Do you suppose there could be two places with the same name?"

Drayton hunched up his shoulders a notch. "It wouldn't surprise me. After all, there are dozens of places named Indigo. Indigo Tea Shop, Indigo Gallery, Indigo Gardens Nursery."

"I guess," said Theodosia. Her frustration was building and she was feeling a little jittery. They were running out of time, after all. Ten o'clock was the deadline and she was nudging up hard against it.

In times of confusion, Drayton tended to resort to logic. He pulled a road map out of the glove box, unfolded it, turned it one way, then the other. "You're positive you have the correct address?"

"I thought so." Theodosia pushed back a hank of auburn hair. "But maybe I screwed up. I *could* have screwed up." She patted her hair, which in the humidity seemed to be taking on a life of its own. Drat those frizzies.

"Maybe it was that asp thing. On your phone," said Drayton.

"App," said Theo. "It's a driving directions app. I *suppose* it could be wrong." Actually, just last week she'd been taken down a road that ended at the Cooper River.

"So now what?" asked Drayton.

"Not much choice," said Theodosia. "I guess I have to check it out."

Drayton looked askance. "You're going in *there*?"

"Just for a quick look-see," said Theodosia. "Because there's definitely something fishy going on." She pushed open the driver's-side door and was immediately struck by the thickness of the night air. It was so humid out here, surrounded by woods and water and swampland, you could almost knead the moist air with your fingers. "But you stay put, okay? Just stay in the car and sit tight."

"You'll get no argument from me," said Drayton.

"But if anything weird should happen . . ." Theodosia glanced at the cemetery then back at him. "Come running."

"What do you mean by *weird?*" asked Drayton. Now he didn't just appear nervous, he was edging into unease.

"I don't know," said Theodosia. "If you hear horrible screams or I get kidnapped by zombies or something."

"That's nothing to jest about," said Drayton.

"Relax," said Theodosia. "I'll be fine. Just one quick look."

Theodosia may have sounded confident, but that confidence quickly eroded once she stepped through the gate and entered the cemetery. Ghostly tombstones, their names and dates long since melted into oblivion, lurched up from moss-covered humps. Kudzu covered an old obelisk, and tilted gray tablets and weathered crosses were barely discernible in the thick underbrush. A trickle of fear ran down Theodosia's spine. It looked like the kind of place where Freddy Krueger or Jason in his hockey mask would be right at home. No doubt about it, Angel's Rest—the cemetery—was spooky, unsettling, and deserted.

But it's not a deserted cemetery, Theodosia told herself. *It's an abandoned cemetery.*

That realization was enough to raise the tiny hairs on the back of her neck and chill her to the bone. Were there really such things as abandoned cemeteries where old graves were simply forgotten? Or was that only in spooky British movies? Or vampire movies?

But a film of ground fog was seeping in, rolling across tilting markers and vague humps like a living, squirming thing. And it would appear no one had brought flowers or tended these graves for a good many decades.

So, clearly, this place was abandoned!

Theodosia clenched her jaw and bounced on the balls of her feet, trying to dissipate her nervous energy. Now what? She was running out of time and tiny little spurts of adrenaline were being insinuated into her bloodstream, triggering even greater feelings of unease.

Standing stock-still in the middle of this overgrown graveyard, with Spanish moss hanging down like rotting cloth, Theodosia decided there was only one thing to do. Call Majel.

Luckily, Majel answered on the second ring.

"Hello?"

"Majel," said Theodosia. "Thank goodness I got you." *And good reception, too.* She drew a deep breath. "Believe it or not, I'm a little lost. I passed through Early Branch and made it as far as Hopper Road. I *thought* I'd ended up at Angel's Rest, but the directions didn't quite work out. So now . . . believe it or not . . . I'm standing in the middle of an old cemetery!"

"Oh, my gosh!" exclaimed Majel, "it sounds like you took a *really* wrong turn and came in the back way."

"There's a back way?" said Theodosia. Her voice sounded squeaky and small among the ghostly, moldering tombstones. "You mean there's another road?"

"Absolutely," said Majel, "Hopper Road also winds around to the front gate of our camp."

"Oh dear," said Theodosia. "That explains it. So I really did miss a turn." Her front teeth nibbled at her lower lip. "And the deadline's in something like ten minutes!"

"Listen," said Majel, "I've got an idea. If you're not entirely creeped out, just continue walking straight through that old place. Go for like another sixty or seventy yards and you'll come to a tall wooden fence . . ."

"Uh-huh," said Theodosia, not liking the idea, but willing to go along with it.

"It's kind of rough-hewn, like an old stockade fence," said Majel. "Anyway, once you hit that fence you'll see a gate. Just pop through the gate and you're at the camp."

Some place for a camp.

Theodosia glanced around as the darkness and night sounds seemed to close in around her. "That's all I have to do? You're sure it's the quickest way?"

"Really, it is. And simple as pie."

"Okay then." *I guess.*

"I'm sorry you're out there all alone," said Majel. "And probably feeling a little intimidated by that old place."

"Yes," said Theodosia.

"But, believe me, you're close. So it's really no big deal."

"Okay," said Theodosia, "talk to you later." She snapped her phone shut and stood there for a long minute. The ground was spongy and damp and she could feel moisture seeping through the soles of her shoes.

Damp. Damp from what?

She didn't want to think about it.

Picking her way between tilting gravestones and around sunken graves, Theodosia walked slowly and carefully. She didn't want to twist an ankle or get caught by the vines that snaked all around her. The ground was mushier here, too, practically swamplike. As if nature were trying to reclaim its due.

Off in the distance came the low, mournful hoot of an owl. And a rustle of branches.

Somebody there?

Theodosia paused in her tracks. No, nobody there. Just the little nocturnal critters. The ones with the yellow, glowy eyes. But they were more afraid of her than she should be of them, right?

Hope so.

Threading her way through a stand of buckthorn that had sprouted up in the graveyard, Theodosia saw the wooden fence loom up directly ahead of her.

Thank goodness something was going to work out. Like Majel had said, just pop through the gate and you're there. All she had to do was take the photo, send it back to the City Charities website, and she'd be out of here.

But when Theodosia arrived at the fence, a seven-foot-high structure of sodden, half-rotting logs that did look like the outer perimeter of some fortress, there was no gate to be found.

Huh. Did I screw up again? she wondered. *Did I not walk the right way?*

Theodosia stretched a hand out and let her fingertips brush against the rough wood, as if to confirm it was really tangible and not just a mirage.

A fence, but no gate. Something changed?

Okay, Theodosia decided, she was going to go off script and switch to plan B. By hook or by crook she was going to hoist herself over that fence and shoot her photo.

Over the fence. How am I going to manage that? Go back and fetch Drayton?

Then she remembered, there wasn't enough time.

Theodosia walked haltingly along the fence line until she saw a possibility. An old gravestone, a square marker almost six feet tall, had heaved out of the ground and tilted toward the fence. If she could scramble up . . . then vault over the fence . . . she'd be home free.

The gravestone was old and crumbly and covered with damp moss. It felt distasteful and furry, but it also gave her some needed traction. She eased up the monolith, half crawling, half climbing, until her hands were able to grasp the top of the fence.

With one mighty heave, Theodosia lurched forward and pulled herself upright so she could peer over the fence.

Success.

But all she saw was . . . swamp. Brackish water and tupelo trees as far as the eye could see.

A swamp?

Theodosia's heart lurched in her chest as she blinked rapidly, not quite believing her eyes. Where were the cabins? Where was the camp with the flag and the campfire circle? What kind of wrong turn had she made this time? And—

There was another more terrifying question, too. Why had she been sent out here on this horrible wild-goose chase?

Behind her, soft footsteps. Like someone walking stealthily through sucking mud. Panicked, Theodosia tried to spin around, struggling to maintain her precarious balance.

But before she could turn completely around, she was struck hard from behind. A terrible crashing blow to her ribs and lower back that brought tears to her eyes and sent a hot, searing pain through her entire body.

And then, like a dream sequence in a horror movie, Theodosia was falling, falling, falling . . .

30

She came to rest with a bone-shattering thump. Aware only of darkness. And then dampness, an oozing, moldering, putrid dampness, that chilled her to the bone.

Can I move? Am I paralyzed? No, I can feel pain, searing pain.

Struggling to move her foot, Theodosia thought she'd managed to twitch a toe. Groaning, trying to fight her way to consciousness, Theodosia concentrated hard on opening her eyes. They fluttered tentatively for a few moments, and then, finally, she was able to focus.

She was staring at a pair of legs.

Whose legs?

"Hello, Theodosia," said Majel. Majel Carter peered down at her from above. A funny, crazy light twirled in her eyes and her mouth was twisted into a feral snarl. "Fancy meeting you here." Majel tossed aside the hunk of wood she held in her hand and dug in her shoulder bag.

"Majel?" said Theodosia, in a quavering voice. She moved

slightly and felt something springy beneath her shift and crack. Like old wood splintering.

Wood? Oh no!

Theodosia twisted around and discovered she'd landed flat on her back, six feet down, in a sunken grave. On top of a coffin? Was that the splintering noise she'd heard? Had to be. She tried to lift her head but was overcome by a wave of dizziness and a flash of shooting pain.

"Oops," said Majel. "Take a bad fall, did we? Isn't that a shame. And look where you landed. Oh well, I suppose there's room for two in that moldy old grave." There was a look of supreme triumph on Majel's face, and then her brain seemed to skip into hyperdrive and she screamed out, "You had to go snooping all over town, didn't you? Sticking your nose where it didn't belong! Asking questions! Now do you see where it got you? What it's forced me to do?"

Theodosia stared up at Majel, who was wailing like a ban-shee, and knew in an instant, almost like a revelation from on high, that Majel was the one who'd killed Parker. That was what had been bubbling around in Theodosia's brain these past few days like some crazy, unknown pot of stew. She'd seen a poster in Parker's office for a fund-raiser that Parker had done for Tuesday's Child. Only it hadn't clicked, the connection just hadn't registered.

But now the pieces were tumbling into place like well-mannered dominoes.

If there was no camp, thought Theodosia, then there was no charity, either. Had that been Parker's sin? His death ticket? Had Parker found out that Tuesday's Child was sim-ply a ruse? That Majel's fund-raising was aimed only at siphoning off funds to feather her own nest? Had to be!

Which meant Majel had lured Parker to his death?

Oh, dear Lord, she must have! What a horrible, murder-ous, evil person she was. And now Theodosia knew that she, too, had fallen victim to Majel. She had been lured out here to this hideous, godforsaken place. But for what end?

All these thoughts spun crazily through Theodosia's muddled head as she lay sprawled in the stinking grave. But this was no time to comb through information. She had to act! She had to . . .

Majel was pointing a small, gray revolver directly into the hole. And although her hand appeared unsteady, she was aiming squarely at Theodosia's chest.

"There's not much to say, is there?" said Majel. She bared her teeth. "Except have a nice rest!" She held the gun out straight in her right hand, hunched her shoulders, and half closed her eyes.

Theodosia flung herself to one side and screamed, just as a tremendously loud explosion ripped through the air and the gun bucked wildly in Majel's hand. There was a splash of gunk and a nasty spray of wood splinters. Then nothing.

Dead? Am I dead? wondered Theodosia.

And then she smelled the fetid stench of the grave and knew she'd somehow escaped being mortally wounded.

Majel missed. She missed me and I'm still alive. In her crazy, twisted, amateur gunslinger mind she thinks she killed me, but she didn't.

And directly on the heels of that thought was, *Is Majel still up there? Is she watching me right now to see if I'm still breathing? Wondering if she should try to drill me with another shot?*

So Theodosia played a game she'd played with Earl Grey. She played dead. She lay in the dark and the rot and the damp until she was pretty sure she heard Majel's footsteps retreating.

When she was fairly sure Majel didn't have another trick up her sleeve, Theodosia pulled herself slowly out of the grave.

She was smeared head to toe with mud and her ribs felt like they were on fire. Broken? She reached around and poked at them. No, but probably cracked.

Theodosia drew a shaky breath. She had to somehow . . .

But another thought quickly interceded. Drayton!

Oh no!

Majel was headed for the cemetery gate. And there was Drayton, scrunched in her Jeep, waiting, a veritable sitting duck!

Theodosia stumbled forward, then broke into a trot. She was disoriented, angry, and in pain, but the thought of Majel taking a shot at Drayton drove her forward. She ran, stumbled, and finally pounded her way across the soft, squishy earth, dodging tombstones, as if she were being chased by seven devils.

Have to get to Drayton! she told herself. *Have to push harder . . .*

Theodosia dodged a tombstone, skipped over a cracked tablet, and spun around a rusted iron cross. She drew upon her grit and fortitude as a lifelong runner and focused on one thing alone. The cemetery gate that loomed directly ahead of her. If she could just make it to . . .

A loud metallic *thwack!* suddenly sounded.

What the . . . ?

Theodosia redoubled her efforts. She stumbled forward, grasping her aching side, pushing and pumping her legs as though her life—or Drayton's—depended on it.

Now the cemetery gate was just ten strides ahead! She raced toward it as branches reached out to grab her clothing and rip her hair. Still, Theodosia ran in an all-out sprint.

Bursting through the cemetery gate, she spotted a lone figure standing by the side of her Jeep!

"Majel!" she cried, in an anguished wail. "Don't!"

"Theodosia!" came the return cry. "Help!" A male voice. Clearly Drayton's!

"Drayton!" she cried. "What's . . . are you okay?"

She stumbled up to him, her breathing reedy and high like an overwrought teakettle. Drayton's face was tense and drawn.

Then Theodosia saw Majel spread-eagled on the ground. Seemingly out cold.

"You got her!" Theodosia shouted. She hugged Drayton tightly and pounded him on the back, relieved, still scared, delirious that he was on his feet and very much alive.

"I heard a gunshot!" Drayton cried. "And then a woman came streaking out of that cemetery! At first I thought it was you, and then when she got closer I saw it was Majel!"

"And so . . ."

"I knew she wasn't supposed to be here! I knew Majel must have engineered some kind of trap. And when she got closer, I saw she had a gun!" He put a hand to his chest and patted it. "Theo, I was so scared!"

Theodosia stared down at Majel, out cold on the ground. Every once in a while her right leg would twitch and she would let loose a little involuntary moan. "But what did you *do* to her?"

"I flung open the car door!" said Drayton. "At the exact instant she ran past. She didn't see me and I . . . well, I guess I timed it just right and clobbered her!"

"You clobbered her," said Theodosia. Car door versus woman with gun. Crazy.

"She just crumpled," said Drayton. "She uttered a weird little *eep*, then collapsed in a heap. And, well, she hasn't moved since."

"Good for you, Drayton!"

But Drayton looked nervous. "You don't think she's going to die, do you?"

"She's seems to be breathing okay. I suspect she'll survive."

"Because the last thing I want is to be charged with involuntary manslaughter."

"Are you serious?" said Theodosia. "Majel tried to kill me! She pushed me into a grave and *shot* at me!"

"Dear Lord," said Drayton. "Are you hit?"

"No," said Theodosia. "I don't think so. No, I'm not. Thank goodness she's a rotten shot." A few hot tears slid down her face and she let loose a shaky sigh. "She's the one who killed Parker, not Buddy Krebs."

Drayton took a step back. "Are you serious?"

Theodosia nodded. "Positive."

"Oh my." Drayton stared down at Majel and said in a voice filled with sorrow, "And then she tried to kill you."

"That's right," said Theodosia. "Which means we better hurry up and tie her hands and feet."

"And then what?" said Drayton.

"Then we're going to drag her back into the cemetery and dump her in a grave. Cover her up and bury her alive."

"Theodosia!" Drayton was shocked. "You can't be serious! Even if she did . . ."

Theodosia gave a faint smile. "It's what I'd *like* to do, what would make my little heart go pitty-pat right now. But what I'm really going to do is call the cops."

"Local officers?" asked Drayton.

"And Tidwell. Gotta bring him in on this, too."

They got some rope out of the back of Theodosia's Jeep and bound Majel's wrists and ankles. Then Theodosia made her calls.

"There's another thing," said Drayton, as they waited. "There's a little red car parked back there in the bushes."

They stomped back down the trail to look at it.

"I guess that's what I caught a glimpse of on our way in," said Drayton.

"A Porsche," said Theodosia. "Awfully nice car."

Drayton scratched his head. "How could Majel afford a fancy sports car on her salary?"

"The same way she could afford her camp," said Theodosia.

"Huh?" said Drayton.

"There is no camp," said Theodosia. "If I had to take a wild guess, I'd say Majel was running a phony charity and siphoning off money."

"No camp?" said Drayton. "You mean she's . . ."

"A total fraud," said Theodosia. "Along with being a stone-cold killer."

Deputy Sheriff John Beall of Hampton County and Detective Burt Tidwell arrived at pretty much the same time—the sheriff driving his khaki-colored cruiser, Tidwell arriving in a black-and-white driven by a uniformed officer of the CPD.

Theodosia did a fast five minutes of talking while Majel, still bound and finally conscious, cooled her heels in the back of the sheriff's cruiser.

Sheriff Beall scratched his head when Theodosia began to run out of steam and said, "So this woman . . . she's part of an ongoing murder investigation?"

"That's correct," said Tidwell. "You heard about the death at the Neptune Aquarium?"

Sheriff Beall nodded.

"We think she's the killer," said Tidwell.

"Plus she knew about the bees," Drayton suddenly blurted out.

"What's this about the bees?" asked Tidwell.

So Theodosia had to explain about driving Aunt Libby to Dubose Bees, getting run off the road, and Aunt Libby getting stung. "It wasn't Buddy Krebs after all," Theodosia told

Tidwell. "I thought it was him because of the black truck, but it had to be Majel. Had to be!"

"You see," said Drayton, "Majel was there at Aunt Libby's tea. She heard them talking about the bee visit!"

Sheriff Beall shook his head in disbelief, then focused on Theodosia. "You're positive she tried to kill you?"

Theodosia's head bobbed. "Yes," she gasped. "She really did."

"We'll do gunpowder residue on her hands, you know," said the sheriff. "And try to dig that bullet out of the grave."

"Be my guest," said Theodosia.

Tidwell gazed across at Majel, hunched in the backseat of Sheriff Beall's car. "She lured you out here and pushed you in a grave." He said it in a tone of almost-disbelief.

"And shot at me!" said Theodosia. She was still shaking with anger.

Drayton pulled himself to his full height and said, in his best Heritage Society orator voice, "Theodosia does not manufacture stories. This is not a case of histrionics. It really happened. I *heard* the gunshot."

Anger finally bloomed on Tidwell's pudgy face. "Good grief," he said. His eyes blazed, his jowls shook with fury. "This woman wasn't even on our radar!"

"She wasn't on mine, either," said Theodosia, "but . . . but there you go." This time they all turned to gaze at Majel, who was scowling and mumbling to herself.

Tidwell adjusted his vest, let loose a loud harrumph, then said, "Let me make a couple of calls."

He went back to his black-and-white and plopped heavily into the driver's seat. Theodosia watched him talking away and nodding occasionally. Then Tidwell glanced over at her, then at Majel and shook his head. When he'd finally concluded his calls, Tidwell sat there for a few moments, tapping pudgy fingers against the dashboard. Then he hoisted his bulk out of the car.

"Well?" said Drayton.

"Majel Carter is under investigation for running a fraudulent charity," said Tidwell.

"Of course she is," said Theodosia. "It's just too bad we didn't figure that out earlier."

"There have been several red flags with the City Charities Review Board," Tidwell continued, "and the state attorney general's office has been called in."

"Does she own a black truck?" asked Theodosia.

"Yes," said Tidwell. "There's a black Ford Ranger registered to Tuesday's Child."

"There you go," said Theodosia.

Tidwell rocked back on his heels as if taking all this under consideration. Then he turned to Sheriff Beall, "What do you want to do with her?"

"You're welcome to take her back with you," said Sheriff Beall. "This is obviously your case."

"True," said Tidwell, nodding. "But this is your jurisdiction and I never like to tread on anyone's toes. My office can always negotiate a transfer later."

"I have to warn you," said Sheriff Beall, "our jail is pretty bare bones. We're not exactly set up for the ladies."

"That settles it," said Tidwell. "You take her." He turned to Theodosia and Drayton. "The hour is late. You two need to get back to Charleston." His voice softened. "Theodosia, you look like you might need medical attention."

"I'm okay," she said. "Bruised ribs is all."

"Better to get an x-ray," said Tidwell.

"I'll make sure she gets an x-ray," said Drayton.

"Of course there's no way you can drive your vehicle home," said Tidwell. "That passenger-side door is completely sprung and entirely unsafe."

"Unless you want to take off both doors and go dune buggy," said Sheriff Beall.

"No thanks," said Theodosia. "Not tonight."

"Tell you what," said Tidwell, "we'll call a tow truck and

have your Jeep hauled to the sheriff's impound lot. Tomorrow morning, you can call your insurance agent and get it all sorted out."

"How are we supposed to get home?" asked Drayton. "Hitchhike with you, I suppose?"

Tidwell cocked a thumb toward Majel's sports car. "Take the Porsche. Miss Carter won't be needing it for a good long while."

"Are you serious?" came Majel's outraged shriek from the backseat of the sheriff's cruiser. "That's *my* Porsche!" Her fingers grasped the steel mesh that separated the backseat from the front of the car and she rattled it like crazy.

"Enough!" Tidwell snapped. Then he grabbed Majel's bag, which had been sitting on the back fender of his car, ransacked through it, and pulled out a set of keys. He tossed them to Theodosia. "Have fun. Try not to break any laws."

A look of surprise lit Theodosia's face as she caught the keys. "Uh . . . okay." She walked back to the Porsche and pulled open the driver's-side door. Gazed in at the cushy leather seats, burled wood steering wheel, and a whiz-bang control panel that practically rivaled a fighter jet. The car was sleek, elegant, and teched to the max. In other words, expensive.

"Don't let her drive that car!" came Majel's muffled squawk. "Excuse me, I'm talking to you people!" Her voice rose in a pitiful shriek. "That's a sixty-five-thousand-dollar auto, if you don't mind!"

Theodosia smiled to herself as she eased herself into the plush interior. "I don't mind at all," she said.

31

❧

"*You're okay to* drive?" asked Drayton.

"I'm okay," said Theodosia. They'd just passed through Parkers Ferry and were headed for Highway 17 and back to Charleston.

"Because I can drive if your ribs are bothering you."

"Better now," said Theodosia. She'd dry-swallowed two Motrin tablets and they'd kicked in.

"You're sure?" said Drayton.

"Have you ever driven a stick shift?" asked Theodosia.

"Excuse me," said Drayton, "I grew up driving a stick shift. Before you were born."

Theodosia smiled in the dark. He was probably right. "This is a lovely car, though."

"Ill-gotten goods," said Drayton.

Theodosia cruised over a narrow bridge, listening to the boards rattle beneath her tires and thinking about what a nimble, responsive little car this was. Maybe, when it was time for a trade-in . . .

"What *is* that irritating rattle?" asked Drayton.

"Not sure," said Theodosia. There was a rattle, but she'd just assumed it was part and parcel of the car. A result of its super-low chassis perhaps? A temperamental exhaust system? Or was the noise coming from inside the car?

"Honestly," said Drayton, "it's starting to drive me batty. Does this auto have a loose tailpipe or something?"

Theodosia lifted her foot off the accelerator and let the car coast down the dark road for a good fifty yards. When she'd bled off some of the speed, she turned her head and ventured a quick look in back. What she saw startled her. "Holy smokes, Drayton. It's the doggone fishbowl!"

Drayton didn't pick up on her reference at first. "With actual fish?" he asked.

"No, no," said Theodosia, hitting the gas again and accelerating. "It's the big glass bowl that's been sitting in the rotunda at the Gibbes Museum for the past month. You know, the charity bowl, where people make cash donations."

"Good Lord," exclaimed Drayton, "Majel was going to abscond with that money, too? Is there no end to the woman's greed?"

"Apparently not," said Theodosia. But following on the heels of their outrage was the thought, *Now what am I supposed to do with this?*

She thought about all the people who'd peeled tens and twenties out of their wallets only to be flimflammed. They'd tossed their money into the fishbowl, confidently expecting it would go to a worthy, worthwhile, aboveboard charity. And it would have all gone to Majel.

So what to do now? How to make it right? Just . . . give the money back to the museum? Or turn it over to the police? Theodosia figured that was probably the most reasonable course of action. Except for the fact that the money would get counted and cataloged and probably sit in an evidence room for the next ten years, doing no good for anybody at all.

That's right, no good at all.

Theodosia drove the next few miles in silence, thinking, mulling over this latest development. It was warm and humming inside the little leather cocoon with its new-car smell. And, pretty soon, Drayton's head began to nod. Not two minutes later, he slumped halfway down in the passenger seat and began to snore gently.

Theodosia drove through the darkness in silence. Thinking about Majel's scam, thinking about Parker's murder. Thinking about how nice it would be to get home. To kiss her dog and crawl into bed. To sleep really late tomorrow. Then cook dinner for Max and tell him all about this. Hopefully share a laugh. Hopefully.

But when the large green sign that said Meeting Street flashed overhead, Theodosia didn't turn off.

As they crossed over the Cooper River Bridge, Drayton stirred slowly and lifted his head. He blinked a couple of times and said, in a creaky voice, "We're not going home?"

"Not quite yet," Theodosia told him. She wore a thin, resolute smile on her face.

"Gotta stop at the emergency room," he said in a sleepy monotone. "You need to get an x-ray."

"We will. But first we're taking a detour. There's something I have to do."

Fifteen minutes later, they were in Mount Pleasant, and a few minutes after that the headlights of the Porsche swept the front of a large, dilapidated building. It had probably once been painted white, but now the paint curled away from the boards in long strips. But there were large, overflowing baskets of bougainvilleas, and over the door was a cheery hand-painted sign that read HEARTSONG KIDS CLUB. Theodosia rocked to a stop and carefully scanned the place. Right in the center of the bright red door was a brass mail slot. Perfect.

"What is this place?" asked Drayton. He sounded sleepy and sluggish as he looked around. Then there was a sharp intake of breath as Drayton registered his surprise. "Oh. Is this . . . are we at Dexter's clubhouse?"

"That's right."

"What are we doing here?" he asked. "Everything looks like it's locked up tight."

"I'm going to make an anonymous contribution to a worthwhile charity," Theodosia told him. She slid out of the car, carefully wiggled her shoulders to get the kinks out, then walked around to the back and jerked open the Porsche's rear hatch. Then she bent forward and gripped the sides of the glass fishbowl. Slowly, mindful of her aching back, she began to muscle the fishbowl out the back.

When Drayton saw what she was trying to do, he was up and out of the car in a heartbeat. "Give you a hand with that?"

"I'd appreciate it," said Theodosia.

Together they grasped the slippery glass bowl and crab-stepped their way across the dirt parking lot to the front door of the ramshackle clubhouse. A spill of light from a street-light was their only illumination. The street was deserted, but a dog barked sharply from somewhere down the block. Then, just as fast as it had started up, it quit.

Theodosia bent at the knees, drew a deep breath, and wrested the bowl from Drayton's grasp. She bobbed her head anxiously toward the front door. "Go over and swing open that metal mail slot, will you?" she asked.

Drayton hastened over to the door. Reaching forward, he pushed the rusted mail slot open. "Now what?"

"I'm going to pour this money in," she told him.

Drayton looked a little startled. "Really? All of it?"

Theodosia didn't hesitate. "Every single penny."

Drayton scrabbled to comply as Theodosia hoisted the enormous glass fishbowl onto her left shoulder, took a few steps forward, then tipped it judiciously. The glass clanked loudly against the front door and the money inside shifted into a frothy puddle of green.

Theodosia strained to tip it a couple more inches. And, just like that, made direct contact with the mail slot.

"Hah!" Drayton cackled.

Theodosia tipped it the last few, final inches. Until, finally, crumpled fives, tens, and even fifties slithered down the sides of the glass bowl and tumbled through the mail slot. A veritable infusion of cash.

It was only after all the money had disappeared through the mail slot and Drayton had let the metal flap bang shut that Theodosia had second thoughts.

"Oh, my gosh," she said, raking fingers through her thick mane of hair. "Do you think we did the right thing?"

Drayton smiled in the dark, a thin ghost of a smile. "What do *you* think?"

Theodosia thought about the kids listening to Charlie Parker and Beethoven and traipsing through the museum to stare in awe at ethereal watercolors by Monet. She decided she liked that image. Liked it very much.

"Yes," Theodosia said, her voice turning suddenly husky, "I'm pretty sure we did the right thing."

FAVORITE RECIPES FROM
The Indigo Tea Shop

Apple Scones

    6 Tbsp. butter
    2 cups tart apples, chopped
    2 cups flour
    ⅓ cup sugar
    1 Tbsp. baking powder
    ¼ tsp. salt
    ½ cup heavy cream
    Sugar to sprinkle on top

PREHEAT the oven to 400 degrees F. Melt 2 Tbsp. of the butter in a frying pan. Add the apples and cook over medium heat, stirring, until they are tender and the moisture from the apples is almost evaporated. Remove from the heat and set aside. In a bowl, mix the flour, sugar, baking powder, and salt. Cut in the remaining 4 Tbsp. butter until the mixture is crumbly. Add the heavy cream and apples and mix by hand until the entire mixture holds together in a ball. Place the ball on a floured surface and knead gently five or six times. Pat the dough into a circle 8 to 10 inches in diameter. Sprinkle with sugar, then cut into 12 pie-shaped wedges. Transfer to a greased baking sheet and bake 20 to 25 minutes, or until the scones turn golden brown. Serve warm with butter, Devonshire cream or whipped cream, and jelly.

Haley's Butter Cake

    1¾ cups all-purpose flour
    ½ Tbsp. baking powder
    ½ tsp. salt
    ¾ cup butter, softened
    1½ cups sugar
    2 eggs
    ¾ cup milk
    1 tsp. vanilla extract

PREHEAT the oven to 350 degrees F. Using an electric mixer and a large bowl, combine all ingredients until smooth and creamy. Pour the batter into a greased and floured 9-by-5-inch loaf pan. Bake for approximately 55 minutes, or until the cake is golden brown and a toothpick inserted in the center comes out clean. Serve with jam as a teatime sweet or top with berries for a dessert treat.

Peach–Pecan Quick Bread

    1 can (16 oz.) sliced peaches
    6 Tbsp. butter, melted

2 eggs
1 Tbsp. lemon juice
2 cups flour
¾ cup sugar
3 tsp. baking powder
½ tsp. salt
¾ cup pecans, chopped
2 Tbsp. peach preserves

PREHEAT the oven to 350 degrees F. Drain the juice from the peaches, reserving ¼ cup juice. Dice enough peaches to make 1 cup, leaving the other peaches in slices. In the bowl of a food processor, combine the remaining sliced peaches, butter, eggs, lemon juice, and the reserved ¼ cup juice. Blend until smooth. Place this mixture in a large bowl and add the flour, sugar, baking powder, and salt. Mix gently. Fold in the diced peaches and chopped nuts. Pour this batter into a greased 4-by-8-inch loaf pan. Bake for 1 hour. Cool in the pan for 15 minutes, then remove and cool on a wire rack.

Maple Pecan Butter

1 cup butter, softened
½ cup maple syrup
¾ cup pecans, finely chopped

USING a mixer, beat the butter on medium speed. Gradually beat in the syrup, then add the pecans. Use this butter to top off your scones or muffins!

Caprese Tea Sandwiches

2 Tbsp. olive oil
4 Middle Eastern flatbreads (pita without the pocket)
½ cup Parmesan cheese, grated
¼ tsp. prepared Italian seasoning
2 Tbsp. vinaigrette
2 cups baby salad greens
8 oz. fresh mozzarella cheese, sliced
1 jar pesto sauce
2 plum tomatoes, sliced

PREHEAT the oven to 400 degrees F. Brush the olive oil on the flatbreads, then sprinkle with the Parmesan cheese and Italian seasoning. Place the flatbreads on a baking sheet and bake for about 8 minutes, or until the cheese is melted. Remove from the oven, place the flatbreads on a cutting board, and drizzle with the vinaigrette. Carefully cut each round into 6 wedges. Top 12 of the wedges with a few salad greens and a slice of mozzarella. Spread a small scoop of pesto atop the mozzarella, then add a slice of tomato. Top each sandwich with the remaining wedges, cheese side up. Serve immediately. Yields 12 sandwiches.

Gobbling Goodness Tea Sandwiches

1 loaf French bread
Mayonnaise
Dijon mustard
Cooked turkey breast

1 jar cranberry relish
Baby arugula lettuce

SLICE the loaf of French bread and lightly toast it under the broiler. Spread half of the slices with mayonnaise and the other half with Dijon mustard. Top the mustard-spread slices with a slice of cooked turkey breast, a spoonful of cranberry relish, and a few leaves of baby arugula lettuce. Top each sandwich with a mayonnaise-spread slice and serve.

Sweet Potato Butter

2 cups sweet potatoes, cooked and mashed
¾ cup brown sugar, firmly packed
½ tsp. ground cinnamon
½ tsp. nutmeg
⅛ tsp. ground cloves
2 Tbsp. lemon juice

COMBINE all ingredients in a saucepan. Cook over low heat for approximately 25 minutes, stirring until the mixture is thick and smooth. Perfect on warm biscuits. Or for a nifty sandwich, cut a roll in half, add a slice of pork, and top with sweet potato butter.

Parmesan Crisps

8 oz. Parmesan cheese, shredded

PREHEAT the oven to 350 degrees F. Line a baking sheet with parchment paper. Then place 1 Tbsp. Parmesan on the baking sheet and gently flatten. Repeat, leaving about 2 inches between each flattened mound. Bake for 4 to 5 minutes, until the edges turn golden brown. Use as toppers for soup or salads.

Charleston Pecan Brownie Bars

1 stick (4 oz.) butter, softened
1 cup brown sugar, packed
1 egg
1 cup flour
¼ tsp. baking powder
⅛ tsp. baking soda
Pinch of salt
¾ cup chopped pecans
1 cup (8 oz.) semisweet chocolate bits

PREHEAT the oven to 350 degrees F. Cream together the butter and brown sugar, then beat in the egg. Add the flour, baking powder, baking soda, and salt, then stir together. Stir in the nuts and chocolate bits. Spread the batter in a greased and floured 7-by-11-inch pan. Bake for 20 to 22 minutes.

Brie and Fig Tea Sandwiches

1 French baguette
1 wedge Brie cheese, softened to room temperature
1 jar fig spread

SLICE the baguette into thin slices and place on a cookie sheet. Toast lightly under the broiler to create crispy crostini. Spread the crostini with Brie cheese, then top with fig spread. Enjoy!

Honeybee Scones

2 cups flour
¼ cup sugar
½ tsp. salt
1 Tbsp. baking powder
6 Tbsp. butter, softened
1 egg
¼ cup milk
2 Tbsp. honey

PREHEAT the oven to 400 degrees F. Sift the dry ingredients together, then cut in the butter until the mixture is crumbly. Mix the egg, milk, and honey, then stir into the flour mixture. Knead gently on a floured surface and pat into a 9-inch circle. Cut into wedges and place on a greased baking sheet. Bake for 13 to 15 minutes or until golden. Brush the tops of the scones with more honey while still hot.

TEA TIME TIPS FROM
Laura Childs

Cherry Blossom Tea

When the cherry blossoms bloom in Washington, why not herald the event with your very own cherry blossom tea? Drape your table with a pink tablecloth and add pink napkins and pink floral dinnerware. Add real or silk cherry blossoms for a centerpiece and use packets of flower seeds as place cards.

Think pink with cream cheese mixed with strawberries to top your scones and tasty crab salad tea sandwiches. Pink macaroons or strawberries dipped in chocolate are great desserts, and tea with bits of cherry is a must.

Shakespeare Tea

Pop in a CD of harpsichord music and hark back to teatime with the bard. Shakespearean sonnets printed on 11-by-14-inch paper make great place mats; books piled in the middle of the table with candles in pewter holders complete the picture. Serve elegant British butter shortbread cookies, a traditional English tea such as Earl Grey or English breakfast, and cream scones with plenty of black currant jam or ginger preserves. Need something more substantial? Think ham and honey mustard tea sandwiches on soda bread, or wonderful creamy Welsh rarebit.

White Tea

For an elegant white tea, ask your guests to wear their favorite all-white outfits. Then drape your table with a pristine white linen tablecloth and use white napkins, white china, a white floral centerpiece, and white tea light candles. Serve a silver needle white tea with buttermilk scones and herb butter. Egg salad with dill is also a great savory. Sweets might include white cake, white chocolate scones, and cinnamon cream cheese on date nut bread.

Sewing Tea

If your friends are into needlecraft, surprise them with a sewing tea. Arrange spools of thread, patterns, pincushions, and fresh flowers in a fun tablescape, then toss in a few fashion magazines. Serve cheese quiche and tea sandwiches of lobster salad or turkey pesto. For dessert, consider lemon bars with meringue, brownie bites, and chocolate truffles. And why not serve a Ceylon tea, the tea that was favored by Coco Chanel, the ultimate seamstress and couturier?

Travel Tea

This is your chance to decorate your table with all your travel-themed bric-a-brac—perhaps an Eiffel Tower, Statue of Liberty, or world globe? Then spread out maps as place mats. You could even make blue passport-themed invitations and ticket-themed place cards. For your tea menu, serve food with an international flavor such as British shortbread, French tea, and Italian biscotti. Heartier fare might include a French croissant with chicken salad, Mediterranean salad, or Italian caprese sandwiches.

Picnic Table Tea

Place your picnic table under a tree that's been strung with colored lights or festooned with ribbons. Use a summery tablecloth (with a floral or toile pattern) and create a tablescape using fresh-cut flowers and felt or furry butterflies and bees from the craft store. Summer tea options might include mint tea or oolong. Pile your scones in a wicker basket and serve savories such as chicken salad tea sandwiches or thin-sliced cucumbers with watercress. If the weather's very warm, serve sweet tea in tall, frosted glasses.

Apple Orchard Tea

When fall nips the air and the apple harvest is in full swing, create your own apple orchard theme. For table décor, go autumnal with a red-and-white-checked tablecloth, baskets piled high with apples, red pillar candles, and bouquets of autumn leaves. Serve cheddar cheese scones and tea sandwiches made with Brie cheese and tart apple slices. For a sweet note, think apple crumb cake, apple fritters, or apple crisp. Source some lovely black tea with cinnamon, clove, and bits of apple. Include honey sticks for sweetening your tea!

TEA RESOURCES

TEA PUBLICATIONS

Tea: A Magazine—Quarterly magazine about tea as a beverage and its cultural significance in the arts and society. (www.teamag.com)

Tea Poetry—book compiled and published by Pearl Dexter, editor of *Tea: A Magazine.* (www.teamag.com)

Tea Time—Luscious magazine profiling tea and tea lore. Filled with glossy photos and wonderful recipes. (www.teatimemagazine .com)

Southern Lady—From the publishers of *Tea Time* with a focus on people and places in the South as well as wonderful tea time recipes. (www.southernladymagazine.com)

Tea House Times—Dozens of links to tea shops, purveyors of tea, gift shops, and tea events. (www.teahousetimes.com)

Victoria—Articles and pictorials on homes, home design, gardens, and tea. (www.victoriamag.com)

The Gilded Lily—Publication from the Ladies Tea Guild. (www.glily .com)

Tea in Texas—Highlighting Texas tea rooms and tea events. (www .teaintexas.com)

Fresh Cup Magazine—For tea and coffee professionals. (www.fresh cup.com)

Tea & Coffee—Trade journal for the tea and coffee industry. (www .teaandcoffee.net)

Elmwood Inn—Tea expert Bruce Richardson has written several definitive books on tea. (www.elmwoodinn.com/books)

Jane Pettigrew—This author has written 13 books on the varied aspects of tea and its history and culture. (janepettigrew.com/books)

A Tea Reader by Katrina Avila Munichiello—anthology of tea stories and reflections.

AMERICAN TEA PLANTATIONS

Charleston Tea Plantation—The oldest and largest tea plantation in the United States. Order their fine black tea or schedule a visit. (www.bigelowtea.com)

Fairhope Tea Plantation—Tea produced in Fairhope, Alabama, can be purchased though the Church Mouse gift shop. (www.the churchmouse.com)

Sakuma Brothers Farm—This tea garden just outside Burlington, Washington, has been growing white and green tea for more than ten years. (www.sakumamarket.com)

Big Island Tea—Organic artisan tea from Hawaii. (www.big islandtea.com)

TEA WEBSITES AND INTERESTING BLOGS

Teamap.com—Directory of hundreds of tea shops in the United States and Canada.

GreatTearoomsofAmerica.com—Excellent tea shop guide.

Tealoversroom.com—Guide to tea rooms in Northern California

Cookingwithideas.typepad.com—Recipes and book reviews for the bibliochef.

Cuppatea4sheri.blogspot.com—Amazing recipes.

Seedrack.com—Order *Camellia sinensis* seeds and grow your own tea!

Friendshiptea.blogspot.com—Tea shop reviews, recipes, and more.

Theladiestea.com—Networking platform for women.

Jennybakes.com—Fabulous recipes from a real make-it-from-scratch baker.

Teanmystery.com—Tea shop, books, gifts, and gift baskets.

Allteapots.com—Teapots from around the world.

Fireflyvodka.com—South Carolina purveyors of Sweet Tea Vodka, Raspberry Tea Vodka, Peach Tea Vodka, and more. Just visiting this website is a trip in itself!

Teasquared.blogspot.com—Fun, well-written blog about tea, tea shops, and tea musings.

Bernideensteatimeblog.blogspot.com—Tea, baking, decorations, and gardening.

Teapages.blogspot.com—All things tea.

Baking.about.com—Carroll Pellegrinelli writes a terrific baking blog complete with recipes and photo instructions.

Lverose.com—La Vie en Rose offers book gift baskets paired with the perfect tea and CD.

Teawithfriends.blogspot.com—Lovely blog on tea, friendship, and tea accoutrements.

Sharonsgardenofbookreviews.blogspot.com—Terrific book reviews by an entertainment journalist.

Teaescapade.wordpress.com—Enjoyable tea blog.

Lattesandlife.com—Witty musings on life.

Napkinfoldingguide.com—Photo illustrations of twenty-seven different (and sometimes elaborate) napkin folds.

Worldteaexpo.com—World Tea Expo, the premier business-to-business trade show, features more than three hundred tea suppliers, vendors, and tea innovators.

Sweetgrassbaskets.net—One of several websites where you can buy sweetgrass baskets direct from the artists.

PURVEYORS OF FINE TEA

Adagio.com

Harney.com

Stashtea.com

Republicoftea.com

Gracetea.com

Bigelowtea.com

Teasource.com

Celestialseasonings.com

Goldenmoontea.com

Uptontea.com

Teavana.com

Davidsontea.com

Svtea.com

Serendipitea.com

VISITING CHARLESTON

Charleston.com—Travel and hotel guide.

Charlestoncvb.com—The official Charleston convention and visitor bureau.

Charlestontour.wordpress.com—Private tours of homes and gardens, some including lunch or tea.

Charlestonplace.com—Charleston Place Hotel serves an excellent afternoon tea, Thursday through Saturday, 1 to 3.

Culinarytoursofcharleston.com—Sample specialties from Charleston's local eateries, markets, and bakeries.

Turn the page for a preview of Laura Childs's
next Tea Shop Mystery . . .

SWEET TEA
REVENGE

*Available in hardcover
from Berkley Prime Crime!*

Rain slashed against stained-glass windows and thunder shook the rafters as Theodosia Browning hurried up the back staircase of Ravencrest Inn. Her long, peach-colored bridesmaid's dress swished about her ankles as she balanced a giant box of flowers that had just been delivered to the inn's back door. It was the second Saturday in June, the morning of her friend Delaine Dish's wedding. Normally, Charleston, South Carolina, was awash in sunshine and steamy heat this time of year. But today, this day of all days, a nasty squall had blown in from the Atlantic, parked itself over the city, and turned everything into a soggy morass. Including, unfortunately, the bride's temper.

Theodosia reached the top step and stumbled, almost catching her heel in the hem of her dress. Then she quickly righted herself.

"Delaine!" she called breathlessly. "Your flowers have arrived."

Delaine Dish rushed out into the dark hallway and threw

up her arms in a gesture of sheer panic. "Finally! And, can you believe it, the power's gone out twice already!"

"I know, I know," said Theodosia, trying to minimize the problem. "They lit candles downstairs for the guests. So all the parlors look quite dreamy and atmospheric." She hustled past Delaine, carrying the cumbersome box into the suite of rooms that Delaine was using for her dressing room. The groom, Dougan Granville, was cloistered in his own suite of rooms down the long, dark corridor.

"How does my bouquet look?" asked a jittery Delaine, as Theodosia carefully opened the box.

"Hang on a minute." Theodosia was practically as nervous as Delaine. All the bouquets had been ordered from Floradora, a florist she had recommended and often counted on to create distinctive centerpieces for her own Indigo Tea Shop over on Church Street.

"So many delays," worried Delaine, as another flash of lightning strobed, giving the room the flickering, jittering look of an old-time black-and-white movie. "My guests must be getting restless."

"Not to worry," said Theodosia. "Last I looked, Drayton and Haley were serving peach and ginger tea accompanied by miniature cream scones. So your guests were happy as clams." She lifted the bridal bouquet, a lovely arrangement of orchids, tea roses, and Queen Anne's lace, from its tissue paper wrapping and handed it to Delaine. "Here you go. And it's perfect."

"It is, isn't it," said Delaine, smiling as she accepted the bouquet. She stepped over to a full-length mirror and peered into its murky depths. "How do I look?"

"Beautiful," said Theodosia. And she meant it. She and Delaine had had their differences over the years, but today Delaine looked positively radiant. Her ivory, strapless ball gown–style wedding dress, with its delicate ruched bodice, served to highlight her dark hair and extraordinary coloring and set off her thin figure perfectly.

Delaine stretched a hand out to Theodosia. "Come over here, you."

Theodosia joined Delaine at the mirror and stared at her own reflection in the pitted glass. With masses of curly auburn hair to contend with, Theodosia sometimes projected the aura of a Renaissance woman captured in portrait by Raphael or even Botticelli. She had a smooth peaches-and-cream complexion and intense blue eyes, and she often wore the slightly bemused look of a self-sufficient woman—a woman who, in her midthirties, had found herself to be a successful entrepreneur, possessed a fair amount of life experiences, and had hooked up with a nice boyfriend to boot. So life was good.

Delaine patted her dark, upswept hair and her eyes glittered. She was a successful business owner, too, with her upscale Cotton Duck boutique. But she was of a predatory nature, always on the prowl for the next new experience or thrill. Theodosia, on the other hand, had found contentment. Her tea shop was cozy, charming, and always stuffed to the rafters with good friends and guests. And Drayton and Haley, her two dear friends, worked alongside her.

Delaine turned from the mirror and shrugged. Her nerves were starting to fizz again and she could barely stand still. She whirled one way, then the other, and asked, "Have you seen my sister? Where on earth is Nadine?"

"I know," said Theodosia. "She's late." Then again, Nadine was perpetually late.

"That woman would be late to her own funeral!" Delaine spat out.

There was a *clump-clump* from out in the hallway, and then an overly chirpy cry of, "Here I am!" Nadine charged into the room, looking damp, self-absorbed, and not one bit apologetic. "Sorry to be late," she chortled. "But did you know Bay Street was actually flooded? My cabdriver had to detour for *miles*!"

Delaine's mouth fell open as she stared in horror at her sister, who was practically a spitting image of her, if not a couple of pounds heavier. Nadine brushed drops of rain from her khaki trench coat as she struggled with the handle of a pink paisley umbrella.

"Close that umbrella!" Delaine cried.

Nadine stopped fussing, frowned distractedly, then stared down at the damp, half-open umbrella that was clutched in her hands. "What's wrong now?" she asked.

"Don't you know it's bad luck!" cried Delaine. "You *never* open an umbrella in the house." Delaine was a big believer in signs, portents, and superstitions.

"Sorry," Nadine mumbled. Then added, in a more acerbic tone, "But in case you hadn't noticed, it's raining buckets outside!"

"I noticed," said Delaine, gritting her teeth. "Really, do you think I *planned* for bad weather? Do you think I called the National Weather Service and asked for the *precise* day on which we were going to have a deluge of biblical proportions?"

Nadine stiffened as she struggled with her umbrella. "You don't have to be so snippy!"

"Whatever," said Delaine, turning away from her.

Not wanting to get dragged into a sister-versus-sister fight, Theodosia continued to unpack the five smaller bouquets made up of tea roses and chamomile. These, too, were perfectly composed. Dainty and fragrant and frothy with blooms.

"Maybe you could take these bouquets into the next room," Theodosia suggested to Nadine. "And give them to the other bridesmaids."

"I suppose," sighed Nadine, whose nose was still out of joint.

When she was finally alone with Delaine, Theodosia said, "Okay, what else do you need?" She was finding maid-of-honor duties to be more trouble than she'd ever imagined. Good thing it would all be over in a matter of hours.

Delaine did a little pirouette, letting her enormous skirt billow out around her. Then she peered into the mirror again. "I really look okay?"

"Gorgeous," said Theodosia, trying to stifle a yawn. She'd been up late, helping to decorate and arrange seating in the downstairs Fireplace Room.

"I do feel we could have used a touch more planning," said Delaine.

"It is what it is," said Theodosia. "You had such a short engagement." *Like about four weeks.*

"Which is why I had to settle for this place," said Delaine, her mouth suddenly downcast.

"It's lovely," said Theodosia. Truth be told, Ravencrest Inn, with its old-world cypress paneling, narrow hallways, and looming presence in the Historic District, was dark and a trifle shabby. The rooms were claustrophobic and furnished with mismatched pieces, and the plumbing clanked noisily. But Delaine had pushed everything ahead at warp speed so she could hastily tie the knot with one of Charleston's top attorneys. It was your basic Southern shotgun wedding without the baby.

"Did you see this place even has a widow's walk?" said Delaine.

"Which makes it quaint," said Theodosia.

"It's a dump," replied Delaine.

"But this is a pretty room," said Theodosia, trying to find one small spark of joy. Delaine was flitting about the room like a crazed hummingbird: dipping, sipping, constantly in motion.

"You think?" said Delaine. She pointed to a shelf of antique dolls that stared blankly out at them. "Look at that. Another silly collection."

"I find it interesting," said Theodosia, "that every room

has been themed with a different collection. Teapots, dolls, angels, leather-bound books, you name it."

"But you know how I feel about dolls in particular," said Delaine, tapping her foot.

"I really *don't* know," said Theodosia. *But I have a feeling you're going to tell me.*

"They're horribly creepy," said Delaine. "With their glassy little eyes and puckered rubber faces. And, look." She pointed a pink-enameled finger at the offending shelf. "There's even a bride doll swathed in ghastly, frayed lace. Makes me think of *Bride of Chucky* or something nasty like that."

"This is not what you should be fretting about on your wedding day," said Theodosia, determined to stay upbeat. "Come on over here and let's pin your veil on."

Delaine ghosted across the room. "You know, I had a fight with Dougan this morning."

Theodosia gathered up a long veil of French lace and held it a few inches above Delaine's swirl of dark hair. "That's probably normal. Frayed nerves and all that."

"Don't you want to know what it was about?" asked Delaine.

Theodosia knew when she was being goaded. "Not really." She centered the veil, then set it carefully on Delaine's head and gently spread the sides of the veil over her bare shoulders.

"Dougan wants to cut the honeymoon short," said Delaine. "Because of work. We screamed and hollered; I'm quite sure everyone here heard us."

Theodosia picked up Delaine's bouquet and shoved it into her friend's twitching hands. "Time to get you married." *Could I be any chirpier?* she wondered. *Could I be in any more of a hurry to jump-start this wedding?* "Let's get you and your lovely bridesmaids lined up at the top of the staircase so we can do any and all final adjustments. Then you, my dear, shall make the world's grandest entrance in front of your guests."

The lights flickered once again and thunder crackled as five bridesmaids, one maid of honor, and a nervous bride gathered at the top of the stairs.

"Remember," Theodosia told the bridesmaid at the front of the pack, a distant cousin of Delaine's who was supposed to lead the procession. "As soon as you hear that first note of music . . ."

Swish, swish, chuff. Someone was hurrying up the back staircase. They all turned, en masse, silk and lace rustling, to look.

It was Drayton Conneley, Theodosia's tea expert and dear friend. Dressed in a slim, European-cut tuxedo with a plaid cummerbund, Drayton's patrician face was drawn and slightly flushed beneath his mane of gray hair. Despite his normally quiet reserve, his eyes were crinkled with worry.

Theodosia hastened over to meet him. "What's wrong?" she whispered.

Drayton put a hand to his chest to still his beating heart. He was edging into his high sixties and not used to bounding up two flights of stairs like a crazed gazelle. "We have a problem."

"No lights?" asked Theodosia.

"No groom," said Drayton.

"Typical." Delaine's voice floated out behind them. "He's probably holed up in his room texting away. Dealing with some important client or political bigwig." She sighed deeply. "That's my Dougan. Always puts his work first."

Before Delaine could get any snappier, Theodosia said, "I'll take care of this. I'll go get him."

"Please," said Delaine, in an arch tone.

"Thank you," said Drayton, turning on his heels and disappearing back downstairs.

Theodosia flew down the narrow hallway to Dougan Granville's room. Interestingly enough, Granville was her next-door neighbor. Her home, her quaint Hansel and Gretel—style cottage in the heart of the Historic District, had once been part of his larger, more grand estate.

She rapped on the door of Granville's suite. "Dougan, it's time," she called out. Theodosia knew he was a hard-driving attorney who was probably working right up until the last millisecond.

Nothing. No movement, no answer.

Theodosia leaned forward and put an ear to the door. Maybe he was . . . slightly indisposed? Could it be that he really was a nervous bridegroom?

"Dougan? Mr. Granville? It's Theodosia. We're all waiting for you."

Still nothing.

Wondering what protocol she should observe for something like this, Theodosia hesitated for a few moments, then decided it didn't much matter. Guests were waiting; it was time to get moving. She gripped the doorknob and turned it, then pushed the door open a good six inches.

"Dougan," she called again, trying to inject a little humor in her voice. "We have an impatient bride who's waiting for her handsome groom."

There was no sound, save the monotonous drumming of rain on the roof and the gurgling of water as it rushed through the downspouts.

Theodosia pushed the door all the way open and stepped across the threshold.

"Dougan?"

The room was completely dark and ominously quiet. Straight ahead, she could just make out a faint outline of heavy velvet draperies pulled across a bay window.

Did Granville fall asleep? He must have. Wow, this is one relaxed guy on his wedding day.

Shadows capered on the walls as she stepped past a looming wardrobe and pieces of furniture. The room had a strange electrical smell, as if an outside transformer had exploded. Theodosia tiptoed across the carpet, her silk mules whispering softly. When she reached the foot of the bed, she stared. A tiny bedside lamp shone a small circle of warmth on a battered bedside table, but there was no one lying on the bed. Nothing had creased the dusty pink coverlet.

What on earth?

Flustered, nervous now that they might have a runaway groom on their hands, Theodosia fumbled with the curtains and ripped them open. Lightning flashed outside, a sharp blade cutting through a wall of purple-black clouds.

Still, this is better. A little more light.

Just as Theodosia turned, something caught her eye. A fleeting image that she couldn't quite process but one that unnerved her anyway. She slowly retraced her footsteps. Back to the sitting room area that had been in total darkness, as thunder boomed like kettle drums in some unholy symphony.

That was when she saw him.

Dougan Granville was sprawled on a brocade fainting couch. His eyes were squeezed shut; his head had fallen forward until his chin rested heavily on his chest. On the small glass table in front of him was an empty glassine envelope and a scatter of white powder.

Theodosia tiptoed closer, her heart hammering in her chest, her brain shouting screams of protest. An unwanted shot of adrenaline sparked by surprise and fear had sent her blood pressure zooming. Still, she was mesmerized, hypnotized, at what she was seeing.

Was Granville just stoned? Or . . . something worse?

Theodosia moved closer and stretched out a tentative hand. The very tips of her fingers brushed the pulse point of his neck. Granville felt ice cold and lifeless. There was no pulse, no respiration.

Revulsion and fear rose up inside her like sulfurous magma from a roiling volcano. Theodosia understood, logically and viscerally, that Granville hadn't just fainted on this fainting couch like genteel ladies of old.

This man was seriously, catastrophically, dead.

BE SURE TO WATCH FOR THE
NEXT CACKLEBERRY CLUB MYSTERY

Stake & Eggs

A grisly murder in a blinding snowstorm leaves the towns-
people of Kindred badly shaken. And right in the middle of
the Fire & Ice Festival, inquiring minds want to know—will
the ladies of the Cackleberry Club dare pursue this creepy
killer?

FIND OUT MORE ABOUT THE AUTHOR
AND HER MYSTERIES AT
WWW.LAURACHILDS.COM.
VISIT LAURA CHILDS ON FACEBOOK
AND BECOME A FRIEND.

FROM *NEW YORK TIMES* BESTSELLING AUTHOR

LAURA CHILDS

Postcards from the Dead

A Scrapbooking Mystery

There's a parade rolling through the historic French Quarter, and Kimber Breeze of KBEZ-TV is broadcasting live from a small balcony on the fourth floor of the Hotel Tremain. Her next subject will be Carmela Bertrand. Carmela has never been a fan of Kimber, but she isn't about to turn down the chance of good publicity for her Memory Mine scrapbooking shop.

But before Carmela's shop gets its five minutes of fame, a killer strangles Kimber with a cord, leaving her body dangling above the parade. Carmela is horrified, but she quickly discovers the nightmare isn't over. Because someone is now leaving strange postcards at Carmela's shop—signed by the dead Kimber. Now Carmela and her friend Ava will have to risk their own necks to find out who's posing as a ghost—and to expose a killer . . .

Scrapbooking Tips and Recipes Included!

laurachilds.com
facebook.com/TheCrimeSceneBooks
penguin.com

M1197T1012

The Tea Shop Mysteries by
New York Times Bestselling Author

Laura Childs

DEATH BY DARJEELING

GUNPOWDER GREEN

SHADES OF EARL GREY

THE ENGLISH BREAKFAST MURDER

THE JASMINE MOON MURDER

CHAMOMILE MOURNING

BLOOD ORANGE BREWING

DRAGONWELL DEAD

THE SILVER NEEDLE MURDER

OOLONG DEAD

THE TEABERRY STRANGLER

SCONES & BONES

AGONY OF THE LEAVES

"A delightful series."
—*The Mystery Reader*

"Murder suits Laura Childs to a Tea."
—*St. Paul Pioneer Press*

laurachilds.com
penguin.com

M314AS0911